Landscape of a Marriage

Central Park Was Only the Beginning

Gail Ward Olmsted

Black Rose Writing | Texas

ISBN: 978-1-68433-721-7
PUBLISHED BY BLACK ROSE WRITING
www.blackrosewriting.com

Printed in the United States of America
Suggested Retail Price (SRP) $20.95

Landscape of a Marriage is printed in Book Antiqua

*As a planet-friendly publisher, Black Rose Writing does its best to eliminate
unnecessary waste to reduce paper usage and energy costs, while never
compromising the reading experience. As a result, the final word count vs. page count
may not meet common expectations.

Cover and Author photos courtesy of Conor Olmsted.

For my family, loving and beloved

Acknowledgements

There has been a great deal written about Frederick Law Olmsted, renowned the world over as the "father of American landscape architecture" for his innovative integration of the natural and built environment. His brilliant vision resulted in over 500 commissions including public parks and recreation grounds, private estates, residential communities and academic institutions.

Despite being married to Olmsted for 44 years, we know little about his wife, Mary Perkins Olmsted. References to her tiny stature, her children and her "inability to suffer fools" are mentioned in several books and articles, but I wanted to know more. At a time when widows with young children had very few options, Mary married her brother-in-law Fred to provide a stable home and financial security for her family. I feel Mary would not be satisfied with a marriage of convenience or her expected role as *the woman behind the man*. I firmly believe she was an inspiration to Olmsted and the guiding force behind much of his brilliant work. I wrote *Landscape* as a work of fiction, feeling that their love story, from Mary's perspective, deserved to be told. I only hope I did her justice.

On the subject of love stories, I am grateful for the love and support of my amazing husband, Deane Olmsted. You are the best person I know, and I am grateful for the wonderful life we have built together.

Researching *Landscape* was both entertaining and rewarding as I read and enjoyed several books, including: *Genius of Place: The Life of Frederick Law Olmsted* by Justin Martin, *A Clearing in the Distance* by Witold Rybczynski, *FLO: A Biography of Frederick Law Olmsted* by Laura Wood Roper and *Olmsted's America: An "Unpractical" Man and His Vision of Civilization* by Lee Hall. If you are interested in learning more about Olmsted and his life, I highly recommend these titles.

For their suggestions, advice, patience and support I would like to thank my friends: Lisa Grele Barrie, Sue Briody, Sandi Coyne-Gilbert, B.J. Knapp, Tracey McKethan, Tracey Ryan and Diane Sabato. I am so lucky to have the privilege of your friendship.

Landscape's beautiful cover results from my son Conor Olmsted's amazing talent. Thank you for turning my vision into something so wonderful!

There are three women without whom *Landscape* would never have been completed:

Anna Bennett, a skillful editor who provided an abundance of support, encouragement and suggestions through rounds of revisions. Your talents and attention to detail made the characters come to life, and I thank you for assisting me in crafting a story that fills me with great pride.

Barbara Wurtzel, who challenged me to dig deeper into the characters and the events that shaped the turbulent second half of the 19th century in America. I am so very grateful for your wise counsel and your friendship.

Laurie Grele Cain, my oldest friend and biggest cheerleader. Laurie enthusiastically read and critiqued several drafts of *Landscape*, offering endless support and encouragement. She believed in Mary's story, and she believed in me. Laurie was killed in a car accident before *Landscape* was published and I miss her every single day. *Tu es ma meilleure amie. Je t'aime toujours.*

–GWO

Landscape of a Marriage

"The landscape belongs to the person who looks at it."
–Ralph Waldo Emerson

Prologue

June 1858

I clung to the ship's rail, staring out at the sea below, mesmerized by the thousands of stars and the sliver of moon reflected on its surface. *This is what infinity looks like.* The only sounds were the thrumming of the engine and the waves hitting the boat. No longer queasy, I had regained my sea legs. This was not my first trans-Atlantic crossing on the *Persia*, and it was unlikely to be my last.

I should return to our tiny stateroom and check on my three children, but they had fallen asleep, and I hated the thought of waking them. I had lain awake for hours on my narrow bunk before deciding to go on deck for some air. I pulled my black woolen shawl tighter as the sea mist sprayed my face. It was a welcome change from the stuffy cabin, and I relished the tangy scent.

I tried to recall what day it was and when the New York shoreline would be visible. We had been at sea for at least a week, so the journey from Liverpool was more than half over. We were almost home. That's what my father-in-law had written to me earlier in the month. "Come home," the telegram implored, and he had wired an ample sum to ensure it would happen.

Home. Where exactly *was* home? After my beloved husband John was diagnosed with tuberculosis, we had traveled all over Europe convinced we could find proper treatment. Our family grew in size, but hopes for a cure dwindled. Despite all of our efforts, we lost him at the age of only thirty-two! Since then, the children and I had continued to travel, staying nowhere for more than a couple of weeks. Heartbroken and lonely, I was unwilling to put down roots lest they, too, be broken. We had lived in a series of meager guesthouses and inns and were running out of money when my father-in-law made contact. Returning to the States made sense, but *where* would we live? The allowance from my grandfather's estate was not enough to survive on and, other than a cousin in Boston, I had no family left.

I had hoped we could stay in Hartford with John Senior for a time, but he was raising a family with his second wife and I doubted there would there be room for us. There was the family farm on Staten Island that belonged to my brother-in-law Fred, but there were tenant farmers living in the farmhouse.

Security was foremost in my thoughts. I knew that we would need to live simply, and as long as there was food on the table, I would be grateful. But someday? The chance to live in a large airy home with lots of sunshine? And a yard for the children to play in? *That* would be delightful. *But how?* Tension filled my shoulders and my arms tightened across my chest. As I imagined dear John looking down at us, I vowed to do whatever it took to keep my family safe.

I was strong, only twenty-eight years old. I was good with figures. Perhaps I could secure a job in an office somewhere. Or possibly a couple of rooms in a private home might be available, and I could help the family by watching their children in exchange for a reduction in rent. Maybe Fred would have an idea or know people that could help. He was planning a big public park in Manhattan and, according to my late husband, was a man "who knows everyone worth knowing."

Ready for another sleepless night, I returned to our room filled with resolve. *I would talk with Fred. Fred would know what I should do.*

Chapter 1

Summer 1859

"Happy is the bride whom the sun shines on," I whispered, smoothing the full skirt of my new gown. It was a lovely shade of lavender — perfect for a second wedding — and I thought it complemented my pale skin, blue eyes, and dark hair. It was a sunny day, and I was about to marry Fred, my brother-in-law. I had never thought my request for his help would result in a proposal of marriage, but here we were. Imagine that!

I had approached Fred for advice after returning to New York last year. He had been very busy with his park project, an 800-acre parcel of land in Manhattan. It was a veritable swamp: rocky, filthy, smelly and rife with both pigsties and slaughterhouses. It was a sow's ear and Fred and his partner, a British architect named Calvert Vaux, were expected to turn it into a silk purse. John and I had shared a private laugh about 'Fred's Folly', as we called the park project, wondering if he would ever complete the herculean task.

Despite constant demands for his time, Fred spent most evenings with us. What a relief to have another adult in the house! I was so lonely as other than Fred, I knew not a soul in New York. He had secured lodging for us on the second floor of an older home in Manhattan, and I looked forward to hearing his booming voice announcing his arrival each night. The children would run to him, begging for whatever treats or trinkets he had stored in his coat pocket. Although he had no experience with children, Fred was gentle and kind, listening to their endless chatter while I prepared supper. Soon it became routine for him to tuck the children in and read to them. On the nights they clamored for me, he washed and dried the dishes and tidied up the kitchen until I returned.

One night, I asked him to join me in a glass of sherry and that became our new arrangement. Fred was eager to give me updates on the park, and I enjoyed the chance to engage in adult conversation. I began to comprehend the sheer enormity of Fred's task. It was far more than just the physical demands of the job, clearing the land and designing the walkways. As superintendent of the park, Fred was caught up in the political upheaval that the project had triggered. Politicians saw the promise of jobs as a means to ensure their own re-election and encouraged their constituents to seek employment. But Fred had high standards and wouldn't allow unskilled laborers on the job site. Although he had already hired close to 3,000 workers, many more were turned away. One night, he had only half-jokingly admitted he feared for the future of the park if those "jackals and miscreants had their way." He said, "and that's just the elected officials." I was proud of how Fred worked long hours to bring the dream of an urban oasis for all New Yorkers to fruition.

Never demonstrative, it surprised me one night a few months ago when Fred embraced me. He told me he was glad I was back home where I belonged and kissed my cheek as he said good night. I must admit I was having romantic feelings by then and I wondered if he could see me as anything more than a needy in-law. I still missed John terribly, but there was something so comforting about being with Fred. He had many of the same mannerisms and speech patterns as my late husband, and I loved to sit by his side listening to him and watching him play with the children. But I had no idea, until that first kiss, how he felt.

Shortly after meeting Fred for the first time, I had overheard him confiding to a friend that "Mary was just the thing for a rainy day. Not to fall in love with, but to talk to." At the time, his words had meant little to me as I was in love with his younger brother. But everything had changed since then.

So, I had begun to imagine a future with Fred and was thrilled when, just a few weeks later, he asked me to marry him. Or rather, stated that he was of the opinion we *should* get married, to which I agreed. Marriage was an opportunity to provide stability for my family. But could it also be a second chance for me? To live *my* happy ever after? I hoped so. But I didn't fool myself with hopes of a passionate union. Fred's love for me was more like that of an older brother, *not* a besotted bridegroom. He was thirty-seven years old, never married, and his engagement to Miss Emily Perkins had ended several years ago. All of his previous romantic relationships had been short-lived, and many in our social circle had assumed Fred would be a lifelong bachelor. And now he was marrying me, a widow with three small children!

From where I stood in the hallway of Bogardus House, a Victorian dwelling on the grounds of the park, I could peek unseen at my fiancé. He was talking with Mr. Daniel Tiemann, the mayor of New York City, who would officiate the ceremony. I heard the opening strains of Mendelssohn's Wedding March and at the organist's nod, I walked slowly towards the front of the room. The wood floor was glossy and recently polished, so I stepped carefully to avoid slipping. I was excited, but tried to appear calm until I heard four-year-old Charlotte telling her younger brother Owen in a loud stage whisper, "Mama is marrying Uncle Fred *right now*." I stifled a giggle, turning to smile at my children sitting together on a single chair. "Be good," I mouthed and continued walking down the narrow aisle. Both men were smiling as I took my place facing Fred and set my simple bouquet on a side table. He looked attractive in his black morning coat and crisp gray trousers. He was only of average height with a slight build, but to me, he appeared larger than life. I had grown very fond of this man with the reddish brown hair and bright blue eyes. I looked forward to spending time alone with him, to falling in love.

Just the thing for a rainy day indeed! I would be the next woman that Frederick Law Olmsted fell in love with. As well as the last!

"You look lovely, my dear. Your gown is also lovely," Fred stammered as he took my hands in his. His palms were damp and his cheeks were flushed. I smiled reassuringly, pleased that I was not the only one who was nervous.

"You look quite smart yourself, Fred. I don't know that I've ever seen you look so dashing."

Fred beamed as Mayor Tiemann cleared his throat, signaling we were about to begin. He spoke in a deep and commanding voice about the sanctity of marriage and the importance of finding someone of the right status and temperament to grow old with. *But what about love?* Marriage without a firm foundation built on love was out of the question to me. A loving marriage and family; *that* was most important.

It seemed the mayor would drone on forever, when his tone suddenly changed and he turned towards Fred.

"Do you, Frederick Law Olmsted, take this woman as your lawfully wedded wife, to have and to hold from this day forward?"

"I do," Fred responded. "Yes, I do."

"And do you, Mary Perkins Olmsted, take this man as your lawfully wedded husband, to have and to hold from this day forward?"

"I do." My heart was beating so loudly that I worried the mayor had not heard me. But he smiled and continued.

"Then by the power vested in me by the state of New York, I hereby pronounce you man and wife. Fred, you may kiss the bride."

Fred cleared his throat and leaned forward as I raised my lips to his. *Kiss me, Fred. I'm your wife. You can kiss me.* And he did. His lips were warm and firm and he drew me closer, his arms encircling my waist. When he pulled away, I saw a gleam in his eyes. *He looks happy. Happy to be married to me!* Warmth flooded through me. I was happy too.

As Mayor Tiemann congratulated Fred, I looked back at my children and saw John and Charlotte still had Owen wedged between them. When they saw me looking, they hopped up and began waving.

"Mama," six-year-old John said, "I've been watching the little ones. Just like you asked."

"You look pretty, Mama," Charlotte said.

"Pretty," Owen echoed, and I thought my heart would burst with joy. *My three darlings.* I rushed towards them and they clambered about, each trying to claim me as their own.

"Now, now, children," Fred boomed, and I looked up to see my new husband smiling down at us. "Let's allow your poor mother the chance to catch her breath," he implored. Seeing a new target for their affection, the children deserted me and climbed into Fred's open arms. They tussled for a few moments like affectionate puppies until Fred set them down and pulled himself to a standing position. "Well, if this is the level of energy that I should expect from the lot of you, I had better ask about a tonic to maintain my strength," he said with a smile. "Come now, children. We can't keep our esteemed Mayor waiting." He took my arm and led me towards the back of the room, where a young woman was setting up refreshments.

"I'm afraid I've started without you, Fred," Mayor Tiemann said with a wink as he raised a glass with a flourish. "To the bride and groom," he proclaimed and brought the glass to his lips.

"Thank you, Daniel. Mary and I are grateful for you being here today." I nodded in agreement, but realized no one was looking at me. I forced a smile and clung to Fred's arm, unsure what to do.

"Think nothing of it, my good man. It's the least I can do, what with you designing a park that will make me the envy of every other mayor in the U.S.," Tiemann said. "So, what is the latest? Bring me up to date, won't you? I can't get a straight answer when I run into your boss. Who's it? Green?" Fred winced at the sound of his supervisor's name, but recovered quickly.

"I'm happy to fill you in," he said. "Let's let Mary and the children have their refreshments and I'll join you in a glass." He poured himself a thimble of sherry and topped off the mayor's glass. They made themselves comfortable in over-sized leather chairs in a far corner of the room.

I wished John Senior had joined us, or that I had thought to invite one of my friends from school. It had been so difficult to maintain contact while traveling with an ailing husband and a growing family. This past year had been quite a change, and since agreeing to marry Fred two months earlier, I'd had no time to reach out to old friends. Until that very moment, I had not realized I could feel lonely on my wedding day.

I assumed the men would be engaged for some time, so I led the children to the sideboard laden with a crystal punch bowl and silver trays of tiny sandwiches and pastries. A white cake decorated with fondant flowers garnered their full attention. John tugged at my hand.

"It's sponge cake," he said. "I would like a big piece as I'm the oldest."

"Can I have a piece with two flowers? Please," Charlotte whined.

"I like cake," Owen announced to no one in particular.

"Sandwich first," I said and watched as the server prepared a plate for each child. They brought their bounty over to a small table and began devouring their meal. The stays of my dress were digging into my sides and I knew I didn't have room for much, but a tiny deviled egg sandwich and a sliver of cake were in order. And a nice glass of punch.

It was time for a proper celebration. It *was* my wedding day, after all.

Chapter 2

That night, after an early dinner, our exhausted children did not protest when we put them to bed. After we tidied the kitchen, Fred turned to me and taking my hand in his, led me to the bedroom we would now share as husband and wife. I felt suddenly shy and trembled as he kissed me and gently stroked my hair. He drew back and cupping my face in his hands, spoke softly, his blue eyes watching me.

"Mary, I won't rush you. If you feel that..." I leaned in and silenced him with a kiss of my own. He reacted by scooping me up in his arms as if I were a mere feather and laying me on the bed. He fumbled with the buttons on my dress and I aided in the effort and soon, we were together, united in our marriage bed. It was heavenly. I had not realized how much I had missed the loving touch of a man, and I responded with an enthusiasm I never knew I was capable of. Afterwards, we lay together, my head on his chest, and I heard the beating of his heart and felt the rise and fall of his deep, slow breaths. The last thing I remember as I drifted into sleep was Fred whispering, "Ah Mary, I love you so."

Those first few weeks, I often blushed while having lunch with the children, daydreaming about the tender, passionate man I had married. Fred's work schedule prevented us from taking a honeymoon, but we managed to eke out private time for ourselves whenever we could. Fred never missed an opportunity to brush against me or bend down to kiss my cheek. His touch made me tingle all over and I began to count the hours until we would be together again in our bed.

But nothing lasts forever, and our love-making, while still exhilarating, became less frequent. *That's natural in a marriage,* I tried to reassure myself, but one morning, only two months after we were married, I watched Fred over the rim of my coffee cup. I was hoping he would present me with an opening to what would be a difficult conversation, but he seemed distracted. Paying more attention to the wall in front of him than to the *New York Gazette,* he had been drumming his fingers on the scrubbed pine table for several minutes. It was nerve-wracking! Wanting to look my best, I wore one of my prettiest dresses in a lovely shade of blue. I had arranged for our new governess to take the children for a walk, so it was just the two of us for what seemed like the first time in days. I worried how he would react. *Was this the right time?*

Despite the sunshine spilling in through the lace curtains, I felt a chill run up my spine. Fred's insomnia had been getting worse. He didn't come to bed most nights until after I had fallen asleep and was often gone by the time I awoke. And now, he had been staring at his coffee cup for so long the coffee had to have grown cold, and his bowl of porridge sat untouched. I needed to know what was on his mind before I shared my concerns.

"Fred," I said. He started, as if the sound of my voice had awakened him from a deep slumber. "Is everything all right?" He put down his newspaper and cleared his throat. I sat forward, aware that whatever was bothering him would soon concern me as well.

"Yes, everything is fine," he said. "It's just that, well, it's been a difficult summer. Wouldn't you agree?" I nodded.

"It's been an adjustment for everyone since you moved in. I'm certain once we settle in our new apartment, we'll be just fine. The children—"

"Yes, the children. Well, for one, I had assumed Owen would be sleeping through the night by now. He's nearly two." I started to assure him Owen's erratic sleeping habits were in keeping with a child so young, but Fred hurried on. "And young Charlotte? The little mite is covered in that itchy red rash and those oozy sores. It's keeping her up all hours of the night. It's no wonder there's so little sleep for any of us these days."

"It's frustrating, Fred, I know. But that new salve is working wonders, and she is improving daily. Everything will be — "

"And what of John, er... Charley then?" Fred said. "His eyes are quite bad. Aren't you worried his condition will keep him from reading? He's due to start school soon." I stifled an urge to inform him I was well aware of the health issues affecting the children and that our oldest son would answer either to John or Charley, the nickname he had chosen. I was the one dealing with all the chaos day after day while Fred was at work. But this is all new to Fred, I reminded myself. He had gone from bachelorhood to being responsible for a family of five overnight. I smiled.

"Yes, Fred. It has been a challenge these last two months. But things are looking up, don't you agree? Miss Curtayne, our new governess, is in residence and it thrills Charley to be starting school." Seeing his frown, I hurried on. "I'm feeling positive about the way things have been progressing. Aren't you?" I hoped he would nod or offer some sign of agreement, but he continued to look glum.

"Mary, I hope you take no offense in what I'm about to say. I've worried about you as well." I sat back, perplexed.

"Me? Why on earth would you worry about me? I should think with the demands of that impossible park project of yours and the health of the little ones, I would be the least of your worries." Fred continued to look uncomfortable and appeared unable to meet my gaze.

I bit my tongue to give him an opportunity to respond, but to fill the awkward silence blurted out, "And what of your insomnia and the impact on my sleeping habits?" Fred looked surprised, but hurried to defend himself.

"I've never been much of a sleeper, Mary. I'll try to move around more quietly so as not to disturb you from now on."

"Thank you. I appreciate that," I said. "So, what has you concerned about me, exactly?"

"It's just that you seem to experience a multitude of anxieties of late. I'm worried about you is all." He leaned towards me, waiting on my response.

Anxieties? Well, indeed! A new husband in and out of my bed after months of sleeping alone. Sick children, a governess to train, cramped quarters, the impending move, lack of sleep. I took a long deep breath and let it out as I tried to collect my thoughts. Fred seemed to take my silence as a form of tacit agreement.

"Perhaps a visit from the doctor is what you need. A tonic of some sort? And of course, you can rest more now that we have arranged care for the children. Do you concur?"

I nodded, but had more to say. "Yes. I appreciate your concern. But the bigger issue, as I see it, is—that is, I fear we are somewhat incompatible. Perhaps we should consider separate sleeping quarters in the new apartment." Fred looked confused and was slow at grasping what I was saying.

"Separate? You mean, you and me? I'm not sure I understand." I took a deep breath and let it out slowly before responding, the words spilling out of me.

"Well, yes. We have never discussed it, but you seem less than thrilled to retire with me each night. Most nights, you delay coming to bed until long after I have fallen asleep and nearly every morning, you rise well before me. Your side of the bed is most always empty." I held back the mounting tears as I willed myself to continue. "It's as if you are eager to escape from our bedroom."

"Escape? Oh, no. That's not it at all. When I can't sleep, it does me no good to remain in bed. And now that I know how much it has been affecting you..."

"I realize all that. But don't you want to be, well, *with* me in our bed?" Fred flushed with color and wouldn't meet my gaze. Clearing his throat, he shifted in his seat as he tried to explain himself.

"We *have* consummated our marriage, Mary. Many times, as I hope you would recall. I just, well, I am unsure how often I mean... what amount of marital relations is normal? I apparently have no clue." Reaching across the table, I took his large calloused hand in mine, stroking it gently as I spoke.

"Dear Fred. Every marriage is different. I would assume that the frequency of... er, *relations* are left up to the two people in the marriage." John and I had been happy to couple often, when his health permitted it. But this was not the time to think of John. "I like it when you are in bed next to me," I said with a smile. Fred looked pleased at this admission, almost preening in his delight.

"As do I, my dear wife. Now that I know your thoughts on the subject, I will plan to be more attentive to your needs," he said. I blushed, happy and victorious.

"Well, that sounds lovely. I shall look forward to it." Fred was watching me. It appeared he still had more that he wanted to say, so I nodded.

"Mary," he said. "I want you to know that marrying you and adopting the young ones has given me a whole new lease on life."

"Oh yes, Fred. I'm certain sick children and an anxious wife are just what you were hoping for," I said, with an attempt at gaiety, but Fred shook his head.

"I realize we are having some issues adjusting to all the changes we have been dealing with. The children will get better and you and I will work all of this out together. I'm certain of that. Why, just this week, I wrote to my father and told him of my joy. I assured him we have a good deal of happiness between the drips, and that's a fact."

My heart swelled, and I thought I might cry. While not quite the romantic declaration I longed for, I felt relieved. Hopeful, even. *Between the drips, indeed!* Uncertain I could speak, I nodded, beaming at him.

Fred took a sip of his coffee and shuddered, realizing it had long gone cold. He appeared ready to clear his place at the table as he folded his newspaper and stuck it under his arm. I moved to stop him as I found my voice once again. "Leave this, Fred, I will get the dishes. You have important work to do," I said with a wink. "Supper will be waiting for you at seven sharp."

Fred smiled and walked towards me with a pronounced spring in his step. Leaning over, he started to kiss the top of my head, but when I raised my face to meet his, he planted a kiss on my lips instead.

"Oh, you spoil me," he said. "This old bach could get used to royal treatment like this every day."

"And many nights," I reminded him. With a wink, Fred strode across the room, gathering up his overcoat and hat as he made his way to the door.

"Yes, indeed. Have a good day, my dear." With a jaunty wave, he was gone. I sat back with a smile on my face. Yes, it would be a good day. And if the children cooperated with help from Miss C., I could feed them an early supper and have time for a relaxing bath before Fred returned home. I had already packed my lilac-scented bath salts to prepare for the impending move, but I knew where they were.

Reminding my new husband of my many charms was on the agenda for this evening.

Chapter 3

Fall 1859

For the past several weeks, we had been sharing a cavernous home with the Vaux family in the former Catholic convent at Mount St. Vincent, next to the Central Park space. I had not been thrilled that we would live with another family, but it had turned out to be a splendid arrangement. I looked forward to daily conversations with Anne Vaux. Fred and Calvert worked long hours, and it was delightful to have another adult to talk with.

Having lost touch with the few friends I'd had over the last ten years, my friendship with Anne was important. One afternoon, with the setting sun providing a lovely backdrop, we sat together in one of the large sunrooms separating our two dwellings. The voices of our children playing in the next room were gay but muted by the thick walls in the solidly constructed building. Eschewing our usual pot of tea, I poured us each a small glass of port. Anne giggled.

"Aren't we the wicked ones?" she said with a grin. A few years older than me, Anne was a gentle woman with a pretty face and a sweet disposition. "Isn't it lovely to have a spot of peace amid all the chaos?" The convent had several large glass-enclosed galleries similar to the one we were sitting in, and the children never complained of a rainy day as long as they could race around and play games inside. Charley, Charlotte and Owen adored having Downing and Bowyer Vaux to play with, as evidenced by the muffled sounds of laughter and shrieks of delight coming from the adjacent room. I smiled back at Anne in agreement.

"Yes, it's wonderful to enjoy adult conversation. And how is our Julia doing today? Does she still have the sniffles? Charlotte is concerned," I said with a smile. Julia, the newest member of the Vaux family, had been born shortly before the move and Charlotte spent a great deal of time each day holding the newborn and comforting her when she cried.

"Oh yes, she's already on the mend," Anne said. "And what is that Fred calls Charlotte? A little mother, isn't it?" I nodded as she continued. "So, I take it Fred got off on his latest adventure yesterday. No delays?" I bristled at the idea my husband's trip was an *adventure*, but chose to ignore it. He was scheduled to visit several European parks at the suggestion of the Central Park Commission. It was reportedly a fact-finding mission and a reward for a job well done, but I suspected the park officials had their own agenda and were trying to get Fred out of the way for an extended period. His talent for design was frequently overshadowed by his penchant for stirring things up with the powers that be. Even *I* could see that.

"Yes, he's well on his way. I accompanied him to see the *Persia* depart. It was so strange viewing it again. Only a year ago, the children and I arrived here in New York on the very same ship. I had forgotten how large it was." Anne's eyes widened as she sat forward in her seat.

"Quite the undertaking with three little ones. I'm not sure I could have managed it."

"Oh yes, it was. But all's well that ends well, am I right?" I said. "So yesterday, I persuaded the Staten Island Ferry driver to circle the ship before they set off. I thought it would cheer Fred up, you know? I waved and waved, but I'm uncertain he saw me."

"Well, I'm sure he appreciated your being there," said Anne. "So will Mr. Green be joining you again this week?"

I groaned, picturing the irksome man to whom both Fred and Cal Vaux reported. Andrew Green was tall and handsome, but I had never warmed to him. To be polite, I had encouraged Fred to ask his new boss to supper a couple of months ago. Since then, Green had been inviting himself to dine with us every other week. I found him rude and disliked the way he interrupted Fred and scorned his passion for the park project. Fred referred to him as "that bean counter" and had determined his new boss lacked both imagination and vision. I had grown tired of hearing the nightly recount of their squabbles, but tried to listen, occasionally interjecting a gentle, "Good for you," or an indignant, "Why the nerve of that man!"

The only silver lining to the dark cloud of Fred's prolonged absence was the thought I wouldn't have to endure Mr. Green's presence in my home for the duration. However, he had sent word earlier today that he was looking forward to dinner later this week. I threw up my hands in frustration.

"I realize I have no right to complain, but the thought of that tiresome man at my table, especially without Fred to keep him engaged, troubles me to no end," I said.

"Well, he hasn't invited himself to *my* table. Perhaps he wishes for something more than a home-cooked meal," Anne said. I giggled.

"You *are* a wicked one. That is preposterous. The idea any man would be interested in me? Well, any man besides my husband that is." I blushed as I pictured Fred. *Oh, that husband of mine.* Ever since I had assured him I enjoyed our time in the bedroom, he had been quite the dutiful and ardent lover.

"Well, forgive me for being so forthright, Mary. The two of you appear—well—close, you know, for a proper married couple."

I felt my cheeks flush a deeper red. It was true we frequently held hands and always greeted each other with a hug and a kiss. Our love life well exceeded my expectations, but I was unaccustomed to such a frank discussion regarding something so private. I looked away, embarrassed to meet Anne's gaze.

"Well, we're still newlyweds. We've been married less than four months."

"Oh, yes. I keep forgetting that. What with three children. You seem like such—"

"It's actually soon to be four," I whispered, my hand moving reflexively to my abdomen. I frequently had to resist the urge to do so, and it was a relief to share the news. Anne set her glass down and leaned forward expectantly.

"What? Am I hearing you correctly? You are expecting another child?"

"Yes, it would appear I am," I said. "It's probably a bit too soon. Owen is barely sleeping through the night and now a baby on the way." It was a blessing, but I had hoped to hold off adding to our family until things were more settled and I worried how Fred would take the news. Anne leaned over to hug me.

"Congratulations! And of course, I will help you in any way I can. Is Fred pleased? Well, of course he is. It is after all *his* first child..." She stopped speaking as she watched me shift uncomfortably.

"I haven't exactly told him yet," I said, my voice barely above a whisper.

"But Mary, you know how happy Fred will be?"

"Oh, I do. I'm certain he will be as pleased as punch. It's just that the timing of his trip has been unfortunate, you know?" Anne grimaced and her voice sounded strained.

"It *was* sudden, wasn't it? And, there was no word of Calvert going along. Not that I would have wanted him to go, what with baby Julia and all. Still, it seemed very odd they would grant Fred paid time off and *my* husband has to report to the park each day," she finished with a frown.

"You know those politicians," I said with a wry smile. "Next it will be Cal's turn." Anne brightened and nodded.

"So, are you going to send word about your condition?" she asked. "Perhaps that would convince him to return home sooner." I frowned and shook my head. Fred's job was very stressful and his insomnia had gotten worse over the last month. He deserved time away to relax and find new sources of inspiration. It was important that he return well-rested and committed to both his family *and* the Central Park project.

"Well, let's get back to more immediate concerns," said Anne. "We need to concoct a menu guaranteed to put an end to Mr. Green's plans to dine with you each fortnight. Cornbread as charred and burned as coal? A joint of beef that's none too fresh?" I appreciated her ability to change the topic so adeptly and grinned, happy to have found such a good friend.

"Sounds divine. And how about we invite all six of our children to join us, with baby Julia at the head of the table? That would put a damper on the evening."

"And we should instruct them to refer to him as 'Uncle Andrew'," Anne said, and we roared with laughter.

We spent the rest of the evening with plenty more sherry and increasingly outrageous suggestions how we could put a stop to Green's visits to my home.

Chapter 4

The months flew by as we settled into our new home. My days were busy with the children and running the house, but Anne and I continued to enjoy our afternoon tea time. It wasn't until late at night when I could indulge myself in missing Fred and re-reading his letters. They were full of details of his travels, and my return letters focused on the children and the goings-on of our busy household. I missed him so much and longed to share the news that I was pregnant, but kept to my pledge to withhold it from him. It was true I wanted him to relax, but a part of me wanted him to return because he loved me, not because it was his duty.

When Fred came home to find me in my fourth month of pregnancy, he was jubilant. He had been gone for three months and the time away had been just what he needed. He had put on some weight and his complexion was once again ruddy, no doubt due to the weeks spent traipsing through the public parks of Europe. Beaming with joy, he held me by the shoulders and looked me up and down, focusing his attention on my very swollen abdomen. I blushed, embarrassed and thrilled in equal measure by the intensity of his gaze.

"I'm positively elated, Mary. A child of my own? You know, of course, I love all of our children equally. But this one? Well, it's something I had almost given up hope of."

"I'm so glad to have you home, Fred. I hoped you would be pleased," I said, sitting down on the sofa.

"*Pleased* does not begin to describe the depths of my happiness. If I had known what was waiting for me, I would have hastened my return. I don't understand why you did not send me a telegraph. Your letters never mentioned your condition. I would have hopped on the next ship home if I had known," Fred said, joining me on the sofa and reaching over to grasp my hand. "And may I say, just for the record, pregnancy becomes you. You are radiant."

"This is *not* my first pregnancy. And you have seen me in this state before," I said with a smile.

"Ah yes, but this is the first time you are carrying *my* child," Fred said with a wink.

Fred described his European itinerary as I leaned against the sofa's plush cushions. Despite the fatigue that accompanied me most days, I was so grateful to have my world traveler back home, and happy to listen to his tales. After three weeks at sea, Fred had spent his first days in Liverpool before departing for two weeks in London. After that, he had traveled to Paris, then on to Brussels and finally, Ireland.

"What was your favorite part of the trip?" I asked.

"Definitely my visits to the People's Park in Liverpool. John and I were there years ago. Do you remember?" I nodded. Shortly after we became engaged, they had set off on a walking tour of Europe.

"Of course I do! At the time, I thought it quite the clever ruse to postpone our wedding. I never thanked you for bringing him home all in one piece. But that's all in the past. Let me take another look at this lovely dress you've brought me."

Fred gestured towards the elegant silk gown spread over a chair.

"I wanted to bring you something special. I had no idea you would have no use for it for the foreseeable future."

I smoothed my hair back before returning my hands to rest atop my middle. It was my fourth pregnancy and my body had ballooned out months earlier than previously. I grinned at him.

"Perhaps this is an indication of the size of this baby. Maybe there is more than one," I said. Fred's expression grew to one of shocked surprise, but he quickly realized I was having a go at him.

"One at a time is fine with me," he assured me. I responded by yawning.

"Oh, how rude. I am finding this pregnancy to be most exhausting," I said. Fred answered with a yawn of his own.

"You know I am a horrible sleeper, and it's even more difficult to get a good night's sleep on a ship. Perhaps if we can count on Miss C. to keep the children busy, we can retire to our bedroom and, well, take it from there, I imagine." His hopeful look turned to one of confusion as he watched for my reaction. "If you think we should."

I stood and, taking his hand in mine, led him out of the sitting room and towards the wide oak staircase that led to our bedroom. "Yes, my love, I think we should."

Chapter 5

Summer 1860

Fred and I were strolling through the southern section of Central Park with the children on a beautiful day in late May. After years of work by up to 3,600 laborers at a time, the park was nearly complete. In keeping with Fred's vision, it featured rolling pastures inspired by the English countryside. Since he returned from last year's trip to Europe, he had been obsessed with every detail and worked long hours six days a week to transform the park into the breathtaking spectacle in front of us.

In my opinion, he had outdone himself, having turned the messy, smelly acreage into a world-class destination. It *was* a silk purse, and a fine one at that. Attendance had grown steadily, reaching two million visitors last year. Despite being in my ninth month of pregnancy, I had insisted on accompanying my family. The sun was shining, and I'd had enough of being housebound. Fred held my arm as the children raced ahead, running along the paths, then skipping back to report what they had seen.

"We're almost at the lake," Charlotte called out. "Do you think there will be swans, Papa?" Fred was about to answer when Charley interrupted.

"The swans are there in the morning, silly," he said. "At this time of day, there will be ducks, dozens of them, I imagine. Isn't that right, Papa?" Fred shook his head good-naturedly.

"I would think both swans and ducks will be present. And Canada geese too."

"Owen, my pet, what do you prefer? Swans, geese or ducks?" I asked.

He looked thoughtful for a moment, then announced, "I like ducks best, just like Papa does." He ran off to catch up with his siblings and I squeezed Fred's arm.

"Your secret is out, my love," I said. "You claim to have no favorites, but we all know how much you love the ducks." Fred chuckled, shaking his head as if to deny it.

"Favorites, heh? Well then, if you know so much about me, answer this. What is my favorite type of tree?"

"Elm, of course," I said, showing with a sweep of my arm the hundreds of elm trees that lined the path. "Ask me something more challenging, please." Fred scrunched up his face as if deep in concentration.

"Bushes that flower or not?" he said.

"No flowers. Too distracting. And paths that curve, like the one we're on. No straight lines for my husband. You're an impractical man, Mr. Olmsted. You never take the easy way out." Fred smiled.

"No, I suppose I don't. I vowed to give this city the beating green heart that it needs to thrive and by God I will make that happen." He pointed to the pasture ahead of us. "That area was the site of the largest pigsty I have ever seen," he said. "And where we're standing? A massive slaughterhouse, I kid you not."

I felt queasy as images of pigsties and slaughterhouses filled my brain. I stopped walking and closed my eyes, trying to rid myself of those awful thoughts.

"Mary, are you all right?" Fred asked as I leaned over to catch my breath. "Come," he said, leading me over to the nearest park bench. I sat and fanned my face with a handkerchief.

"I'm fine. Winded is all. These winding paths of yours are lovely, but quite challenging to navigate." Fred sat beside me and held my hands in his.

"It's wonderful being here with you. Can you imagine the next time we walk through the park we'll be a family of six? Less than a year ago, I was living the gay life of a bachelor and here I am, with a wife and family. I am a lucky man, Mrs. Olmsted. You've made me very happy, my—" He stopped at the sound of the children running towards us, Charley yelling at the top of his lungs.

"Pub-lic drunk-en-ess is pro-hib-it-ed," he called out in a sing-song voice. "And loi-ter-ing too."

"I see my community outreach program is working," Fred said with a frown. The level of attendance at the park had brought with it a new set of problems. Arrests for drunkenness, assault and loitering had skyrocketed, and they had charged Fred with developing a solution to reduce the number of crimes. They had posted a series of signs encouraging proper decorum and discouraging littering, public intoxication and other disreputable behavior.

"Now darling, the problems here at the park are hardly unique. We must educate the public on the behavior expected of them," I said. Fred shook his head.

"And what sort is *not*," he said.

The children collapsed in a heap on the grass, laughing. Fred smiled and nodded to a pair of uniformed men walking past.

"Did I tell you we've hired more security staff?"

"Yes, dear. Initial reports appear to bode well for the safety of all."

"I suppose so," he said. "I say, why don't you rest and I'll accompany the children to see my favorite ducks."

I smiled, certain that I needed to stay off my feet for a few moments before heading home.

"Thank you, that sounds wonderful." Fred kissed me on the cheek and got to his feet.

"Come children. Let's head to the lake." They jumped up and ran ahead, Charley pulling his younger brother along while Charlotte skipped alongside them.

"Oh, and Fred?" I called out. Fred turned with a smile.

"I should bring you back a lemon ice, my love?"

"That would be perfect." I watched as my wonderful family disappeared from view, heading down the hill towards the lake. I was blessed.

Chapter 6

"Well done, Mary." Fred kissed the top of my head, and sat down beside me. I was lying in bed, jubilant and exhausted, having just given birth to a son.

I tried to raise myself up, but realized I was far too sore. Each successive pregnancy had yielded an increasingly larger baby and a more arduous birthing process. I closed my eyes and lay against the pillows.

"Do you need anything?" Fred asked. I was about to ask for water, when the doctor spoke up from the corner of the room.

"A fine baby, Olmsted. And a healthy weight. Nearly ten and a half pounds," he said in a booming voice. "Good job, Mrs. Olmsted."

I winced when I heard our son was so large. I had gained more weight than usual and suspected this would be a good-sized baby, but over ten pounds!

"Goodness gracious," I mumbled. My firstborn had been barely six pounds. John and I had joked that the last chicken I roasted had been larger than our newborn. *Don't think about John now*. I needed to concentrate on our new son, born one year and one day after my marriage to Fred.

"We missed our anniversary," I said, but realized Fred was no longer by my side. He and Doctor Sinclair were now congratulating each other. I motioned to him and he rushed back over.

"All his fingers and toes. Everything present and accounted for," he reported. I managed a weak smile, but it must have appeared as more of a grimace. Fred looked nervous as he asked, "What can I get you? Are you in pain?"

I wanted to tell him my bottom half felt like it was on fire and how I couldn't imagine being able to leave the bed ever again, but merely asked for a glass of water, which he delivered with a flourish. I took a couple of sips as Fred watched me. I patted his hand.

"I'm right as rain. Or at least I will be within a few days. Don't worry about me. But the little pugilist needs a name. Have you thought anymore about it?"

"I like John. It is a sound name for my first son who will grow to be a strong man, like his late uncle and his grandfather." I groaned at his suggestion.

"But Fred, it will be confusing. My — I mean, *our* — eldest is already named John after his father. His late father," I quickly added. He shook his head.

"It will be fine, Mary. You'll see. We call John Charles 'Charley', so a baby named John will not be confusing. Our bigger concern should be breaking the news to Charlotte. You know how convinced she was that she would have a sister."

"Well, I like Cyrus as a middle name," I said. It had been my grandfather's name. "John Cyrus," I repeated. Fred smiled.

"As you wish, Mary," he said, as the doctor approached with a clean, well-swaddled infant, now shrieking and red-faced. "I will let you get acquainted with the newest member of the household. Edward," he said as the doctor placed the baby into my arms, "let's go find you a drop of something suitable before we round up the children to meet their new brother." He and the doctor left the room as I stared at the crying baby on my chest.

"Hello, baby John," I whispered and pulled him closer. He was a beautiful boy with pale skin, the slightest amount of reddish hair and large gray eyes. Would they turn blue like Fred's and mine? He seemed to be watching me, and I smiled. "What do you see, little one?" I murmured as I closed my eyes. Just a quick nap and I would be ready to face the day.

Chapter 7

"Mary, we need to move along. They won't hold on to the horse much longer. I gave my word we would arrive by one o'clock. And it's almost that now." Fred paced the floor as he watched me packing a bag.

"I'm almost ready. I just need to add a couple more diapers and—" Fred threw up his hands in frustration.

"We will be gone for an hour, two at the outside. How many diapers does one tiny infant require?" I shook my head and continued organizing everything necessary for an afternoon out with an infant. I had traveled across Europe with three little ones in tow. Today's outing was a walk—or, more aptly, ride—in the park by comparison.

"Perhaps you can notify Miss C. we are going to leave shortly," I said, smiling sweetly at him as he left the room. I wanted to suggest that he channel some of his restless energy into something more productive than second guessing my every move, but held my tongue. He had been on edge and slept less and less each night.

"We're off on an adventure, my little one." John was such a delightful baby, sleeping for long periods of time and feeding enthusiastically several times a day. My heart swelled holding my sweet boy. "At the rate you're growing, you'll be larger than Owen within the year."

I caught up with Fred, pacing in front of the door. I dropped the bag at his feet and pulled a shawl from the coatrack. "Let's go then, Mr. Slowpoke," I said, and we left home and began walking down the street.

***

Later that night, I sat alone in the darkened parlor, head in my hands, eyes red from crying. It had been the worst day of my life. I closed my eyes, willing the images of the tragic accident to disappear. Instead, it played again in my head, every terrifying detail. It had happened so fast. One minute we were traveling in an open buggy through Upper Manhattan. The weather had been perfect and the horse's energetic canter magnified the light breeze. Fred was an experienced horseman, and he held the reins loosely as the horse trotted down the street, pulling us in the borrowed buggy. I was about to encourage him to purchase the horse, envisioning the family outings we would enjoy. Just as I started to speak, I turned to look at Fred, who had grown silent. His head had dropped to his chest and his eyes were closed. Horrified, I realized that he had fallen asleep, just as the horse began to gallop.

"Wake up," I had shrieked.

Fred had dropped the reins and the horse, accustomed to getting more direction, had panicked. I scrambled to grab the reins with my free hand as I held the baby even more closely. I couldn't reach them, but my screams woke Fred, who quickly realized the perilous situation we were in. By then, the horse was galloping down the middle of the street, causing passersby to jump out of our way. Even as I tried to come to grips with the danger we were facing, I could see the look of shock on the faces of those we barely missed.

"Help, help," I screamed in desperation as the horse continued to pick up speed. "Fred, stop him, please." Even in my terrified state, I heard Fred yelling for the horse to stop. The baby was now wide awake and screaming. I tried to comfort him while holding on to the carriage for dear life. Gasping for air, I squeezed my eyes shut to block out the petrifying vision of hurtling to a certain death. *Someone, anyone help us, please!*

Just as Fred was able to grab the reins the buggy tipped, launching him into the air and smashing him against a large rock on the side of the road. The baby and I tumbled out, and I screamed as we hit the pavement and rolled to a stop. Breathing heavily and still gripping John, I tried to take stock of the situation, scrambling to check him for cuts and scrapes. He appeared unhurt, but the fall had startled him and he continued to howl. I tried to calm him as I searched for Fred. *Where was he? Was he hurt?*

My mind was racing until I saw him lying still and silent some twenty feet away, his left leg twisted at a most unnatural angle. I tried to stand, but was overcome with a bout of dizziness. I closed my eyes and tried to comfort my baby, now shrieking in terror. A strange man rushed over to help and told me that someone had called a doctor.

"Please, Missus. Lie still. You should try to not move," he said.

"My… husband," I whispered hoarsely. "Please see to my husband."

"I'm afraid he's — well, we should wait for the doctor," the man cautioned. "I'm just a shopkeeper," he said, gesturing at a storefront. "I'm no doctor, but even I can see your husband…" His voice trailed off, and he shook his head. "I'm sorry, Missus…?"

"Olmsted. Mrs. Frederick Law Olmsted." I was frantic as I struggled to my feet, clutching John. "My husband is a very important man in this city. He is also father to four little ones. Please, can't you do something?"

The shopkeeper nodded. "I'll be right back," he said and hurried over to check on Fred, who did not appear to have moved. A small crowd had gathered and over the baby's cries, I could hear snatches of their fevered chatter. "He's gone, I'm afraid," a deep male voice thundered. "That poor man," a woman sobbed. "Do you suppose that baby is his? The poor little mite, growing up without a father."

I hugged John even closer as my tears continued to fall. Could they be right? Was Fred dead? We have four children and now must I bury yet another husband? My head spun, and as the doctor approached, I fell into his arms and everything went dark.

After a noxious dose of smelling salts revived me, the doctor had accompanied us home. They carried Fred, lying prostrate on a large wooden shutter which the well-meaning shopkeeper had removed from his store's entryway. Even after being tucked into our bed, he had still not regained consciousness. Doctor Sinclair had assured me that Fred was still alive, but his tone was grave and he could not meet my eyes.

"We will know more in the morning," he said. "If he lives through the night, we can better assess the situation. He remains unconscious, but that's his body's way of dealing with the trauma." I nodded, desperately trying to make sense of what I was hearing.

"The fall severely damaged his leg," the doctor said. "We may very well need to consider amputation. Regardless, if he survives, it is unlikely he will ever walk again. As long as he has a desk job, he may provide for you and the infant," he said, attempting to comfort me.

"Four children," I reminded him. "We have four children, and my husband *never* sits behind a desk. He's always on the move, overseeing hundreds of workers. Why, he's more active than most men half his age."

"Well, yes, of course. I understand. First, he needs to make it through the night and regain consciousness. Let's not put the cart before the horse," he suggested, then frowned, realizing how inappropriate that comment was.

Tears slid down my cheeks as I struggled against an overwhelming sense of despair. I barely heard the doctor as he shuffled out of the room, promising to return in the morning.

Miss C. was a godsend, feeding and bathing the children with help from Anne Vaux while I sat by Fred's bedside long into the evening. Fresh tears fell as I reached out as I took his hand in mine. *Such firm hands.* I squeezed his calloused fingers and held them to my cheek. He looked so peaceful, as if he were in a deep sleep, a sight I was rarely privy to. I stroked his forehead.

"Oh, Fred," I whispered. "Won't you please come back to me? That doctor doesn't know just how much you have to live for," I told him with a fierceness I had not known I was capable of. I drew in a deep breath, exhaling as I wiped away my tears. *I am made of sterner stuff.* My grandfather had told me that after my parents died, and I desperately wanted to believe it was true. I *was* made of sterner stuff, and so was Fred. "You are the strongest man I know. You're going to beat this and we're going to prosper. We will prove him wrong. If I have to push you in a wheelchair myself, you and Mr. Vaux will complete the Central Park job and it will continue to draw millions of visitors each year. 'Why, Mr. Frederick Law Olmsted of New York City designed this lovely park' they will say. You'll see," I whispered, hopeful he had heard me.

Rising slowly, I made my way into the hallway. After checking on my four sleeping children, I collapsed on our bed. Bringing my hands together in prayer, I spoke silently, mouthing the words. "Please, please God. I beg you. Don't let him die."

Around dawn, I willed myself to get some sleep. Tomorrow would be here before I knew it and my family would need me.

Chapter 8

I jolted awake with a start. I had been dreaming I was on a ship in the middle of the ocean, but as my eyes adjusted to the darkness, I realized I was at home in my bed. The sight of the large walnut dresser comforted me from my childhood bedroom and by the sound of Fred snoring. Despite the doctor's prediction that it was unlikely he would survive, Fred had continued to make progress in the week since the accident. His left knee had shattered and his leg was broken in three places. Talk of amputation had ended after Doctor Sinclair determined Fred was too weak for surgery. There was no mention of his being able to walk again, but I remained hopeful that he would.

It was clear he was in pain, even with heavy doses of morphine. He slept for hours at a time and would awake needing a sip of water. His fevered eyes followed me everywhere and when he spoke, it was to ensure baby John and I were doing well. His concern encouraged me and I viewed this as a sign he would make a full recovery.

I relaxed back into my pillows, relief flooding over me. My own injuries were minor, mainly cuts and bruises already beginning to heal. And, the only silver lining to the accident, was that baby John had not even a scratch on him.

Coming out of my reverie, I panicked suddenly at the thought of my son. He had been cranky last night. I had tried to feed him, but he had refused and fussed in his crib for hours before falling into a restless sleep. I had gone to him in the wee hours of the morning to soothe him back to sleep. He had felt warm and appeared flushed, but after a few minutes of cuddling, I left him in his crib and returned to bed. Now it was a few hours later, and I felt an urgent need to check on him. Throwing a shawl over my nightgown, I made my way down the dark hallway to the nursery. The quiet comforted me, but the smells emanating from his crib stopped me in my tracks. My poor baby boy was lying still on sheets soaked with loose feces and dark-colored vomit. As I reached him, he curled up in a fetal position and cried as if in great pain.

My heart was pounding as I reached for him, pulled him close and paced back and forth. Instead of curving into me as he usually did, his body remained stiff and unyielding. The foul odors emanating from his tiny body were almost overwhelming. I knew I should settle him back in his crib and contact the doctor, but was unwilling to leave him for even a moment. Taking a deep breath, I forced myself to think straight. I had to alert the Vauxes for help.

Holding him in my arms, I descended the stairs and made my way across the sunroom separating our living spaces. The skies were brightening as I banged on the door. Seconds later, Calvert Vaux appeared, astonished to see me. He blinked and ran his fingers through his disheveled gray hair.

"I need your help," I cried out, my vision blurring from the tears. "John is quite sick."

"Come in. I'll go for the doctor," he said. He turned and called for Anne, who appeared in the foyer almost immediately. She took in the sight of us and reacted just as quickly as her husband had.

"Mary, we need to get the little mite cleaned up. Come with me." When I didn't move, she spoke more sharply. "We have to examine him more closely and it is impossible in his current state." Without waiting for a response, she led me towards the back of the house. Entering the kitchen, we heard Cal call out he was leaving to fetch the doctor.

Anne started heating a large stockpot of water. After getting me settled in a chair, she produced a stack of clean towels. Dipping one in the warm water, she dabbed at the soil covering every inch of the baby, focusing first on his face. Checking to see if he had swallowed any of his own vomit, she pried him from my arms. Laying him down on a towel, she undressed him. As more of his bare skin was revealed, she drew in a sharp breath. Instead of a healthy pink or even the red flush of fever, my baby's skin was a death-like shade of blue.

She wrapped him in a clean blanket as I watched, silent and shocked. *This is not happening. This cannot be happening.* Anne spoke in a whisper.

"Would you be more comfortable having the doctor come to your apartment Mary?" I nodded and holding the baby, Anne led me back to our living quarters and into the nursery. Once I got settled in a rocking chair, Anne placed him in my arms and said she would be right back. I sat, staring at my baby, my eyes riveted to his much-memorized face. *Sweet, sweet boy. What on earth is wrong, my pet?* Surely a quick dose of medication will have him back to rights in no time.

A few minutes later, Anne bustled back into the room.

"I spoke to our governess. She'll watch for Cal and the doctor and tell them we're here. And she and Miss C. are going to bring Fred to you." I nodded again, but couldn't form the words "thank you." Several minutes later, the two women appeared in the doorway dragging a chair, to which Fred was hastily tied, into the room. As soon as I saw him, I burst into tears. Clearly in pain, Fred waited as he was untied. He welcomed John into his arms as I crumpled to the floor, my head in his lap.

"Oh my darling," Fred said. "I wish I could relieve you of this terrible burden. Our boy," he began, before he dissolved into loud sobs, the force racking his entire body.

***

In the hour before the doctor arrived, John alternated between bouts of screaming and periods of stillness, the latter prompting me to place my ear on his tiny chest to ensure he was still breathing. Fred, his damaged leg stretched out in front of him, dozed in his chair, oblivious to the sound of his son's distress. John's cries grew weaker as the morning wore on, and although he had regained a healthier pink tone to his skin, he was now burning up with fever. Finally, Cal and the doctor rushed in and Sinclair began his examination of the baby. I sat by the crib, my eyes closed, and prayed.

When he finished and John was swaddled in clean clothes and a fresh diaper, Fred motioned for me to hand him the baby. Holding John close, he murmured assurances to all within hearing distance that his son was going to be fine, just fine.

"Cholera Infantum" Doctor Sinclair pronounced gravely, after wiping his brow. I burst into tears and, snatching the baby from Fred's arms, began to pace back and forth. *Cholera?* I couldn't believe it.

"Forgive me," Fred said. "I'm not sure I understand. I had always heard cholera was a disease suffered by the poor. Those living in slums and crowded tenements. Surely —"

"And contaminated drinking water, isn't that true? Are you certain our John has cholera?" I shrieked, my hysteria breaking loose. I held my breath, hoping for some sort of reassurance, but the doctor shook his head.

"There are many rumors surrounding cholera, I'm afraid. We don't know everything about the cause or how to cure it. There are hundreds affected in this city alone. I recommend a small amount of opium injected just below the skin. It will relieve the poor thing of the pain," said Dr. Sinclair. As if on cue, John screamed in pain and loose stools soaked his diaper.

"What are you telling us?" I tried in vain to clean him. "Will this shot cure him or just quiet him?" Before the doctor could respond, Fred spoke up.

"Mary," Fred said. "Let's let the doctor do what he deems necessary. Please come sit beside me for a bit, won't you?" Wordlessly, I handed John to the doctor, who injected the opium into his tiny left thigh. The calming effect was almost instantaneous, and after Anne and the doctor cleaned him up, they placed John back into his crib. I watched helplessly, then stumbled a little as I went to Fred's side and knelt before him.

"Please, please my husband. I need your strength today, of all days. And the children —" I stood and started to leave the room in a panic. "What if they are sick as well? I have to check on them, too..." Anne stood in the doorway to block my exit, and I collapsed against her and sobbed. She wrapped her arms around me, uttering reassurances.

"Charley, Charlotte and Owen are playing with my children. I have checked on them myself, I promise you. They are being well cared for by Miss C. and my Emma," she said. "They know what to watch for and I told them to come for me immediately if any of the children exhibit any symptoms." Dr. Sinclair agreed with Anne.

"Mrs. Olmsted, your immediate concern should be this little fellow here. I won't sugarcoat it. He is not experiencing any pain but believe me. He is gravely ill." I nodded mutely, but insisted on a quick visit to see my children with my own eyes. The doctor agreed to go with me and we returned to the nursery a short while later.

"Your older children are doing fine, Fred," Sinclair said as he entered the room ahead of me. I nearly ran into him as he halted at the sight of Fred sitting, slumped down in the chair, head to his chest. His shoulders were heaving with silent sobs. As we approached, Fred drew in a deep breath and spoke, stumbling over his words.

"Sinclair, I must know. The accident? Was that it? Did it cause my son's condition? Was he weakened from the fall? Did I..?"

"God, no Fred. Cholera is a disease that strikes randomly. John's age is responsible. He is only two months old. That's what makes him so susceptible. There's nothing you could have done to prevent this," he said. Fred shook his head.

"A father's job is to protect his family at all costs. I let my son down. I failed to protect him." Fred's head slumped forward, and he was silent, not even a sob racking his still frame.

I bent to hug him before returning to keep vigil beside the crib. It's not your fault, Fred, I wanted to reassure him, but I was spent. The little energy I had left needed to be directed towards my baby. It was in God's hands. Surely, he would be merciful and let us keep him here on Earth. I closed my eyes and continued to pray.

***

"He's gone. I'm very sorry." Doctor Sinclair spoke softly as he turned away from the crib to face me. The room had long grown dark, but I could make out the shape of him as he approached me. I stared straight ahead, not wanting to believe what I had heard.

"No, surely there's something…" I tried to stand, but I was too weak. My limbs felt leaden and there was a tightness in my chest. "Please…" I begged before dissolving into tears. Anne pulled me into her arms and I sobbed into her shoulder as I felt my entire world being ripped apart. Nothing made any sense. *My beautiful boy was gone.* I don't know how long I sat like that, Anne anchoring me and holding me close. Finally, I drew in a great shuddering breath. "Fred?" Anne nodded in his direction and I saw him just a few feet away. He sat slumped forward, staring down at his hands. "Fred," I said again, and he looked at me. His eyes were dull and his face was slack.

"I'm sorry, Mary." He spoke in a dull monotone, his voice barely above a whisper. "I'm so very sorry." With Anne's help, I stood and stumbled towards him. I collapsed against him and we held each other as the first streaks of dawn appeared in the sky.

Chapter 9

Our loud and boisterous household had grown silent since we lost baby John. Despite an unaccustomed level of freedom with only Miss C. to supervise them, Charley and Charlotte had been withdrawn and refused all offers to visit the park or play with the Vaux children. Since hearing of their baby brother's death, they had taken to reading to themselves or to Owen. Not truly able to comprehend his infant brother had died and would no longer be part of the family, Owen asked repeatedly where John was and upon being told he was gone, would shake his head and refuse to listen. It wasn't until Charley told him he was once again the baby of the family that he seemed to understand, and then he, too, grew silent.

I was inconsolable. Grief and excruciating headaches had kept me confined to my bed for the past week. Refusing the additional morphine Dr. Sinclair offered me during his daily visits to check on Fred, I lay in bed for hours at a time, staring up at the ceiling. Although I craved the mindless stupor that the drug would provide, I clung to the idea I somehow deserved the anguish I was suffering. I fought the urge to console Fred, who had also suffered this terrible loss and was doing his best to recover from his own injuries. But despite the doctor's assurance the accident hadn't caused my baby's death, I was racked with guilt and, in my heart, felt that either Fred or I was responsible for all of this. I should have stayed home that day. What had I been I thinking? *My poor baby.*

Occasionally Anne would sit by my bedside and, although her attempts at conversation were unsuccessful, she was persistent in reminding me I had a husband and three children who needed me.

"I think Charley has grown an inch or more this summer," Anne said one morning. "He is likely to be taller than you by Christmas if this keeps up, my friend." She always enjoyed teasing me about my tiny stature. "And Charlotte is quite the little mother to Owen and my Julia. She has such a gentle way about her." When I failed to respond, she hurried on. "And of course, Fred is back at work. Now that's wonderful news, isn't it?" I remained silent, still staring unblinking at the ceiling. "Well, yes, of course it is. Who would have thought just a month ago Fred could get around as well as he is? Calvert asked for volunteers to carry Fred to the office, and now they do it every day. I can't remember their names, two Irish lads. Big, strapping fellows they are. They show up each day and after I fortify them with strong coffee and biscuits, they link arms and scoop up Fred as if he was just a child and off they go. Apparently, they continue all day, with Fred instructing them where to take him. And then they bring him home and I give them a bite of supper and off they go again."

Suddenly a look of understanding came over Anne, and she snapped her fingers. "It's Will. Will and um, Jack. Yes, of course. Will and Jack. Jack told me his given name is John, but everyone calls him Jack, because John is…" Realizing I had turned and was now staring at her, Anne stumbled over her words. "John is… his father's name," she said. "So, they call him Jack." My eyes filled with tears at the sound of the name. First my husband and now my infant son. I reached for Anne and clasped her hands in mine. Hearing his name spoken, the sobs I had been holding back let loose. I cried against her shoulder until only dry, racking hiccoughs remained. Finally, I pulled away and wiped my eyes with a handkerchief left on the nightstand. I started to climb out of bed, steadying myself as I stood for the first time in days.

"Thank you, my friend, for your many kindnesses these last days. I could never have gotten through all of this without you." Anne demurred, but I continued. "I must see my children and spend time with my husband when he returns home from work. I have lost a child, it's true, but my husband has lost his only natural child," I said. "My family needs me now," I said as we left the bedroom. My grief would take time to lessen and would never disappear, but I could not allow my loss to take me away from my family. *You are made of sterner stuff.* That is what I would tell my children. I would be there for them and together, we would find our way out of the darkness.

Chapter 10

Spring 1861

"Today is the day," Fred said. "Today I will deliver my letter of resignation to that self-important bean counter I have had the misfortune to report to these past years." My heart raced as I pressed my hands to my swollen abdomen, trying to slow my breathing. *Oh, no Fred. Not now!* I had hoped with the news I was once again pregnant, Fred's obsession with quitting his job had been put on hold. It had been weeks since I heard him refer to the letter he had started writing last winter. I knew better than anyone just how dreadful Fred's job had gotten over the past year, but worried he was acting irrationally. Though not the amount he deserved for all the effort he put into the job and the headaches it produced, his salary was generous, allowing us to live comfortably. And with another mouth to feed soon, a steady source of income was more critical than ever. I looked at Fred, who appeared to be waiting for my response.

"W-well," I said. "If you think it best..." Fred crossed the room to sit next to me at the kitchen table, waving a stack of papers. I recognized those papers well. Earlier in the year, Fred had asked me to assist him in writing the letter to ensure it delivered the message he wanted to convey. He looked perplexed as he reached for my hands to pull me closer to him.

"Dear Mary, if not now, then when? I have gone to the Park Commission on countless occasions to tell them the cause of all the delays we've been experiencing. I can't seem to get it through their heads just how irresponsible that dunderhead Green has been and how truly ineffectual he is in the job. I have begged them to allow me to report directly to them, by-passing that oaf. I have to run everything by him and by the time he makes a decision, weeks have passed, and we have missed opportunities. I'm not sure what else there is to do."

"It's all right, Fred. Everything will work out." I realized my words sounded hollow, but I had tried to help when he started writing the letter, alternately agreeing with him and playing devil's advocate, trying to get him to look at the big picture. *Why today?* He hadn't complained about Green since I had told him we were expecting another child two months ago. But I had known things were not going well for him, even without him saying a word. He was sleeping only a couple of hours each night and his diet consisted of black coffee and a few hurried bites of supper. His tweed jacket hung on his too-thin frame. I shook my head sadly.

"I know you love the park, Fred," I said. He nodded and pointed to the first paragraph on the top page.

"Of course, I do. It's right here. I wrote, '*I love the park which will most surely last long after I'm gone.*'" Fred stopped and, placing the page on the table in front of him, drew out a handkerchief and wiped his face. He grinned. "It's his birthday. Green? It's his birthday, so why not give the man what he wants most in the world? To get rid of me. Right there on the last page, I said if things did not improve, I would take my talents and energy to Washington and help with the war effort." He let out a chuckle and slapped his hand on the table. "Be careful what you wish for, Andrew Green," he said. He stood, and stuffing the papers in his coat pocket, made to leave for work.

"Wish me luck," he called out as he hurried towards the door, blowing a hasty kiss as he left.

"Good luck," I said and with a sinking feeling in my stomach, pushed my chair back and stood slowly. It was time to go over the shopping list with the cook and plan meals for the week ahead. Perhaps tonight's dinner should be a special one. If Fred were to make good on his threat to join the war effort in Washington, this might be our last evening together for quite a while.

***

Fred came home early that evening, long before supper was ready. From his smile, it was obvious things had gone well, but he held up his hand to stop me when I asked how the letter had been received.

"All in due time, my love," he said with a kiss on my cheek. He headed down the hall to spend some time with the children, while I rearranged place settings and inspected the water glasses for spots. The waiting was driving me crazy. It must be good news. Maybe the Park Commission had agreed to fire Green. Or perhaps it was bad news and Fred didn't want to tell me. Could he have resigned on the spot? A short while later, I helped Sarah bring platters of meat and roasted vegetables to the table. I rang the sterling silver dinner bell and watched as Fred came in, Charlotte clinging to his back like a monkey and Charley and Owen attached to his legs. What a sight!

"Mary, I'm unable to locate the children. I've searched everywhere, but I fear they are lost, possibly forever," Fred announced sadly. "Whatever will we do?" Charlotte giggled, and both boys jumped up and down in front of their father.

"We're here, Papa," Owen called out. Fred continued to look forlorn and pretended to be searching for them.

"If only our missing children were to turn up at the table, I would know all was well," Fred said with a wink. All three children scurried to find their seats and seconds later, Fred announced, "They've returned. It's a blessed miracle I say." I shook my head at their foolishness and took my seat. Once Fred had seated himself at the head of the table, I passed around the food, encouraging everyone to help themselves. Charlotte assisted Owen by cutting up his meat into bite-sized pieces and slathering butter on a biscuit for him. After it was clear the children had eaten an appropriate amount, we excused them and they rushed off to play in the hour before their bedtime. Fred, who had been intent on helping himself to another serving of roasted turnips and carrots, smiled as he watched them.

"Lovely family we have here, Mrs. Olmsted." I beamed at him in response.

"Yes, Mr. Olmsted. Now are you going to keep your poor wife in suspense much longer? When you handed Mr. Green that letter, what was his reaction? Did he contact anyone at the Commission?"

"Well, of course, he tried to hide his surprise, but I saw right through him, that old phony. He turned as red as a beet when he read the part where I said how much I loved the park. I thought he would have a fit. This entire ordeal was almost worth all it has taken from me, just to see Green's reaction. He huffed and puffed and finally spoke up. 'Well, Olmsted, this comes as a shock. All of us on the Board of Commissioners assumed you have been well satisfied these last months on the job,' he informed me with a straight face. I reminded him I had been years on the job, not months, and that those years felt more like decades. Getting questioned at every turn. Being forced to beg and account for every penny. Why that—" I was growing impatient, having listened to a litany of complaints about Fred's job as Superintendent and Architect-in-Chief of the Central Park project for too long. I leaned forward and glared at him.

"I've heard quite enough about that most obnoxious man. What happened when he delivered the news to the Board of Commissioners?" Fred shrugged his shoulders and adopted a casual tone.

"Well, it seems the overwhelming opinion that I have been doing an admirable job has never made its way to me. Green may have attempted to strip me of any actual power, but the Board thinks I have made… wait, let me read you their exact words." Fred smoothed out the letter he had been holding. "They put this in writing so there could be no question about their offer. Let me see. Oh yes, 'made demonstrable progress' and that I am 'a man of honor and honesty,' and finally how I 'can't be sacrificed for long even for the greater good.'"

Did this mean he'll stay here? He won't be getting involved with that dreadful war? I felt a glimmer of hope that was dashed as soon as Fred continued.

"They are granting me an indefinite leave of absence to meet with officials in the capital over the next few weeks to determine how I can assist in the war effort. I believe I can contribute significantly to that new organization that's forming."

"Which organization? The housing one?" I asked, barely masking my frustration.

"Mary, we discussed this last week, I'm sure of it. It's the group charged with improving the morale and living conditions for our brave men in uniform."

"For goodness' sake, Fred. I can't keep track of all of your whims. I remember you mentioning something—"

"How else would you see me contributing to the war effort, then?" Saddled with one leg nearly two inches shorter than the other because of last year's buggy accident, Fred was realistic enough to know his contribution to the war effort would require the use of his mental faculties and leadership skills instead of his physical strength.

"Of course, I understand. If you feel so strongly about this…" Fred hugged me close and I vowed to support him. All around us, families were making sacrifices during these troubling times. If I had to get by for a few weeks without Fred, well, that was the price we would pay. It was reassuring the Park Commissioners recognized his efforts and, regardless of the outcome of his trip to Washington, he could return to the park in some capacity. Despite all the backstabbing and delays, I knew he wanted to see the project through to the end.

"Perhaps you will meet our new president during your visit," I said with a hint of a smile.

"Well, yes," Fred said with a twinkle in his eyes. "I will pass on your best wishes to him and Mrs. Lincoln." He stood and walked over to where I sat. Putting a finger to his lips, he led me down the hall and we poked our heads into the room where the children were playing. Charley was reading to his siblings from a well-worn copy of *The Merry Adventures of Robin Hood,* and all three appeared enthralled with the story, despite having read it dozens of times. "It would seem our children can survive without us for a bit. Now that we've got everything settled, perhaps this is the time for us to say a proper goodbye… in private."

"Why, Mr. Olmsted," I whispered in his ear. "That sounds like a wonderful idea., it's the very least I can do for a dedicated soldier before he heads off to serve his country." Together, we tiptoed up the stairs, and enjoyed a lovely respite where there was no war and no long separation looming. It was just Fred and me. Together.

Chapter 11

I sighed and rubbed my temples. I refolded the letter that had arrived earlier that day from Fred, but decided to read it one more time.

My dear wife at home,

Washington, D.C., is a dreary place. Now that the cherry blossoms have faded, all is gray and bleak as far as the eye can see. I am discouraged by the lack of support I experience from elected officials. Most are happy to pass the buck and tie up even the smallest of expenditures in miles of red tape. It almost makes me wish for an honest bureaucrat like my old friend Mr. Green. At least he does not even pretend to be supportive. But, as the newly appointed Executive Director of the Sanitary Commission, all I can do is to alleviate suffering and bring some small comfort to our soldiers. I believe it is my duty, although I recognize how difficult this sacrifice is for you. I look forward to being with you as we welcome our newest child into the world.

My stay at the Willard Hotel has been pleasant enough, but sleep continues to be elusive when you are not by my side. I hope the funds you received last week were helpful in calming your fears about our household finances. When I return to New York, I will sit down with Mr. Green and complete payment arrangements for my leave of absence and work out a date to return to the park on a full-time basis. I'm certain the news will be of great satisfaction to Calvert Vaux and will make your lovely blue eyes sparkle with delight. I am counting the days, my loving wife.

Daily inspections of the living conditions at the camps continue. I regret things have improved only slightly. Most soldiers remain poorly clothed and packed five-deep in stuffy little tents. I hate to offend your sensibilities, but I confess the sight of the latrines, horrible thirty-foot trenches, is appalling. The stench is sickening and there have been frequent outbreaks of dysentery. I remain committed to improving the lives of our troops, but progress is slow. I cannot fight alongside of them, but I can lessen the challenges they face.

I head out at dawn after a breakfast of strong coffee and a plate of pickles. By the time I am on site, a fresh crew of women volunteers is arriving to help the wounded soldiers. After I am satisfied that they are receiving care, I continue my day in a series of meetings with directors, doctors and nurses at various field hospitals and hospital ships. Yesterday, I spoke with several ambulance drivers, and rode with one of them on his route. I am sorry to say the young man they charged us with transporting did not survive the trip to the hospital, but at least they afforded him the dignity of a proper burial. I pray Charley and Owen will not have to fight in a war such as this and that Charlotte is never to experience the heartbreak of losing a husband or a son to the calamities of war.

To compensate for, and perhaps ease, the stress of the sickness, injury and death that surrounds us each day, my colleagues gather most nights and drown their sorrows with port or whiskey. Though a light drinker myself, I understand the occasional excesses of others. The bar and the public rooms at the hotel are swarming with politicians and lobbyists, dense with tobacco smoke and vibrant with clamorous voices. I have made the pleasant acquaintance of a nurse, a Miss Katherine Wormeley. She is of British lineage and most agreeable. We often take a stroll late in the evening and discuss literature. She is a breath of fresh air from all the swaggering men I am surrounded with. You would be happy to make her acquaintance someday. After a busy day and my evening constitutional, it is a relief to return to my solitary lodgings with its peace and quiet.

It has grown late and I pray writing this letter and thinking of you and the children have calmed me sufficiently to allow for a modicum of sleep. Tomorrow, I will resume my patriotic duties, but for now, I will sign off and remain,

Your loving husband,
Fred

I refolded the thin pieces of parchment, and returned them to their envelope, which I carefully placed in the pocket of my robe. Fred had been gone for five weeks. When would he be returning home? And just who was this Miss Wormeley to Fred? I missed him so. My pregnancy was progressing, but it exhausted me much of the time. I had taken comfort in the assumption that he would return soon, but this letter had mentioned no specific plans.

The children had stopped peppering me with questions about their father, having grown accustomed to his absence. Tomorrow, I would read them an edited version of the letter, omitting any references to injury and death. My next step would be to compose a very clear request to my husband to return home where he belonged. I would include notes and drawings from the children as a reminder of all he was missing. Certain that my plan would put an end to all of this foolishness, I finally fell into a sound sleep.

Chapter 12

Fall 1861

Summer had finally ended, and with the welcome relief of cool, crisp autumn days, Fred returned after five months in Washington. I was thankful as running a household with three active children, even with the help of a governess, was proving more than I could handle in my current stage of pregnancy. I desperately needed sleep these last several weeks, while the cooler weather also stimulated my appetite. I joked to Fred that if anyone was looking for me, I would most likely be at the kitchen table or in bed.

With my due date just two weeks away, thoughts on the new baby's name were on all of our minds and everyone had an opinion. If a girl, I was in favor of a traditional name like Elizabeth, which Fred vetoed, fearing the child would be called Lizzie. Charley and Owen were lobbying for the names Todd or Abraham, after the Lincolns. Charlotte preferred Emily and wouldn't even consider her new sibling might be anything *but* a sister. Fred was the most vocal on the subject and while he appeared convinced the child would be a boy, he favored the name Content.

"Content is a fine name for a girl. My grandmother Content Pitkin Olmsted bore the name proudly. But you," he chastised me with a dramatic flourish, "don't seem to understand the importance of family lines when naming a child. Perhaps it would please you if we named the poor child Nelly or Sadie or some such common-sounding moniker."

I smiled, helping myself to another portion of apple cobbler. As long as the baby was healthy, I would be happy. And I got my wish.

Early one morning in late November, I went into labor and several hours later, gave birth to a daughter. The latest member of the household was healthy and possessed all the requisite fingers and toes, along with a powerful set of lungs she exercised frequently. She had a fine halo of ginger-colored hair and a nose Owen compared to a button. I was euphoric. That evening, Fred broached the subject of the baby's name.

"Mary, about the name," he said just as Charley, Charlotte and Owen rushed into the room.

"Papa, did you see? I have a sister at last," Charlotte shrieked as she climbed onto the bed and gazed at the baby. Charley and Owen appeared less than thrilled, but both smiled at her obvious delight.

"Papa," Charley said as he dug into his pocket. "Please tell us how you met the president won't you?" He pulled out a letter Fred had written before returning home. "Tell us more," Charley said. Fred removed a thin piece of parchment from the envelope and handed it to him.

"Why don't you read it to us, my boy?" he asked, and nine-year-old Charley, who had been reading at a level well beyond his age for years, eagerly grabbed the letter. He read the carefully written text.

Dear Charley,

I hope you are fulfilling your duties as the man of the house while I am serving our country. Your mother and I count on you to set an example for your siblings. It has been an experience to be living and working in our nation's capital these many months, but I am counting the days until I can return to my family in New York.

I had a very memorable experience that I will share with you. I went to the White House and saw our President Lincoln. He is very tall and states plainly what he is thinking. He is rather serious, but when he laughs, he laughs very loud.

Charley put the letter down and looked up at his father. "Really, Papa? Our President Lincoln laughed, and you heard him?" When Fred nodded, the boy continued. "But how does he sound? Like this?" He drew in his breath and emitted a deep chuckle. "Is that what he sounds like?" I laughed aloud at his silliness. Before Fred could respond, Owen chimed in.

"I think he must sound like this, Papa," and he chortled. Regaining his breath, Charley cut him off.

"Of course not, Owen. Our president would have laughed more like this," and he struggled to guffaw. I winked at Fred, who shook his head at their foolish antics.

My merry men, I thought with a smile. When I looked down, I realized Charlotte and the baby were huddled together and sleeping soundly. I was growing drowsy and struggled to stay awake as I watched Fred put a finger to his lips. He motioned for the boys to follow him out of the room, and I closed my eyes as they were leaving.

"Come boys. Let's let your mother and the girls get some rest. We'll go see what we can pull together for our supper. And you can continue practicing your presidential laughs," he said as they headed for the kitchen.

It was early the next day when we decided on a name for our daughter. We would call her Marion, after the maiden who stole the affections of the legendary outlaw Robin Hood. It was perfect for the little girl who had already captured our hearts.

Chapter 13

Winter 1861- 1862

I finished going over dinner menus for the week with our cook and was on my way upstairs when I overheard Fred and Charlotte in the dining room. His usual booming baritone was soft as he spoke to our seven-year-old daughter, whose giggles and high breathy voice responded eagerly as he quizzed her on her spelling. Outside the wind was howling, and I pulled my shawl around my shoulders and stood listening, out of sight in the hallway. I loved how Fred always made time for the children, despite the demands of his job.

"Good job, pet. Now, can you spell horse?" Fred asked.

"Oh Papa, that's easy. H-o-r-s-e. Horse. Ask me something harder, won't you?" Charlotte asked.

"Hmmmm. How about elephant?"

"E-l-e-p-h-a-n-t. Elephant. Easy peasy. Even Owen can spell that. Something harder."

I peeked in the room to see Fred scratching his head as if in deep thought. He looked up and caught me watching, but I put a finger to my lips to stop him from revealing my presence. He turned his attention back to Charlotte.

"Can you spell soldier?" Her sweet face scrunched up in concentration as she sounded out the word.

"Soldier? Ummm, it's s-o-l. Wait. S-o-l-j-u-r. Soljur!" she cried. Fred seemed about to correct her when she hurried on. "Like the soljurs you helped in Washington, right Papa? Mama said you wrote letters for them, but that's silly. Soljurs are big men. Surely they can write their own letters."

"Well, it's more complicated than that, my pet. Some soldiers were sick, and they wanted to write to their loved ones back home. But they were too weak to hold pen to paper, so we helped them. I started doing it myself, but it got to be too much for just one man, so I instructed the nurses and other volunteers." He stopped and sighed. Charlotte smiled at him.

"You taught them to write, Papa?" she asked. Fred chuckled at her.

"Oh, my silly girl. They already knew how to write. I taught them to listen." Charlotte jumped up from her seat and crawled into Fred's arms.

"Read," she said, and pressed her tattered copy of *A Wonder-Book for Girls and Boys* into his hands.

"Your wish is my command, Lady Charlotte," Fred assured her and began the story of Pandora opening the box filled with all the world's troubles.

Turning to leave, I felt a lump in my throat as I recalled Fred's last letter, which had arrived just two days before his return last week. I was so touched with his efforts to aid the families of the dying soldiers.

I can't describe to you just how satisfying it is. Much of what I do is administrative; drawing up rules on the chain of command, directing the time and content of the meals our enlisted men consume, how to process patients… but this one task, training our nurses and volunteers to record a dying soldier's last words, is beyond description. Our ability to preserve for a mother or a wife the priceless whispers of the dying is gratifying beyond measure.

The thought of him documenting a young man's last words had brought me to tears when I read the letter. Now I climbed the stairs to our bedroom and kneeled down to pray. *Please God, if Charley or Owen are wounded fighting for our country, please have someone kind enough to hold their hand.* The only thing worse than receiving that kind of letter would be not receiving one at all.

Chapter 14

Spring 1862

I was enjoying a second cup of coffee one morning in early April, turning the pages of today's edition of the *New York Times*. Fred had returned to Washington a month ago, and the children were outside with Miss C. I basked in the quiet, until I heard a sudden pounding on the door. *What on earth?* I rushed to see who it was. I was not expecting anyone and besides, none of our friends would make such a fuss, especially in the presence of a perfectly good doorbell. Through the glass, I could see three men in police uniforms and I yanked the door open before they could begin knocking again.

"Good morning," I said. "How can I help you?" The tallest of the men pushed forward and approached me, reading from a document of some sort.

"Mrs. Olmsted? Mrs. Frederick Olmsted?" he asked.

"Yes, that's me. What is all of this about?" I was a bit cross. "Are you seeking a donation for a benevolence fund or something?" The two officers standing back exchanged grins, but the one in charge shook his head.

"No, nothing like that. We're sorry to trouble you, ma'am. We've been dispatched from the Park Commission. We have orders to evacuate these premises by the end of this month."

"What on earth? That's less than two weeks and this is our home. There must be a mistake."

"No, ma'am. I'm sorry, but our instructions are clear. This building, Mount St. Vincent, is to be turned into the Central Park Hospital for the Union wounded. I'm afraid you are going to have to leave. This is an official notice of eviction," he said, waving the document in front of me.

"Eviction? But I have children to care for. And what of the Vaux family? They also reside here." The police officer looked at the letter again.

"Yes, I can see that. Olmsted and Vaux. Both families." I sagged against the doorway.

"But I don't understand. Why was no advance notice given? How can you expect two families to just up and leave with such limited notice?" The officer frowned and looked once more at the letter.

"Several notices were sent to Mr. Olmsted. The dates are right here." I was shaking my head, annoyance having given way to fear.

"But that's ridiculous. My husband travels frequently. He's in our nation's capital on very important business." The officer shrugged.

"Perhaps the notices were forwarded there? I don't know ma'am. But our orders are very specific. I have to ask all of you to leave."

Just then, Cal and Anne Vaux came around the corner. Their leisurely stroll ended when they saw me talking to men in uniform.

"What is the meaning of this? Who is leaving?" Cal Vaux asked.

***

An hour later, Anne and I sat in the sunroom, untouched cups of tea in front of us. We had been silent for several minutes, and I was about to suggest a glass of port when Anne spoke up.

"I don't understand. This has been our home for two-and-a-half years. Where are we to go?" She looked dumbfounded, and I shook my head.

"I honestly don't know. I'm still shaking. Those rude men—"

"They were just doing their job, Mary. But at least Cal negotiated a temporary reprieve."

"Yes, one month is better than being tossed into the street in two weeks," I said. "But honestly? How will we go about finding a new home?" *And one that we could afford?* Anne's tone was curt, bordering on angry.

"I don't understand how Fred could have missed all those notices. He should have alerted us to all of this." I bristled at the notion Fred was responsible. *I* could be upset with him, but he was *my* husband and I would defend him with all my might.

"Instead of assigning blame, we should focus on the problem at hand," I said. Anne nodded in agreement.

"You're right. Cal is right now pounding the pavement in search of lodgings. I wish you would let him look for something for you." I had told Cal not to bother; it was Fred's responsibility, after all. This wasn't a task to delegate to a business partner or even a friend.

"I'm certain it's temporary. Fred will return and straighten all of this out," I said, feeling the hollowness of the words as soon as I spoke them. *Damn you, Fred. Just for once can't you please put your family first?* I had defended him to Anne but, in my heart, I was furious.

***

Over the next couple of weeks, I had to scramble to find affordable lodgings. Money was tight as delays in processing Fred's paychecks were compounded by the fact that funds had to be transferred to New York before I could access them. The ever-responsible Calvert Vaux had a ready source of income and several influential contacts and secured lodging for his family in a rented brownstone nearby. He offered me the top floor of their building, but I had decided to strike out on my own, tired of sharing my home with another family. I considered moving the children to Tosomock, the Olmsted family farm on Staten Island, but learned the current lodgers had a lease and no plans to vacate the premises.

Next I had thought of seeking refuge at the home of my father-in-law, who lived in Hartford with his wife and their children. But that, too, meant living under the same roof with another family, so I settled on a short- term lease for a cramped rental on the Upper East Side, a few blocks from where I had lived with the children before marrying Fred. And here we were back again, our lives once more in a state of flux.

Too proud to ask for help, I struggled to create a home for the children. My last two letters to Fred had gone unanswered and, even in my own mind, I could no longer defend his actions. He had surely abandoned us. I put on a brave face for the children, but at night, alone in my bed in a strange house, I gave myself over to despair and sobbed into my pillow. I repeated my mantra; *I am made of sterner stuff.* Sometimes, though, it wasn't a question of whether I was strong enough. It was a question of whether *I* was enough.

Finally, a letter arrived, which I read and re-read with growing concern. Apparently, Fred had written several times and not received a response. I did not recognize the return address, but he wrote there had been a fire in the boardinghouse where he had been staying and he had moved twice. I saw he had used our old address. How was it possible he did not know we had moved?

I responded to his letter at once, in part to allay his concerns and to communicate my wish to reunite our family. I was still angry and while it wasn't truly Fred's fault, this wouldn't have occurred had he been home where he belonged.

Dear Husband,

It has been some time since we have seen you in person. We were forced from our home and had to secure temporary lodgings. Given our precarious financial situation, I had no choice but to uproot our children from their once happy home and separate them from their friends. The Vauxes have settled happily, from what I hear, into a large spacious flat with plenty of light. If only that were the case for your children. There is no "green beating heart" anywhere near our mean lodgings, of that I can assure you. I pray daily we will not be accosted on the street or murdered in our beds by any of the miscreants and ruffians we now call neighbors.

My only consolation is the thought you will return to post-haste or you will send for your family so we can be reunited in our nation's capital. If the latter, Charley (who has informed me he now wants to answer to his "real" name, John) has requested we schedule a visit with President Lincoln. He is certain he and young Master Tad Lincoln would be the greatest of chums.

I must end this letter now as I am out of parchment and my budget will not allow the purchase of additional writing supplies for some time. Please send word as to your plans to return.

I remain,

Your loving wife and the mother of four young children who need their father,

Mary

Chapter 15

Fall 1862

Fred returned home shortly after receiving my letter, and while I had not totally forgiven him for abandoning us, it thrilled me to see him. He appeared shocked that I had not exaggerated our dismal living arrangements and promised to remedy the situation. He spent hours each day with the children, taking long walks and reading to them. We enjoyed a weekend on the beach in Long Island and returned sunburned and in good spirits.

After a couple of weeks in New York, Fred returned to the nation's capital with one goal in mind: to find a home for us for the duration of his time in Washington. Within a week, he located lodgings at an affordable price. He signed a six-month lease, believing the war would end soon.

Miss Curtayne, the children, and I quickly relocated to Washington. To my dismay, the house was only about the size of the cramped one we had just left, and it upset me to note Fred's habits of working non-stop had returned. He had gotten into the habit of sleeping in his office, and his work schedule became a constant source of disagreement. He swore he would cut back his hours, but I had worried he was using work to avoid his family. Did he regret marrying me and taking on the responsibility of a wife and children? Had his time away from us been more pleasure than pain? Could he have met another woman?

Early one morning, he opened the front door and let himself into the small sitting room, almost tripping over me where I sat on the floor in the middle of the room. He regained his balance and stared at me as if I were an apparition of some sort.

"Mary. What is it? Is it the children?" My voice was low and my demeanor calm as I looked up at him in the semi-darkness.

"Good morning. I wanted to make certain in the off chance you were to stop by, you could not miss seeing me. To what do we owe the honor of your company this fine day?" Fred winced, knowing what was coming.

"I'm sorry. I couldn't get away, and then I thought I would try to catch a few winks on the sofa in my office. I woke early and realized I needed a fresh shirt—" At my glare, he hurried on. "And to see you, of course. To see all of you."

I drew myself up to my full height of just less than five feet and raised my gaze from his Adam's apple to his tired blue eyes. Glaring at him, I spoke in measured tones.

"Who is she?" Fred appeared confused.

"She? I'm not sure I… she?"

"She! The woman! Surely there is a woman involved. Perhaps you met someone new." I hadn't really thought Fred had developed feelings for someone else, but anger at being left alone and the exhaustion of moving twice in less than three months got the best of me. The idea took hold. "What about that Miss Wormeley you were so keen on? Katherine, yes? I admire your patriotism, but if you think for one moment that I believe there is *not* another woman keeping you from us? You don't think me that big of a fool, now do you?"

Fred grew flustered as he tried to reassure me.

"Never would I ever entertain such thoughts. My God woman, that is preposterous. Katherine Wormeley is a friend from my early days at the Sanitary Commission. I would no sooner… You are the only one for me. Why, ever since I met you, I—" I cut him off, growing furious.

"Just the thing for a rainy day, hmm? Isn't that what you thought? I'm not the type to fall in love with though, am I? And heaven knows we've been in a bit of a drought of late."

"Mary, I do not understand what you're talking about. Please—" I stamped my foot.

"The day I met you at my grandfather's home. I heard you describing me to a friend of yours. I was 'someone to talk with.' 'To while away a rainy afternoon with.' But not someone to love." Hot, angry tears rolled down my face. Fred nodded.

"Yes, now I remember. I was talking to Knightsbridge or Brace. I'm not sure which. I remember saying those words. I suppose I meant them at the time. I knew very little of love in those days. I was a fool. But since you agreed to marry me and build a life together, you're the only one for me. I married you out of a sense of duty, that is true. But you've thoroughly captivated me, and I've fallen hopelessly in love with you. Ours is a genuine marriage in every sense of the word. Please believe me." Fred hung his head and rubbed at his temples. He whispered, almost as if to himself. "I was afraid of bringing you here. I thought this might happen. That the demands of work would get the best of me. I hate the thought of you sitting here alone. At least in New York, you..."

As I watched him, I grew convinced that what he was saying was true, and suddenly my worries seemed ludicrous. What had I been thinking? Of course, he's not involved with another woman. The very idea was preposterous. I collapsed against him in relief.

"We're together as a family should be, Fred. I know you would never get involved with someone else."

"My love, I swear to you. I'll try harder. Please be patient with me," he begged. I smiled to reassure him.

"I will always wait for you, but I ask you to think about what you are missing. I sit here day after day, playing endless card games with the children, darning your socks and cooking meals you are never present for. This must stop at once. Your children want their father and I want my husband. Fully present, at the supper table and at night, in my bed. Your patriotism is commendable, but your first duty is to your family."

Fred nodded, seeming grateful at the level of my understanding, but exhausted from hard work and too little sleep. He held out his arm, and I took it gladly, my own exhaustion hitting as the adrenaline from our argument abandoned me. "You are right, as always. I promise to put our family first. For now, perhaps after a quick nap, we can have a late breakfast with the children. Sounds good, doesn't it?"

Relieved to hear Fred's declaration of love, I knew I had married an honorable man who loved me. I allowed him to lead me towards the stairs.

"Yes, my dear, very good." If I had any lingering doubts that Fred fancied anyone else, we quickly put them to rest. My husband had returned home and the only thing he seemed to desire was me!

Chapter 16

Winter 1862-1863

Despite my concern I would miss our friends and worries it would be a dull holiday season, I enjoyed our first Christmas in Washington. True to his word, Fred spent most evenings and every weekend with us. The more we explored the city, the more I found to like. I was pleased it was not as cold as it could be in New York, and, despite John and Owen's grumblings that there was not enough snow for a proper snowball fight, we spent many happy hours outdoors and even more in front of a roaring fire drinking hot chocolate. Several neighbors extended invitations for cozy suppers and parties, which it pleased us to attend. Both Fred and I enjoyed the smaller, more intimate gatherings where the conversations following the meal were the most enjoyable part of the evening. One night, a few days before Christmas, we were strolling home from such an evening at the Hills who lived a couple of blocks from us. I had forgotten my gloves and was glad when Fred took my hand in his as we crossed the street.

"You're so much warmer than I am," I complained good-naturedly. "I'm always so cold." Fred regarded me fondly.

"My little turtle. They're also cold-blooded." I snorted at that.

"How romantic! Comparing your wife to a turtle." Fred chuckled.

"Well, if you are seeking compliments, I'm happy to report the trifle you serve is far superior to Susan Hill's. I think her hand was a bit too generous with pouring the rum."

"I thought so too," I said, then grew serious, remembering a conversation that had begun over dinner. "But Fred, on a more serious note. What did you think of the notion President Lincoln will be soon putting an end to slavery?"

"Oh, I am certain of it. Lincoln has always been against slavery, but honestly? What sane, thinking man would not be?"

"Do you think he will abolish it altogether?" I asked.

"I do. Word has it he'll be making an official announcement soon."

"Perhaps before Christmas," I said with a smile. "What a wonderful gift that would be."

***

On January 1, 1863, invoking presidential wartime powers, Abraham Lincoln decreed all persons held in bondage within the Confederacy were free. Fred read the news of the Emancipation Proclamation to the children that morning at breakfast.

"This is a great day for our nation," Fred said. "And for the future of all citizens."

"There are four million slaves living in the United States," nine-year-old John reported to his siblings. It confused Charlotte.

"But what will they do now they are free?" she asked. "Will they get jobs and buy homes? And will their children come to school with us? They would like our school, I think."

"Is Sarah a slave?" asked five-year-old Owen. The question about our Irish cook shocked me.

"Of course not, Owen. Why on earth would you even imagine that? Sarah is like a member of the family."

"But she's not," John said. "Her last name isn't Olmsted, and we pay her to live with us."

"And cook our food," Owen said. John gave his brother a withering stare.

"Of course to cook our food, dummy. That's her job."

"Is it her job to bandage our knees when we fall down?" asked Charlotte.

"Or read to us sometimes," said Owen. Fred shook his head.

"We pay generous wages to Sarah to keep us well-fed. The first aid and the reading? That's how she shows us she cares."

"But don't slaves cook, too?" asked Owen.

"Sarah is not a slave," Fred told them with a note of finality. "She is here because she wants to be with us. Slaves are not paid and are not free to come and go as they please. That's why our president abolished slavery. It's wrong and we can't let it continue."

Everyone nodded in agreement, and I enlisted Charlotte's help to clear the table. It was Sarah's day off and I had served biscuits made with sorghum and drizzled with honey.

"I'll leave the dishes to soak," I said, realizing the honey had already hardened on the plates. "Let's get bundled up. We need to hurry if we are to arrive at the Smithsonian when it opens!"

The dinosaur exhibit at the Smithsonian Institution Building was the latest in a series of showings over the past year, and we were eager to view it. While the announcement of plans to visit to the museum often resulted in loud groans of protest from the boys, they were very excited to learn more about the prehistoric beasts that roamed the earth millions of years ago. And so were we!

Chapter 17

Spring 1863

With no signs of abating, the Civil War raged on. In his official capacity as General Secretary of the United States Sanitary Commission, Fred was packing his bags for a trip with stops in Cleveland, Cincinnati, Chicago, St. Louis and Louisville. It disappointed me that his work was taking precedence over our family. Furious at the thought of another lengthy separation, I wasted no time telling him how I felt.

"Why is it always you?" I asked. "Why must you make the sacrifice, leaving your family to pay the price?"

"It is a day for heroes and we must be heroes along with the rest," Fred said. I threw up my hands in frustration.

"But why now? What is so important it can't wait?" Fred frowned and shook his head.

"I've tried to tell you, Mary. Relationships between the Washington office and the western operations have grown strained. I plan to visit the most critical field offices and present my findings to General Ulysses S. Grant."

"Oh, well then. If it's Mr. Grant you'll be seeing, be certain to schedule your meeting with him early in the day to find him upright and sober."

Fred assured me he would heed my advice and having said all I needed to, I left the room. I did not offer to help him pack, as was my normal practice. Less than an hour later, he let himself out of the empty house and took off on foot for the train station. Still angry, I had taken all four children for a walk without giving him an opportunity to say goodbye. I realized I was acting childishly, but I can be very stubborn.

I peered around the corner and watched his stooped figure limp towards the train station. I wanted to call out to him, to blow him a kiss, but I resisted the urge. Charity begins at home, I reminded myself. Fred needed to learn that lesson, and soon!

***

Fred returned home several weeks later, and it was obvious things had not gone well. I tried to talk to him, but he brushed off my efforts. His insomnia had gotten worse, and he frequently complained of headaches. I tried to be patient, but worried about his mental state. Finally, I decided it was time to discuss whatever was troubling him. I returned to the sitting room after ensuring the children were settled to find Fred sitting on the sofa, a discarded copy of the *New York Times* at his feet. I sat next to him and patted his knee.

"Darling, what is it? And please don't tell me all is well. It's clearly not. You barely ate a thing, and you toss and turn all night. Please tell me what is going on?" Fred turned to face me.

"I'm sorry, Mary. Perhaps I should drag a cot into—" I cut him off in exasperation.

"Whatever it is Fred, I can assure you, it will *not* be solved by you spending even less time in our bed. Talk to me, please."

"I just don't see myself working with the Sanitary Commission much longer. I accomplished a great deal during my recent travels, but I don't know if it was enough."

"But what about your meeting with General Grant? Did that go according to plan?" *Or was he drunk as a skunk?* Fred smiled.

"Despite Grant's obvious state of inebriation—which he tried to hide by clinging tightly to a chair while we spoke—I conveyed my thoughts on what needed to unite the various factions within the organization. And I can't say I wasn't warned," he said with a twinkle in his eye.

"Then what is the problem? I don't understand."

"Knowing there is a problem and being able to repair it are two very distinct variables. The changes are, perhaps, greater than I can assist in. There is talk of changing the name of the organization to the

American Red Cross. They must make plans to prepare for the post-war efforts. This war can't go on forever," he said.

"But you began with the USSC to help with the challenges they faced."

"Yes, exactly. And I have accomplished just that. I helped streamline ordering procedures and instituted controls to improve the living conditions of our soldiers." I looked at him in amazement.

"You are far too modest. You affected tens of thousands of lives, not just for our troops but for their families. Why, it was little more than a clearinghouse for supplies when you began." I was about to list the many improvements made during his time with the USSC, but he held up his hand to stop me.

"It was a group effort and while I support the opportunities being discussed, I wonder if this is the right time to move on. The bureaucracy in an organization the size and scope being discussed is..." he groaned. "You know me. I have no tolerance for any of that. I might as well be back in New York, working on maintenance budgets and getting chewed out by endless committees and begging for every penny."

I nodded in understanding, knowing Fred was no fan of red tape and delays in decision-making. He was much better suited to being his own boss, with little or no interference from above.

"And what is the latest from Central Park?" I asked. Returning to New York would suit me just fine. Fred shook his head.

"My salary has all but dried up. But..."

"What is it? Are we returning? I'm so relieved. I've never hid from you how l dislike living here. To be going home is the best—"

"No, Mary. Not New York. Not now anyway." I swallowed hard before I responded.

"Then where? Boston? I could contact my—"

"No, Mary. Please let me finish." I frowned, feeling his sharp tone was uncalled for. We were just having a conversation. I let out a long breath and nodded.

"Please continue. I'm eager to hear what you have to say."

"Thank you. Let me begin by asking you, have you read any of Horace Greeley's writings?" I shook my head. When I could find precious time to read, I preferred women authors, like Louisa May Alcott or Jane Austen. What could this Mr. Greeley have to do with the future of my family?

"Well, I have been following him for some time. He's of the opinion the Gold Rush is more than temporary. He thinks gold mining is an intelligent long-term opportunity for this country What do you think of that?" I connected the dots. Ever since the discovered gold in California a few years earlier, the desire to take part in the lucrative Gold Rush had tempted thousands of men to travel to the West Coast.

"What are you saying? You want to travel thousands of miles from home and pan for gold? That has to be the most hare-brained scheme you've ever..." Fred threw his head back and roared.

"You can't imagine that I, with my game leg, could survive as a miner." He wiped his eyes and smiled at me.

"Then what? What is all of this talk about discovering gold? You aren't making any sense."

"Mary, they've asked me to manage Mariposa Estate. Horace Greeley says—" I was tired of this conversation and lashed out at Fred.

"You told me what Mr. Greeley has to say on the subject. I don't care. Who are *they* and what do you know about managing a gold mine?" Fred looked hurt, but tried to explain.

"*They* are the owners and investors. Apparently, my work at the park has not gone unnoticed. Based on my reputation as a shrewd administrator and a man of vision, they've offered an annual salary of $10,000 in gold. That's worth at least twenty percent more than greenbacks, with the effect of wartime inflation. And during each of my years of service, I will also receive $10,000 in company stock." I continued to stare open-mouthed at him as he continued. "They are seeking a five-year commitment. This is an excellent opportunity to put my skills and experience to good use. I'll be my own boss with little or no daily supervision from the off-site owners. And after many lean years, the generous salary and annual bonus will serve this family well."

Fred finished and watched me expectantly. My mind was racing as I tried to organize my thoughts. "I'm sure you have questions, Mary. I realize this is a big move. I am expected to be on location as soon as I can—" I cut him off, eager to talk.

"How soon can we join you?" I asked. "How does one even get to California?" I peppered his face and neck with kisses. Fred grinned in delight and hugged me. I wriggled in his arms, unable to contain myself. Fred pulled back to watch my obvious delight.

"Oh Mary, you never cease to amaze me. Let me tell you what I know. I would travel on a ship heading south along the Atlantic seaboard. Then a short train ride across the Isthmus of Panama, and finally a steamer heading north to San Francisco. The entire trip will take between three and four weeks. It's much quicker than traveling down to Venezuela."

I tried to process the exciting news. As a girl, I had longed for adventure and found it as a young bride travelling through Europe with my first husband. Now, as the mother of four, my life had become routine. I had all but forgotten when every day held exciting possibilities. The prospect of sailing ships, California and gold? And a chance to leave Washington? I let out a breath I wasn't even aware I was holding.

"It sounds wonderful, Fred. But when do we join you? Please say it will be soon."

"Depending upon our financial situation, I'll arrange for you and the children to travel the same route," he assured me. "It's much more costly, but the dangerous trek through Venezuela is to be avoided at all costs, from what I hear."

"Just please don't delay sending for us. I'll be counting the days." I was positively beaming. What an adventure this would be!

"As will I," Fred said as he hugged me. I pulled away as he was about to kiss me. In my sweetest voice, I posed one last question.

"Can we spend a few days in San Francisco before heading to Mariposa? My cousin Louisa was there last year and reports it is a delightful city. It would be a wonderful opportunity to enjoy some family time, seeing the sights and doing some shopping, don't you agree?"

Fred nodded, and I clapped my hands in delight.

California, here we come!

Chapter 18

Winter 1863-1864

Fred wrote to us nearly every day as he settled in to his new position managing the seven gold mines that comprised the 44,387-acre Mariposa Estate. He had taken up lodging at the Oso House, the lone inn serving the area. His small, dark room had walls made of canvas. Since the Oso House did not own a single chair, he ate his meals perched on a rickety stool. He assured me we would move to more spacious accommodations once reunited.

He attempted to visit as much of the operation as he could, to familiarize himself with the requirements of a successful mining enterprise. Despite all the accolades he had heard, it disheartened him to find several of the mines in disrepair and many at a standstill. He grew concerned as he pored over the financial records and learned the previous profits of up to $50,000 a month had disappeared and current losses averaged $80,000 monthly. "This cannot continue," he wrote. "I must turn this dire situation around."

Fred blamed the ongoing drought as mining required running water to power the mills that crushed quartz into powder. Further processing would eventually reveal bits of gold. He explained how he shared his concerns with the owners in New York and after weeks of waiting, found his request for funds to repair the mills denied. "Further capital improvements," they wrote, "depended on increased gold production."

"I ask you, Mary," he wrote. "How can we increase gold production without repairing the mills?"

His most recent letter was disturbing and as I read it, I felt a tightening in my chest. Could our California adventure be over before it even begins? I read it again, trying to stay calm.

My Dearest Mary,

I do not wish to alarm you, but the more I learn about Mariposa, the greater is my concern this is not the viable enterprise they led me to believe. We should delay your travel with the children until I can favorably predict it will turn around. Things are worse here than I dare say to anybody but you.

On the bright side, I have had success establishing a reading room for the miners. Many former colleagues in the publishing world have agreed to provide editions of their magazines and newspapers, now delivered weekly. While the men only drift in occasionally, I am certain they will soon realize the reading of current events and world affairs will ease some loneliness they are experiencing. I have to institute a 10% decrease in their daily wages from $3.50 to $3.15 as the entire operation will soon be bankrupt unless we cut expenses and increase output. Please join me in prayers for copious amounts of rain to end this drought.

I am pleased your former teacher has agreed to serve as governess for the children. I hope her upbringing in England will not spoil her for daily life in this most uncivilized corner of the world. On a sadder note, I understand Miss Curtayne's decision to marry and leave us has been difficult for the children, especially dear Charlotte, who is such a gentle soul. I worry so about her mood swings. I hope you will tell her that Papa loves her and will see her soon.

Please wait to hear from me before making any final travel arrangements. I would not want the six of you to make this arduous journey until I am more certain of the future.

I am reminded of the fact it is Christmas Day, although we will not see any snow nor experience much in the way of holiday cheer. I pray you could make the day special and will make this up to you soon, God willing.

I remain your loving husband,
Fred

I sat back and groaned out loud. There were no two ways about it. Moving to California was on hold for the foreseeable future.

Chapter 19

Spring 1864

The drought finally ended and conditions at the Mariposa mines improved, so Fred gave the go ahead to finalize our travel arrangements. After a series of delays, Miss Errington, the children and I set sail from New York, arriving in San Francisco in mid-March. At Fred's insistence, I had been doling out daily doses of quinine to prevent malaria, also known as the Chagres Shakes after a river in Panama. Fred met us at the pier and after a couple of days of resting, exploring the city, and stocking up on supplies, we set out for Bear Valley. Fred kept us entertained with keen observations of our travels and predictions of what we would see along the way.

Once we reached the estate, we settled in to our new home, a suite of rooms above the Mariposa Company general store. The children adjusted quickly to the freedom afforded them in exploring the small mining town. Soon after we arrived, the three older ones were assigned a trio of donkeys, which they named Fanny, Kitty and Beppo and rode everywhere they could.

Although his workdays were long, Fred attempted to spend time with us. While the long-term future of the mining operation was still uncertain, the mining crew was once again earning full wages and producing quantities of ore. Fred was sharing the good news with me one rain-soaked afternoon. We were standing in the doorway of the general store watching the children riding their donkeys around the lot. Charlotte and Owen rode alone, but John was good-natured and held little Marion as she sat side-saddle in front of him on Beppo.

"The children will catch their death, Fred. We should tell them to come in at once," I said. The children had been housebound all week and had begged to go riding. I was glad to see them enjoying themselves, but the light drizzle of a half hour ago had progressed to a steady rain and the dusty road on which they rode in circles was covered in mud.

"Nonsense, Mary. They are having the time of their lives. The rain is so critical to the success of the mines. Surely a few drops won't cause any ill effects. And the donkeys? They are as sure-footed as can be. Let's let them enjoy a bit of a breather. I must go back to the mines. You can towel the children off and stick them in front of the fire and I'll return Franny, Kitty and—"

"It's Fanny, dear. Owen picked the name himself." Fred nodded good-naturedly.

"Of course. I'll return them to the barn and head out. I should be back in time for supper." I smiled and reached up to touch his cheek.

"I adore it when you are home with us in the evenings. Family time is my favorite part of the day, reading and enjoying each other's company."

"And teaching new card games to John and Charlotte," Fred said. "Are you telling me moving lock, stock and barrel to California was a good move for the family?"

"Oh yes. I think it's one of our best moves yet. This is such an adventure. I miss Anne and New York, but I am enjoying our time here."

"I hope we can stay for a long time," Fred admitted, drawing me close and kissing the top of my head.

"Yes, a long time," I said.

***

When they weren't off exploring, the children spent a good deal of time in lessons with Miss Errington, most of which she conducted outside. I discovered my equestrian skills were still intact, and Fred and I got into the habit of nightly rides around the estate after the children were asleep. Our relationship grew stronger than ever after months of separation, and we looked forward to a family trip to the Yosemite Valley.

Fred had first spotted Yosemite while traveling the outer edge of the estate and had written to share his thoughts on its natural beauty, with mountains, lakes, meadows, and glaciers. The most striking feature was the bare granite cliff, El Capitan. Yosemite was one of several destinations planned for our camping expedition, and preparations were finally complete. Joseph Ashburton, a mining consultant, and his wife Eleanor would join us. With a guide and a housekeeper named Martha, we required a caravan of eight saddle horses, six mules and two carriages.

After traveling forty miles of rugged terrain, we arrived at our first stop where we would spend the next two nights. Eleanor, Martha and I set about preparing a hearty meal, while Fred and Miss Errington took the children on a hike. Eleanor and I headed towards the river in search of firewood while Martha unpacked the food supplies. I had collected a large bundle of sticks and was about to tell Eleanor I was heading back, when movement across the river caught my eye. A dozen brown-skinned, scantily dressed Indian women and children were standing on the riverbank, watching our every move. Although I couldn't make out their words, the children were gesturing excitedly and everyone seemed to talk at once. Fred had told me we would probably encounter members of a few local tribes at some point, but I hadn't expected a welcoming committee on our very first day. I wondered where the male members of the tribe were and I dropped the wood at my feet, preparing to run if need be.

"Eleanor," I called out softly. "Don't look now, but we seem to have attracted an audience on the other side of the river." The other woman turned and looked, letting out a strangled cry. She rushed towards me, her eyes wide with fright.

"What should we do? Do you suppose we're in danger?" I tried to imagine the excited group swimming across the river to attack us and laughed nervously.

"I'm certain we're fine," I said and put my arm around her shoulders. "Let's head back to the camp and wait for everyone. Our guide will know what to do." I picked up the sticks I had dropped, and we hurried away. As we left, I turned and noticed the group had doubled in size in just a few minutes. How many of them are there? And where were the men? Had they already made their way across the river to investigate our arrival? Had Fred and the children crossed their path? Breathless with fear, I hurried with Eleanor back to the campsite. "Don't say a word to anyone," I said.

As we approached the clearing, I saw everyone had returned. Relieved, I rushed over to Fred and dropping a pile of firewood at his feet, hugged him close. "You're back," I whispered, relieved to take in his familiar smells of pine trees and tobacco. Fred was the first to pull away and frowned.

"What on earth? You're positively trembling, my love. What is going on?" he asked, starting to sound annoyed.

"I have to tell you something. It's important, maybe even a matter of life and death." Fred followed me and we headed back towards the riverbank. Once we were out of sight of the others, I hurried to tell him the danger we were facing.

"Indians, Fred. I was collecting wood down by the river and I saw them. They have been congregating on the opposite shore and are growing in numbers. There must be three dozen of them by now." Fred looked surprised but recovered quickly as he tried to reassure me.

"I'm sure there is nothing to worry about, but let me look into this. I warned you it was likely we would encounter many indigenous tribes on this trip. Most are peaceful. Perhaps Ashburton and I can initiate a meeting to get to know them. I'm certain our guide has experience. How does that sound?"

I nodded and tried to look brave as we returned to the campsite. The children were chattering excitedly as they shared what they had seen on their walk and their impressions of the trip so far. Although I agreed with everyone that food tasted better when eaten around a campfire, I could only manage a few bites of stew. I nibbled at a biscuit, fashioned by wrapping dough around a long stick and toasting it over the fire.

"If there are any leftover biscuits, I'll serve them for breakfast," Martha promised. "Wait until you taste them stuffed full of my blackberry preserves." Everyone thought that sounded wonderful, and soon after, Miss Errington had the children tucked in their bedrolls in the largest of the tents. I went to kiss them good night and considered joining them, as I was bone-tired and my muscles ached from so many miles spent on horseback. But I needed to be certain we were safe, so I emerged from the tent to find Martha storing leftovers and Eleanor, sitting on a large rock, staring at the fire. Like me, she had eaten very little and had hardly spoken a word all evening.

Fred, Joe and the guide, a young fellow named Thomas, were deep in conversation and I joined them. Too nervous to sit, I circled them and listened carefully. Thomas had been alerted by Fred and had gone to the riverbank after we ate. He had just returned to tell us what he had discovered. He estimated there were fifty Indians living on the other side of the river which narrowed to only a hundred yards about a quarter-mile upstream.

"They're Miwok," he said. "I saw the markings on their horses. That's good. They're a peace-loving sort, thanks be to God. We should have no trouble, but we should make contact at daybreak as a sign of respect." The men agreed and Fred led me to our tent. Despite worries I wouldn't sleep a wink, I fell asleep immediately and woke several hours later to a breathtaking sunrise and the smell of coffee. The men had already departed, so I poured myself a steaming mug and breathed in the familiar aroma. Sipping slowly, I tried to calm my nerves by focusing on the beauty of the morning until the children woke up to distract me.

By late morning, the children grew bored, confined as they were to the small area surrounding the campsite.

"I want to go exploring," John said, but I refused to let them out of my sight and suggested building a small log cabin with excess firewood. We were preparing the noontime meal when the men returned and I rushed over to hear what they had learned.

They had crossed the river on horseback to meet our neighbors, who approached them as they reached the shore. Communication was limited with only one member of the Miwok tribe understanding a little English, but the meeting went smoothly. They had traveled from their permanent home some distance away in order to stock up on fish for the tribe. The Indians had promised us a quantity of fresh fish as a trade for a bag of grains. After a hurried meal, the three older children and I joined the men as we prepared to meet the Miwoks. I rode sidesaddle with Fred, holding on to Charlotte for dear life as we crossed the fast-moving river, watching as John rode with Joe and Owen with Thomas. Before we left, I hugged and kissed Marion, making Miss Errington swear she wouldn't let her out of her sight. Despite my fear, I trusted Thomas and believed Fred wouldn't let anything happen to us.

The Miwok were warm and welcoming, and I relaxed on a colorful woven blanket spread out on the sandy shore. Everyone was barefoot and wore their dark, coarse hair long. The men were dressed in rectangular pieces of hide tucked over a belt, so the flaps fell down in front and behind. The women were also scantily dressed and several of the children were nearly naked. I found making eye contact with them somewhat challenging. Everyone stared and one child approached me and touched my cheek almost reverently. I doubted any of them ever seen a white woman before. I smiled a lot and nodded whenever anyone spoke in my general direction. *Wait until I tell Anne how I spent my afternoon!*

The children spent hours at play with their new Indian friends after establishing contact with funny faces and much laughter. I watched them, along with several Indian women I judged to be about my age. Although we exchanged no words between us, there were plenty of warm smiles and when we prepared to return to our campsite, it pleased me when one woman reached out to hold my hand in farewell. *They're mothers, just like me.* We all want our families to be safe and happy. Only yesterday, I had feared them as savages, but now considered them friends. Waving and smiling, we bade our hosts goodbye and headed across the river to spend our last night before heading out at first light.

The trip was off to a splendid start and we set out bright and early, our next stop scheduled for Mariposa Grove with upwards of six hundred giant sequoia trees! I vowed to enjoy every single moment.

Chapter 20

The six weeks we spent exploring the Yosemite Valley were some of the happiest of my life. I rode daily with Fred through the beautiful countryside. Our favorite vista included a wooded valley bracketed on one side by El Capitan and Half Dome on the other. Another memorable destination was Yosemite Falls, reported to be the highest waterfall in North America with a dramatic drop of nearly a half-mile. I was awestruck by the greenery as I pointed out the various ferns and wild flowers to the children on our walks.

"Despite the grandeur, there is something quite gentle about this valley," I confided to Fred one night as we relaxed in front of the campfire. "Didn't you say the Merced River reminded you of growing up in Connecticut?"

Fred's weathered face broke into a wide grin. "It does. As a lad, I spent countless hours traipsing through the woods and the sight of the Merced brings back memories. John and I loved to explore all around the Hockanum River..." He grew silent and appeared pensive.

"Fred? What is it," I asked, although I guessed saying John's name aloud had upset him.

"It's just, well, it's the first time I've spoken my late brother's name in years," Fred said. I squeezed his hand, understanding. I, too, had thought of and said John's name less and less over the years. I no longer had to urge myself to not think of John when things got difficult.

"You and John had many carefree days together. Now it is our turn, you and I. John prayed for this, he wanted us to be together." Fred put an arm around me and pulled me close.

"And together we are."

"I love you, Fred. With all of my heart. You've made me very happy."

"And I love you, dear wife. And I always will." Before long, we stood and after ensuring the campfire had died out, climbed into our bedrolls and fell asleep under the canopy of the two hundred-foot Grizzly Giant sequoia.

***

Returning to dusty Bear Valley was a letdown, but after the arduous trip it was a comfort to sleep in proper beds and eat meals around a table instead of a campfire. I assumed we had heard the last of Yosemite for now, but the very next day, Fred received word they had named him to a newly formed committee to preserve the entire valley. A recent bill passed by both houses of Congress deeded Yosemite and the nearby Mariposa Grove to the state of California. Preserving a piece of land for its scenic beauty was a novel idea, and Governor Frederick Low had written up a list of names for a steering committee, including Fred and Joe Ashburton. As his name topped the list, Frederick Law Olmsted became the *de facto* chair of the committee. Although the work would take him away from us at times and there was no salary associated with the post, it thrilled me.

"This is cause for a true celebration. The governor could not have chosen a worthier man," I said. As I hugged him, I tried to recall how much poultry remained in the larder. Was there enough for a steaming pot of Fred's favorite cock-a-leekie soup, or would I be forced to serve plain leek soup to my family? *Not very celebratory.*

Fred was excited. Running a mining operation could be very lucrative, but he had ofttimes confided the work had never inspired him in the same way the Central Park project had.

"Perhaps I *should* consider a future building parks. With you by my side, I can do anything I set my mind to. Let me tell you where I am with Yosemite. Just this morning, I was reflecting on our visit. What with my game leg, it was a most challenging destination. My first proposal would provide for a more conveniently located campground. What do you think of that?" Before I could agree, he continued. "And how about a carriage circuit connecting Yosemite, the Mariposa Grove and other nearby sites?" Fred continued on, talking as if to himself.

I smiled and located a quill pen and a piece of parchment. Someone would need to keep an accurate record of these ideas. It was certain to be a late night.

Chapter 21

Spring 1865

General Robert E. Lee's defeat at the Battle of Appomattox would be the last major battle of the Civil War. I was overjoyed that the war would be over and prayed for all the mothers that their sons would return home, safe and sound. There was no time for celebration, however, as less than a week later President Abraham Lincoln was assassinated while attending a performance of *Our American Cousin* at Ford's Theater in Washington, D.C. They pronounced him dead on April 15, 1865. Fred was in San Francisco when he got the news and sent word to us in Bear Valley.

I knew full well how unbearable the death of a spouse could be, and I grieved for Mary Todd Lincoln. "At least I could suffer in private when my husband died," I said to Miss Errington. "Our president's poor widow has all the country watching her."

A few days later, Fred returned from his business trip. Meeting with the banks had been unsuccessful, and he could not secure a loan on behalf of the mining operation. Publicly, he was optimistic about the future of Mariposa, but he confided his concerns to me.

"I'm sorry to tell you, but I believe our days are numbered," he said with uncharacteristic glumness.

I had been thinking about Mary Lincoln and assumed Fred was making a statement about how brief life is and how it could be taken away without a moment's notice.

"You mustn't think like that," I said. "Every day is precious, but we must live life to the fullest. Why, when we lost baby John, I—"

"Good God woman, what are you going on about?" Fred asked. "I am trying to tell you my days here are ending. The operation is on its last legs and so are we." My mouth opened in surprise and for a full moment, I could not speak. I stared at Fred with growing horror. *What on earth?*

"Our last legs? But Fred, you said..."

"I said a lot of things, my dear."

"But what—" Fred cut me off, as he moved closer to me.

"As manager, it is my job to keep the morale up for my men." Now it was my turn to be cross.

"Fill their heads with false promises, you mean. How does that help a man send money home to his wife and children?"

Fred's tone was conciliatory as he tried to comfort me. "I'm sorry. I shouldn't have shared this with you. I'm exhausted from a long and difficult trip home. There is still a chance that things will turn around. A few weeks of rain this spring and we'll have the mills at full capacity. I'll take the children mining for gold again. Do you think they would enjoy that?"

He was not telling me everything, and I longed to press him on the matter, but he would tell me more in time. I agreed it was a wonderful idea. "Why, Owen was just mentioning he wanted to try his luck panning for gold." I took his arm as we made our way to bed. "Don't give up on Bear Valley yet," I said.

Fred assured me he would not.

Chapter 22

Fall 1865

One night, at the end of a hot and dry summer, Fred announced the sun-parched mines were ceasing operations. Funding had dried up, and it had forced him to lay off all the workers. We spent hours discussing our options, with me insisting we could make a life for ourselves in California.

"I'm certain returning to New York makes no sense for us, Fred. Won't we have wasted all this time if we were to head East with nothing to show from nearly two years of hard work?" Fred looked surprised at my characterization of our financial situation.

"The mines may have gone belly-up, but we are far from destitute, I can assure you. We still have some savings and our return will be in the grandest of styles." He shared that despite not being paid a salary in months, he had barely had to dip into our savings to cover the shortage. Our only expenses were food and Miss Errington's salary, as we were living rent-free in company housing.

"So, we won't have to travel home through Venezuela?" I asked with a mischievous gleam in my eyes.

"Let's not get too far ahead of ourselves," Fred said. "But I do have a decision to make. I'm considering going back into journalism. Even after all these years, I still have connections with some very prestigious publications."

"I heard you telling Joseph Ashburton you would consider managing oil refineries or vineyards if the mining operation went bust," I said.

"Oh, Mary, that was just an idle thought, but to be honest with you, the Yosemite project has thoroughly whetted my appetite for building parks. I only wish they could afford to pay me a living wage to stay on." Fred looked glum, but I continued excitedly.

"If you truly love parks, why not join Calvert Vaux? I know he continues to write to you these past months. He wants to build on your success as park planners and landscape architects. Brooklyn, Chicago and Buffalo are all interested in hiring both of you to build parks rivaling Central Park." Fred looked at me, shocked by my admission.

"Have you been snooping, Mary? Going through my private correspondence?" He tried to hide his smile, but I frowned at his attempt at levity.

"I have. Our family's future depends on your willingness to take an honest look at our options and decide which makes the most sense. I did what I had to for our family."

"You're right. Of course you are." Fred admitted grudgingly.

"How about a compromise?" I suggested. "We return to New York and after a year, if working with Cal doesn't suit you, start looking for another opportunity. Maybe in journalism? It'll give us a chance to build up our savings and I know you want to get back to work you really love." And I would get to see my dear friend Anne. Fred nodded.

"That sounds sensible. I'll write to Vaux tonight and let him know we will pack our things and return to New York."

"Ask him to please find us a suitable house to lease. And by suitable, I mean large enough in a desirable neighborhood. And that won't come cheap," He shook his head when I added, "And tell him to hurry. We'll be there in just a few weeks."

"I'm afraid it will be longer than that. For the seven of us to travel so soon, we won't be able to spend the extra money on the Panama route. The sensible arrangement is to go through Venezuela, adding a couple of weeks to the trip." He looked disappointed, but I was quick to reassure him. I didn't want him second guessing his hasty decision to move us back East.

"The different route will be an adventure for the children. When else will we get this opportunity again?" I asked. "They're great travelers, and they'll view the extra time on the ship as an exciting journey. Perhaps we can convince John to keep a journal of the voyage. He could end up a writer like his father."

"Then we must stash away a supply of parchment and pens."

"And doses of quinine," I said.

"Ah, Mary Perkins Olmsted," Fred cried out as he hugged me. "What on earth would I do without you?"

"I will not allow you to find out," I promised him, right before I kissed him soundly.

Chapter 23

Winter 1865-1866

I sat back with a smile. The Vaux family had joined us for a holiday meal and although the china was mismatched and chipped and the menu was more appropriate for a weekday supper than a festive banquet, there was plenty of food and even more holiday cheer. We had been living in a pricey boardinghouse since returning to New York in late October, but plans to move to a large house on Staten Island were progressing. The only holdup was the delay in receiving the shipment of our furniture and household goods, reportedly making the slow circuit around Cape Horn.

Fred and Calvert sat side by side, swapping stories and engaging in plenty of back-slapping. The two years apart seemed to have done some good, and the last couple of months had been among the most productive of their partnership. Their proposal to build Mount Prospect Park in Brooklyn was nearly complete and the influx of requests for public parks, private estates, colleges and universities was encouraging.

It delighted John, Charlotte and Owen to reunite with the Vaux children. Our youngest daughters became fast friends, spending hours giggling and playing with their dolls. All eight children sat crowded around a makeshift table in a corner of the sitting room, and spirits were high.

"Did you ever think we would be together again? It seemed you were gone forever," Anne said. "I had grown so accustomed to living under the same roof with all of you. After they evicted us, I swear, I went looking for you nearly every day. I kept imagining I heard your sweet voice." My eyes misted over as I squeezed her hand.

"Oh, Anne, I felt the same. Every time one of the children said something clever or when we saw Yosemite for the first time, I would think, 'Anne would love this, Anne would understand, Anne would tell me what to do.'"

"I'm so glad you didn't become best friends with an Indian woman," Anne said with a twinkle in her eye. "You might have never returned home." I chuckled and shook my head at her foolishness. Anne's sense of humor had brought many a smile to my face that last year in New York. The accident, losing baby John, Fred's struggles to support us; all made more bearable with her by my side. A tear rolled down my cheek, and I brushed it away. Determined not to allow melancholy to ruin the day, I changed topics quickly.

"And what do you think of the fashions here in New York?" I asked. "Let me tell you, the latest trends were the last things on our minds out West. We spent countless hours on horseback and sleeping on bedrolls in crowded tents. Even when we were home in our flat above the general store, what we wore was of little or no interest, believe me."

"That must be why we spent so much time shopping during your first few weeks back. I swear Owen barely fit in young John's hand-me-downs, and John and Charlotte's clothing was all but threadbare. And little Marion just about swam in Charlotte's discards." Anne's grin widened. "Even you and Fred need new wardrobes. Please tell me your clothes being shipped from Bear Valley are a bit more presentable for life in New York."

I shook my head. "No, I am sorry to report what is in transit is basically more of the same." I looked down at my shabby burgundy gown. "As soon as they pay our husbands their year-end bonuses, we will need to schedule another shopping trip." Never a slave to fashion, I was looking forward to purchasing a few gowns and much needed undergarments. "If you can imagine, my knickers are being held up with a length of twine from the butcher's shop."

Anne's burst of raucous laughter caused Fred and Calvert to look up from their end of the table.

"Everything all right, my dear?" Calvert Vaux inquired as he and Fred studied us.

"Just ducky," we said in unison, right before we started laughing again.

Chapter 24

Spring 1866

Fred's mood was jubilant after he and Cal received word that the Prospect Park commission had chosen them to design their park. The new project held a powerful appeal as it was in Brooklyn, the third largest city in the United States, and would not require any overnight travel for the two landscape architects.

We had moved to a spacious home in the Clifton section of Staten Island a few months earlier and Fred commuted to Manhattan by ferry. When he left the offices of Olmsted, Vaux & Company in the late afternoon, he had rushed home to share the good news.

Despite being in my fourth month of pregnancy, I hurried to greet him. He roared at the top of his voice as he entered the room, "We got it. Prospect Park is ours!" He tried to lift me with the goal of swinging me around, but the extra weight of pregnancy combined with his game leg prevented him from doing anything more than lifting me a few inches and setting me down seconds later.

But even evidence of his physical shortcomings failed to subdue his triumphant return home that evening. After the children settled in their beds, I begged him to share some design ideas that had resulted in the prestigious commission. Never superstitious by nature, Fred had been uncharacteristically tight-lipped about the proposal and for weeks had been answering my questions with an enigmatic, "We'll see."

"Tell me, Fred. I'm dying to hear more. All I remember is it's no longer at the originally proposed Mount Prospect, and it's roughly the shape of an arrowhead." I recalled John drawing pictures of arrowheads in order to show his siblings how their papa's new park would look.

Fred's smiled at me. The glass of claret he had consumed appeared to have gone straight to his head. "Do you recall there'll be a man-made lake with a waterfall or has our unborn child robbed you of your ability to remember any of our conversations?" I ignored his teasing, eager to hear more details of the design aesthetic.

"It has been ages since you shared any of the details with me. With Central Park, you told me everything. I feel you're holding back on this project," I said with a pout. My eyes welled up, and I brushed away unshed tears. This pregnancy had been a difficult one. At thirty-six, I had been feeling I was too old to carry yet another child. I was all too familiar with the nausea associated with pregnancy, but these mood swings were another matter altogether.

"I'm sorry, I never meant to shut you out. It's been worrisome, these past weeks waiting to hear. I didn't want to keep harping about our finances and you have your hands full with the children."

"I realize things are tight, but all the more reason to share how the design is progressing. It's exciting to me and we're partners. Share your burden with me. I'm stronger than I look."

"I'll try, Mary. I promise I will."

"Go on. Tell me more." Fred nodded, happy to resume the sharing of his design.

"The lake will be our most daunting job. We must pump hundreds of gallons of water through a series of streams that will converge into a ravine flowing over a waterfall and emptying into the lake itself." His eyes shone with delight as he imagined the task ahead.

"What else?" I asked, eager to hear more.

"Naturally there'll be paths for carriages, horseback riding, and visitors on foot. And don't forget the unlimited amounts of fresh air for the residents. It will be an oasis of tranquility apart from the crowded city streets," Fred said with practiced aplomb. The contribution the park would make to residents and visitors from around the world was important to him.

"And the views? What of the views?" I asked sleepily. I closed my eyes as I listened to him rave about the opportunity to see the city of

New York and the harbor, and the New Jersey Palisades and even the city of Newark from various points in the park.

"We break ground immediately, Mary. It will be a very busy summer for Olmsted, Vaux and Company."

"Busy summer," I mumbled and sighed happily as he lifted my feet and covered me with a woolen throw. I felt his soft kiss on my cheek as I snuggled into the contours of the sofa, utterly content.

Chapter 25

Fall 1866

Waking from a morphine-induced haze, I could barely make out the sight of Fred, Doctor Sinclair and Anne talking softly just outside the darkened room. Whatever had happened was not good. I should be holding a crying baby in my arms. Where was my baby? Did we have a new son? Daughter?

"I can give her more morphine. Just say the word," Sinclair said. "Given the circumstances, it would be a blessing. The labor was long and very difficult. She was in a great deal of pain right before the baby came." What circumstances? *Where is my baby?*

"I still don't understand what went wrong," Fred whispered. He sounded so sad, so weary. What had gone wrong?

"Mary would want to be told what happened sooner rather than later," Anne insisted. "I'm uncertain over-medicating her is a good idea." She turned to Fred. "What do you suppose Mary would want?" Fred's voice was clear as he responded.

"She would want to hold her child and love him until her last breath. She would want to see him christened and grow to be a respectable man. How could this have happened? He seemed fine until he just... stopped breathing," Fred said, as sobs overcame him and he sagged against the doorway. Horrified, I watched as he disappeared down the hall supported by Anne and the doctor. I gave birth to a baby boy. He died soon after he was born. I never got to hold him. My mind reeled, then darkness overcame me.

***

Over the next several weeks, I recovered physically, but inside I was bleak. Despair left me exhausted. Trays of food remained untouched, and I had all but stopped speaking. I spent day after day in bed, staring out the window, seeing nothing. The leaves had fallen from the trees and snowflakes swirled around. But while I noticed the change of seasons, I never mentioned it. Not to Anne, who visited regularly. Not to Miss Errington, when she shepherded four children in to see their mama after they completed their lessons for the day. Not to Fred, who spent evenings at my side attempting to regale me with stories of his days at Prospect Park. He had returned to work soon after our baby boy had died. I understood his need to surround himself with work. I wished I had his determination, but barely had the strength to use a chamber pot without help. Fred had hired a nurse named Eliza, but the young woman spent more time playing with the children than tending to me.

I had grown accustomed to everyone talking about me as if I wasn't in the room and felt no need to respond to comments about my health or appearance. Conversations frequently took place in the doorway, not ten feet from where I lay.

"Poor Mrs. O. I can't help her. She won't let me," Eliza said to Anne one day. "I offered to help her out of that filthy chemise and she turned away from me. I don't know what to do."

"Let me see if I can help, Eliza. Why don't you check if the children want their snack? I'm sure they would enjoy your company." Eliza hurried down the stairs, grateful for a reprieve. Anne crossed the room and perched on the wooden chair next to my bed. Even with my eyes closed, I felt myself being studied. No doubt Anne could see the stains on my undergarments, remnants of the afterbirth from weeks earlier. I was aware the smell of sweat and unwashed skin clung to me as I had resisted offers of sponge baths. It was no wonder Marion had to be dragged in to my room each day and left minutes later in tears.

I had lost all the baby weight and many pounds more and was literally skin and bones under the mounds of gray sheets. My lips were cracked and dry and my normally neatly coiffed, long brown hair lay in greasy strands across my pillow.

"Oh, Mary," Anne said, and I opened my eyes to see tears streaming down her cheeks. I turned away. *What do you want from me? My heart is broken and I can't bear to see the sadness I am causing to everyone around me. My grandfather was wrong. I'm clearly not made of sterner stuff. Just please leave me be.*

Anne sat by my side until Eliza returned and she sprang into action.

"Gather up a set of clean sheets and a stack of towels. I'll locate a bar of Mary's special milled soap. Then help me fill a washbasin with hot water." The girl scampered off, eager to help. Once everything was ready, Anne lifted me while Eliza stripped the bed. I lay still as they removed my chemise and they gave me a sponge bath. The stack of clean towels disappeared as first my face and neck, then my underarms and torso were scrubbed clean. Anne was gentle but thorough, and minutes later, she settled me back into a freshly made bed wearing a clean shift. My hair was pulled back and braided neatly.

When they were done, Eliza left the room carrying the washbasin full of damp, filthy towels. Anne followed, but turned back to me. She approached slowly and knelt by my side. "I realize you require this time to heal. But we miss you and need you with us." Her voice broke and her eyes filled with tears. "Please, Mary," she begged.

I nodded and sat up in the bed. My voice was barely above a whisper when I spoke and I averted my eyes, unable to make direct contact with Anne.

"Do you suppose this is all some form of punishment?" Anne's response was swift and certain.

"No, Mary. Of course not. You probably didn't hear Dr. Sinclair, but he swears it's an act of God, a blessing even. The poor little mite just wasn't meant for this world." I grew frustrated and shook my head.

"No! That's what people say when there's nothing else they can say. What I mean is, with Fred and me? Maybe we shouldn't have married. It seems like we've had nothing but sorrow since we got together. Maybe our marriage was a mistake."

"How can you say that? You two were destined to be together."

"Anne, please. Look at the facts. John died and Fred married me out of obligation. It was to be a union in name only. But I wanted more. I wanted love and a genuine marriage. And I got it in spades. And ever since, we've had nothing but heartache. The accident that crippled Fred. Losing baby John to cholera. And now more loss. Losing another son? I am certain I cannot handle any more heartache." I leaned back against the pillows and closed my eyes.

I heard Anne gather up her things before she approached the bed again.

"Regardless of his reasons for marrying you, Fred is deeply in love with you. And you have John. He's growing up to be such a fine young man. And Charlotte? Your dear 'little mother' is missing you so much. And did you hear Owen and Marion are apparently the closest of pals? They have adopted a secret language all their own. You have five people who love you and want you back. And if that's not enough, you have me. I miss my best friend. Who else can I talk to about my marriage? My children? My life? Mary, I need you."

"I miss all of you. You're the best friend I could ever hope for. And please don't worry. I'll come back to you and my family soon. I promise." I closed my eyes and lay back against the pillows.

"God be with you, my dear," Anne said as she left the room.

Chapter 26

Spring 1867

I made good on my promise to be there for my family and joined them for meals. I had little appetite and spent most of the time pushing food around my plate. I rarely spoke, but enjoyed listening to the children talk to Fred about their day. One night, little Marion piped up.

"Mama, why are you playing with your food? Miss Errington won't let us play with our food." Fred laughed, but stopped as he realized I was about to respond.

"Why you're right, my love. Playing with food is not proper. I guess I shall have to eat mine instead." With that, I stabbed a square of the roast beef on my plate, shoved the fork in my mouth and chewed noisily. "Mmmm, so good, Marion. Can you clean your plate like Mama?" All four children forced meat and potatoes in their mouths, chewing loudly. Fred feigned surprise as he stared at us in amazement.

"I thought I was enjoying supper with my family, but it looks like I am dining with a bunch of little piggies instead. I suppose I will have to become a piggy myself." He scooped huge forkfuls of food into his mouth and for a time, it was the gay household it had always been.

That night, Fred came to our bedroom and knocked softly. He had taken to sleeping in a spare room so as not to disturb me. I was already in bed and had let down my hair. I looked up in surprise.

"Fred, do come in. This is your room too," I said. He cleared his throat and limped over to the bed. "Is your leg bothering you? It's the damp weather, isn't it?"

"No worse than usual. But yes, dampness causes my old bones to ache and none worse than my bum leg," he said with a wry smile. "But

I'm not here to talk about me." I sat up straighter and leaned towards him.

"What is it, Fred? Is it the children?"

"No, no. The children are right as rain. I want to talk about you." I grew wary as I watched him.

"What about me, Fred? I'm trying. I've been—"

"But I would like to help. I have an offer for you."

"An offer of what?"

"You remember my old friend Charley Brace? He went on the walking tour of England with John and I right before..."

"Right before John and I got married. Yes, I remember him." I frowned, remembering how upset I'd been when John told me we needed to delay our wedding. "That was right after they diagnosed John with tuberculosis. He thought the air in England would be just what the doctor ordered. But what of Charley? I haven't heard his name in years."

"Well, that's the thing. It's been far too long and he and his wife Letitia would like us to visit their country home upstate for a holiday of sorts. It would be good to get away for a bit. Lots of fresh air and it's so peaceful away from the city. I can leave the park in Vaux's capable hands and Miss Errington and Sarah agreed to—" I cut him off.

"You've already talked to them about this trip? Before you mentioned it to me?" Fred nodded somewhat reluctantly.

"Yes, I needed to be certain they could take care of the children," he explained. "I didn't want to get our hopes up and then find that we could not travel." I was nodding, and he broke into a wide grin, realizing he didn't need to continue apologizing.

"When would we go?" I asked. "It sounds wonderful."

"As soon as you're able. I can send word to Charley we can be there in a week's time. Would that work?"

"Sounds divine." I leaned back against the pillow. "Now come to bed. We'll have lots to do to get ready for our trip." Fred smiled as he walked over to his side of the bed.

"With pleasure, my dear. With pleasure."

Chapter 27

We enjoyed a much-needed vacation at the Brace's lovely country home. The fresh air agreed with me, and I regained my curves as a result of large portions of home-cooked food. My skin glowed after afternoons spent walking the grounds of the large estate with Letitia Brace. There was always time to play cards, read, or even indulge in a long nap. We spent our evenings by the fire with a glass of port. She and I exchanged smiles as Fred and Charley expounded upon their exploits as younger men one night.

"Well, if memory serves, it was you, Olmsted, who insisted we remain in Liverpool for several extra days during our infamous walking tour. I was never sure if it was the public parks that drew your attention or the comely serving wenches at the tavern." Fred chuckled and held his glass high.

"A toast to the lovely parks and the lovely women of Liverpool," he said. "May they remain even half as beautiful as our memories."

"To beautiful parks and to my oldest friend making a living building them," Charley said and everyone drank to that.

The next morning Fred received word from Cal Vaux, demanding he return to work. The message was brief, but his intent was clear. The office was inundated with requests for personal visits to private estates and bids for municipal parks in a dozen locations, including Philadelphia; Newark; Fall River, Massachusetts and Bridgeport, Connecticut. The parks they had created in two of the largest cities in America had created a frenzy, and they needed to develop a plan to capitalize on the demands for their time and talents.

While I hated to end our vacation early, I knew Fred should return at once. It took little effort on his part to convince me to stay behind, and I agreed to remain for another week.

"It will do you good. There is no sense in both of us having to cut short our time with the Braces," Fred advised as he prepared to leave. We had spent most of the morning in bed, relishing the intimacy a child-free haven provided. I stretched luxuriously as he packed his suitcase. I watched him for a short while, but after refolding most of the clothes he was packing, ordered him to sit down and let me finish.

"You don't have to pretend to be so disappointed about going back to work," I admonished him with a smile. Fred looked shocked.

"What do you mean? Of course I would rather be here with you," Fred said.

"Oh Fred, do you think I don't know you are itching to get back to your parks?" He tried to protest, but I continued. "Don't worry. Your secret is safe with me. As far as our friends are concerned, you are brokenhearted at having to rush back."

"Ah, Mary. You know me so well. I have enjoyed relaxing with you, but Vaux needs me to prioritize all this work that's appeared out of thin air." I kissed him on the lips and then pushed him gently away.

"Go say your goodbyes and I'll finish up here." Fred hesitated on his way to the door and looked back at me.

"I love you Mary and that's a fact," he said with a wide grin. Then he turned and headed off in search of our host.

***

By the time I returned home, Fred had reviewed a dozen proposals from various municipalities and outlined itineraries for Cal and himself. Both men turned down requests to design outdoor spaces for several private estates, agreeing their focus needed to be building parks for the masses to enjoy, not indulging the whims of a few rich clients. There was plenty of work available, and if they were awarded contracts for even half of the pending projects, they would be busy for two or three years. Within a few weeks, two jobs were confirmed and sizeable sums were deposited into the firm's account, a result of

Vaux's insistence that earnest money be received prior to any work being started. Several new employees were hired and the future of Olmsted, Vaux and Company was looking very bright.

I resisted the urge to remind him it had been my idea to return to New York. One night, when Fred filled me in on the day's accomplishments, he expressed his desire "to change the face of modern America." I grasped his hands and kissed his cheek.

"I'm so proud of you. You are doing the work you were put on this earth to do."

"And I owe it all to you, Mary." I demurred, but Fred pulled me close. "And don't think for one moment I don't realize how much you are dying to say 'I told you so,'" he whispered.

Oh, this man of mine. He knows me all too well.

Chapter 28

Winter 1867-1868

The holidays were a blur of parties and extravagant gift-giving. Emboldened by the financial success of the Olmsted & Vaux partnership, Fred encouraged me to spoil the children. In the weeks leading up to Christmas, I shopped and planned get-togethers for our friends, both new and old. We were invited to so many functions, I joked to Miss Errington that I needed a social secretary to keep track of everything.

Today I was attending a luncheon with the wives of the Park Commissioners. My interactions with these women had been limited, and I surmised they were a cliquish group. Perhaps today I would break into their inner circle. I had chosen my dress with great care. It was one of my favorites, an emerald green taffeta that always drew compliments. Although it was a couple of years old, I believed it was timeless and perfect for a daytime event. I drew my cloak a little tighter and continued up the street towards the huge brownstone. Minutes later, I knocked on the mahogany door decorated with a large wreath of evergreens and scarlet ribbons. A housekeeper in a black dress and crisp white apron opened the door and beckoned me inside.

"Thank you," I called as she hurried down the hall with my wrap. I looked around the cavernous foyer and almost gasped. Why, it was the size of my entire parlor! The wallpaper featured huge cabbage roses in pink and lavender and the oriental rug was plush with an elaborate design in soft muted tones. The overall effect was exquisite. I turned when I heard someone approach. It was Cassandra Elliott, and I smiled, approaching her with outstretched hands.

"Hello! Thank you for inviting me. Your home is lovely." The other woman nodded, but did not take my hand in greeting. Her features were attractive, but she looked as if she had just smelled something foul.

She turned and walked away, calling over her shoulder, "Please join us in the drawing room. We're having a glass of sherry." I hurried after her, trying to keep up. I wondered if I should refuse the sherry, as I had not eaten breakfast and a single drink would affect me on an empty stomach. But I accepted a glass from a uniformed server to have something to do with my hands.

I puzzled over the chilly welcome. *Perhaps Cassandra is dealing with an unexpected guest or there is a problem in the kitchen.* But as I watched, she approached a trio of women in the center of the room and whispered something to them. It must have been a joke, as all four women laughed together. I looked around for a familiar face. There were a dozen women clustered in small groups, and I considered joining the closest when one of them approached.

"Mrs. Olmsted, is it?" a tall, pinched-face woman drawled, sizing me up and down with an amused look.

"Yes, I'm Mary. It's nice to meet you, Mrs..?" The other woman cleared her throat.

"Franklin. Mrs. Theodore Franklin," she announced. "My husband is the *chairman* of the Parks Committee." I had heard Fred mention his name.

"Oh, of course. So nice to meet you," I repeated. My throat was dry, and I took a quick sip of sherry, then almost spat it out when the liquid burned my throat. "Oh my, it went down the wrong, um, I just..." I coughed and dug around in my skirt pocket, hoping to find a handkerchief. One of Owen's marbles fell out and rolled away, and I remembered collecting it from the stairs before leaving the house. I felt all eyes upon me as I scrambled to deposit my glass on a tray and collect the marble wedged at the base of a large grandfather's clock. As I neared it, the clock's chimes announced the hour, and I started in surprise. I caught myself from falling by grabbing hold of the arm of a horsehair settee. *What a sight I must be.* I attempted to smooth back my hair and adjust my dress. I deposited the marble back into my pocket as another member of the household staff rang the bell, announcing it was time for luncheon.

Cheeks flaming with embarrassment, I followed the other women into the well-appointed dining room and found my name written on a creamy card, propped on a china dinner plate. I sat, turning both ways to see who would be next to me. The place setting to my left did not have a name card, but the one on my right had "Mrs. Benjamin Foster" written in cursive. I hoped she would arrive soon, as the other women were already seated and everyone seemed to be deep in conversation. But the chairs on either side of me remained empty, and I silently made my way through the soup course, a fresh-tasting celery broth, followed by a plate of sliced beef, roasted potatoes and steamed carrots. Feeling the need to freshen up, I excused myself to go to the washroom where I lingered for a few extra moments, trying to understand why no one had attempted to bring me into the conversation. I chided myself for being so sensitive and walked down the hallway. I approached the dining room, stopping short when I heard my name.

"Mary Olmsted? Cassandra, please tell me why she and that husband of hers are on every guest list of late. Some country bumpkins from Connecticut, as far as I can tell." I stood quietly, shocked at what I was hearing. What did we do to deserve to be talked about like this? Surely one of the other guests would take the speaker to task.

"He's just a middle class farmer. Probably has dirt under his fingernails," another responded and several women giggled. Tears welled in my eyes and I rubbed at them angrily. Should I attempt to locate my cloak and leave quietly? Before I decided, the conversation started again.

"She's some nobody from Staten Island raising a whole passel of children. And I hear they're *not all his*," the speaker said and sounds of shock followed.

"And what about those dresses? Do you think she stitches them herself? Why, she showed up at the Greeley's home wearing a dress that was positively ancient." I had heard enough. As regally as I could, I marched into the dining room. By the looks on several faces, it was clear they realized I had overheard them.

"Cassandra, I'll need my wrap. Threadbare as it is, it will keep this poor country girl warm as I attempt to make my way around the big city." Cassandra Elliot's face was beet red as she instructed her maid to comply. She turned to face me.

"I'm sorry, Mary. No one meant any—"

"Thank you for a lovely meal," I said, cutting her off. "I didn't realize you would serve sour grapes for dessert, and I need to get home. My passel of children will be waiting. And you were right. Fred is their late father's brother, and he adopted three of them, and now we're just one big happy family." Taking my shawl, I left the room. "The happiest of holidays, ladies. I hope you get what you deserve."

I didn't breathe until I was halfway down the block. *I can't let Fred know how little regard these women have for us. Did their husbands feel the same?* I headed for Anne's, just a couple of streets away. As I got closer, I almost ran the last block.

Minutes later, I was sitting in Anne's cozy parlor with a pot of tea and a plate of almond wafers.

"Whatever is the matter, Mary?" Anne inquired gently.

Taking a tentative sip of tea, I determined it was still too hot and returned it to the saucer. My cheeks flaming with embarrassment, I recounted what had taken place that day. Anne looked horrified, but didn't speak until I had told her everything. She shook her head angrily.

"Those women should be ashamed of themselves. If that is high society, give me everyday folks any day of the week. That must have been just awful. I would have run from the room and never looked back."

I was feeling better. The ordeal was over, and going forward, I would do my best to avoid those women.

"And what will Fred say about all of this?" Anne asked.

"I won't tell him," I said.

"But why? Surely he—"

"I *can't* tell him. It would break his heart to think his colleagues and their wives hold us in such low esteem."

"But this is just a bunch of two-faced social climbers with nothing more to occupy their time than to disparage lovely people. I'm sure their husbands do not share their views, nor would they appreciate their uncouth behavior." But I shook my head.

"I cannot take the chance. It would devastate Fred. You know how insecure he is about his lack of a formal college education. One year at Yale doesn't measure up to some of these men, with their degrees and their fancy pedigrees."

"But Fred can—"

"My husband is of superior intellect, degree or not." I pictured his dear face and flushed with pride. I knew his worth, and so did many others. Who cared what a couple of dried-up society matrons thought, anyway? "Fred has more vision, more creativity than the entire commission put together."

"I'll honor your decision, and I'll add this to the growing list of 'things I can't talk about with Cal,'" Anne said, and I relaxed against the plush contours of the sofa.

"Thank you. And now, perhaps I can trouble you for some sherry?"

"I will, as long as you promise not to spit it out," she said, and I chuckled.

"I promise."

Chapter 29

Spring 1868

After weeks of planning, Fred traveled by train to Chicago for a series of meetings on a proposed park project. He planned to spend at least a week there, detouring to Buffalo, NY on his way home. The prospect of a huge commission in Chicago was intriguing to Fred. With a population of approximately 300,000, it was the fifth largest city in America.

"Can you imagine?" he had asked as I helped him pack. "The city is ripe for a wonderful park for local folks and tourists to enjoy."

"A beating green heart, my love. I'm so proud. Your passion, your vision! Don't forget this," I said, handing him his muffler.

"I won't need that, Mary. It's springtime in Chicago, the same as here in New York," he said. I responded by wrapping the scarf around my wrist several times, and stuffing it in his valise.

"Humor me," I said. Accustomed as I was to his need to be away for lengthy periods of time, I still needed to exert *some* influence on his day-to-day habits.

***

Fred was enthused by what he learned in the first few days of meetings. He wrote of his vision for Riverside, a stretch of prairie nine miles west of the city.

My loving wife,

I am seeking to celebrate the area's sweeping generous curves with nary a sharp corner in sight. It will remind one of the purpose of a public park — a place of leisure and tranquility. I hope you will accompany me the next time I travel here.

I read the letter to the children, which prompted John to beg for an outing to Central Park. I agreed, and we boarded a ferry headed to Manhattan. John was boastful as he pointed towards the city skyline.

"Someday, I will help Papa build more parks. We will be the greatest park builders in the world," he vowed.

"Me too," Owen said. "I want to build parks." John protested, but I assured Owen that *Olmsted and Sons* sounded lovely, silencing John with a single look.

"Come now, children," I said as the ferry reached its destination and we made our way onto the dock to spend the afternoon exploring Central Park or, as the children called it, *Papa's Park*. This was not the life I had ever envisioned, but on days like these, I could imagine nothing better.

Chapter 30

The next time I heard from Fred, he was on a train heading towards Buffalo. It surprised me he was choosing to keep the appointment as scheduled, because if they accepted the Chicago proposal, it would stretch him thin. But he kept to his original plan to detour on the way home. He wrote:

My grandfather used to say 'make hay while the sun shines'. I assume that is where my work ethic stems from. I would prefer to return several days sooner, but will honor my commitment and spend a few days in Buffalo to determine how much hay Vaux and I can make.

Several days later, I received another letter detailing his progress on the Buffalo project.

I met with the parks committee headed by former President Millard Fillmore. They asked me to choose between three sites, but I made a bold statement and integrate all three into a park system. The Park is the largest, a 350-acre tract of land four miles north of the city featuring Scajaquada Creek, dammed to create a lake. The Front, a smaller site overlooking the Niagara River, would a promenade and a waterfront terrace. The third site, the Parade, would offer breathtaking views of the city and Lake Erie. The three sites create the shape of a baseball diamond with downtown Buffalo at home plate, the Parade at first base, the Park at second and the Front at third. The distance between the "plates" ranges from two to three miles, and would feature with parkways and tree-filled avenues.

I re-read the letter with much excitement. This was an ambitious project, but I could picture just how amazing it would be. What would Cal think of this? Fred's partner was notoriously conservative and would no doubt want to veto the whole thing. But, to be fair, Cal understood what he was getting when he begged Fred to work with him. I remembered Fred telling Cal when he returned from California that he had "no interest in replicating the same design repeatedly."

A few days later, my prediction proved accurate when Fred described just how strongly Cal disagreed. Fred's audacity to commit to such a project without seeking his approval outraged him.

The next day, I had a visit from a visibly shaken Anne. Always well-groomed, she appeared to have left her home in a hurry, failing to tidy her hair or button her cloak. About to offer her a cup of tea, I decided something stronger was in order and minutes later we were sitting in the parlor. After I poured each of us a glass of sherry, I sat back.

"What has you so upset? I've not seen you looking so disheveled, not since we shared…"

"Fred is out of control, Mary. You must talk some sense into him. He needs to be more moderate in his business dealings. This Buffalo plan of his, well, it's pure folly." Anne took a gulp of her drink. I was shocked at her outburst.

"I have no idea what you are talking about. Out of control? Surely you—"

"He's acting foolishly, and Cal is afraid his extravagances will sink the firm. He feels betrayed, and I thought it best if I begged you to counsel your husband. Make him see the error of his ways." After another gulp of sherry, Anne slumped forward and cradled her head in her hands.

I was in favor of the Buffalo project and was proud that Fred had conceived such a glorious design. Taking my time before responding, I tried to grasp the situation.

"I think you may have overestimated my influence," I said. "We have always seen my purview as extending to our family and our home, but decisions relating to his professional life were his to make. I can't see how a park in Buffalo is that concerning."

"Three parks, Mary. Three! Connected with miles of parkways. And it's a baseball diamond or something. I don't pretend to remember all the details. But Cal is beside himself with worry about overextending the company's resources. He didn't even have a say. And it's his company, too. His name is on the door, the same as your husband's. It's wrong of Fred to treat him this way."

Ah, so that's it. This was more about ego than about a risky business strategy. Fred's was the face of the company; he was the visionary whose talents were in demand. Next to him, Vaux a bookkeeper, tracking inquiries and requests for proposals and fretting over every expenditure.

"This is a conversation *you* should have with *your* husband. His concerns appear related more to his own shortcomings than any actions taken by my husband."

"Your husband's actions *are* the problem. Don't you see that? Isn't that why you returned from California with nothing more than the clothes on your back? All a result of your husband's ill-conceived actions?"

"That is truly none of your business, and I'll thank you to not disparage my husband in our home. If that is all you have to say, it's best you take your leave. I'm certain you have more important things to do." I stopped and watched Anne slam her glass of sherry down so hard the remaining red liquid splashed over the edge. She hurried from the room, stopping to gather her cloak from the front hallway, before she rushed out the door and down the steps. I followed and watched as my closest friend disappeared from view. I wanted to hurry after her, but what could I say? I would need to fix this somehow.

Chapter 31

After reading to the children and getting them settled, I talked to Fred. He had gone to bed early, exhausted from his trip, but he would likely toss and turn for hours. I made my way through the dark towards Fred's side of the bed. He was still awake and as I perched on the edge of the bed and he spoke in a hoarse whisper.

"Mary, what is it? Is it one of the children?" I reached for his hand to reassure him.

"No, dear. The children are fine. But I need to speak with you." As he protested, I stopped him. "And no, this can't wait until the morning. I want to talk to you about Buffalo and Cal." Looking confused, Fred struggled to sit up.

"Whatever are you going on about? Buffalo? Cal?"

"Your plans for Buffalo. Cal thinks they are unrealistic, that you've stretched the resources of the firm too thin. He's upset, and it's affecting my relationship with Anne."

"Oh, for goodness—" I cut him off.

"Fred, she is my closest friend. If I'm honest, my only genuine friend. You can understand how important Anne is to me. With you traveling so often, I get so lonely and she is like a sister, until today. There must be some way for you to repair things and allow me to have this relationship. When you were ill, when we lost little John and the baby, I had Anne to turn to. I'm begging you to resolve this issue soon. There will always be more parks, more projects. People are more important. I don't ask for much and I would never influence you in your professional leanings, but I'm asking you now. Please, make your peace with Cal to restore a sense of balance in our lives." He was silent, and I wondered if I had gone too far. Then he cleared his throat and squeezed my hand.

"You're right, Mary. I promise I will make peace with Cal. Now won't you come to bed? It's late and you—" I planted a kiss on the top of his head and jumped up.

"There's something I need to do. Don't wait up." I blew him another kiss and hurried downstairs to write a quick note to Anne. Tears welled in my eyes as I recalled the angry words that had passed between us and I wrote.

My dearest friend,

I've taken the time to give our discussion some additional thought, and I am appalled at how quick I was to dismiss your feelings. I have asked Fred to repair his relationship with Cal, in order to protect not only the future of their partnership, but our friendship. I pray they will reach a reasonable compromise, allowing you and I to gain back our relationship, which I cherish more than you can realize.

Your friend,

Mary

Feeling calmer about the day's events, I went to check on my sleeping children before heading to bed.

***

I waited anxiously to find out how Fred's conversation had gone with Cal. It was a dreary day, and the rain kept us cooped up in the house. By late afternoon, I was a nervous wreck, and I almost wept with relief when John took his siblings upstairs to read to them. A few minutes later, Fred arrived home and as soon as I saw the smile on his face, I knew things would work out. He pulled me close and kissed me and before he even took off his coat; he started speaking.

"Cal's on board. Once I showed him the Buffalo design, he supported it completely. I drew the whole thing out, and he agreed it was do-able. He said it had sounded more complicated, but seeing it in print helped him realize that I hadn't lost my mind." I gave a sigh of relief.

"Thank you, Fred. And please keep that in mind next time. No more rushing into things. Please try to communicate more clearly, that's what partners do." I said with a wink to let him know he also needed to be more up front with me. Fred understood.

"Sage advice, my love. From now on, I shall do my best to seek support from *both* of my partners."

Now I needed to make amends with my friend. I would reach out to Anne in the morning and invite her for lunch. I was hopeful we would be back on speaking terms before we even lifted a fork.

Chapter 32

Winter 1868-1869

On Christmas morning, I unwrapped a gift from Fred. It was a copy of *Little Women* by Louisa May Alcott. He looked thrilled to have surprised me with a gift I would enjoy.

"Apparently it is all the rage," he said. "My contacts in publishing seem to agree on little these days, but the word is Miss Alcott is the new belle of the literary ball. And Miss Wormeley said you would enjoy it." *Oh, that woman again!* Her name was always popping up in conversation ever since he had run into her in Boston a couple of months back. Pushing petty thoughts aside, I beamed as I reached for him.

"Thank you, dear. This is a most thoughtful gift. I cannot wait to read it." After Fred kissed my cheek, we regarded the chaotic scene. All four children had been unwrapping gifts for the better part of an hour and wrapping paper and ribbons covered most every surface in the room. Normally I would be the one encouraging the children to clear away the clutter, but I was content to sit back and let Fred attempt to restore some order.

"Let's get this straightened up, shall we?" he asked. "The Vaux family will arrive soon with a new pile of gifts." Amid groans and protests, the three older children gathered up their presents.

"We'll bring these to our room, Father," John promised and headed toward the stairs, his arms full of gifts. Owen and Charlotte followed suit, leaving little Marion sitting amid her own presents.

"Charlotte, please come back and help your sister," Fred called out before he turned back to me. "We have once again spoiled these children," he said with a smile. I responded by crossing the room to stand by his side. He opened his arms and embraced me.

"Ah, Fred, don't you see? We have created a wonderful family. Our children are kind and loving and we should be proud. And thankful, too, today of all days."

John and Owen returned, and began gathering up the wrappings, taking turns tossing paper and ribbon into the fire blazing in the stone fireplace.

"I see what you mean and, as usual, you are correct," Fred said.

Early in the afternoon, the Vaux family arrived, bringing more gifts for the children. After a lively meal, Anne pulled me aside as our husbands engaged in a discussion about plans for Olmsted, Vaux and Company.

"I realize we don't usually exchange gifts, but just this once, I wanted to honor our friendship with a small token of my appreciation. You mean so much to me," Anne murmured, handing me a parcel tied with a gay red ribbon.

"But I have nothing for you. Although I believe there is one more serving left of wild berry trifle. I'm afraid that is all I have to share."

"Your friendship is all I need," she said and encouraged me to open her gift. It was a pale violet shawl. I pulled it over my shoulders and hugged Anne.

"It will be perfect to keep me cozy and warm as I read my other favorite gift this winter," I said.

"Don't tell me you received a copy of *Little Women* from your husband. But of course, Fred would have counseled Cal on such a thoughtful gift," she said. "I should have guessed. Gifts from my husband tend towards the more practical. Last year was a set of crockery. I had assumed I would unwrap a soup tureen this morning."

"I received Miss Alcott's latest." Then I frowned slightly. "Apparently our *Miss Wormeley* highly recommends it." With eyebrows raised, Anne regarded me closely.

"Indeed," she said. "And just how is Miss Wormeley these days? And when, pray tell, will you finally get to meet this paragon of virtue?" My frown deepened.

"I can't put into words exactly why their friendship is so irksome to me," I said.

"Perhaps because she is an accomplished war nurse, author, and sought after translator for those French novels you enjoy," Anne quipped. "But at least we get to benefit from her excellent gift suggestions, *n'est-ce pas?*"

We shared a laugh and dropped the subject, instead hustling towards the kitchen, hoping to share the last portion of trifle before the children could claim it.

Later that evening as I sat reading, wrapped in my shawl, my thoughts drifted to Fred. I knew I had no reason to doubt him; he was a passionate lover and a wonderful husband. But every so often I wondered what it was like for him, travelling and being away from his family. Was he tempted by other women? Was this Wormeley woman just a platonic friend? I shivered and pulled my shawl closer. I was tired after a long day and my mind was taking me to places I did not want to go.

Go to bed and curl up next to your husband, you silly woman. Fred had already turned in after a long day of playing with the children and entertaining our friends. 1869 was promising to be a very successful year for Olmsted, Vaux and Company, but he had promised to spend as much time as possible with us. As I trudged up the stairs, I imagined afternoons of sledding and ice skating, followed by cocoa and games of cards. In the springtime, we would row in Central Park or take a drive and enjoy picnics on the Long Island shoreline. It would be wonderful, and I wanted to enjoy every moment. Starting now, I decided as I crawled into bed next to my husband.

Chapter 33

Spring 1869

Fred was reading his newspaper at the breakfast table. Over the past months, he had kept his word, making more time for us. He had just directed the children to get ready to go ice skating in Central Park. "We must beat the crowds," he warned. Daily attendance at the park would be well into the thousands, even on an overcast day like today. "Last year the park welcomed ten million visitors," he said. I smiled at this oft-repeated claim of Fred's. It was true and a point of well-deserved pride. I was choosing to remain at home and looked forward to a warm bath and an opportunity to write letters to a few friends.

"Mary, did you see this?" Fred asked, pointing to an article on the front page. I put down the dishes I had been carrying and returned to stand by him.

"How can I know anything about what's going on in the world, with you hogging the newspapers?" I asked.

"What do you hear about the suffrage movement?" Fred asked. I racked my brain, but couldn't think of much. I had been hearing snippets about women's suffrage since the first Women's Rights Convention in nearby Seneca Falls twenty years earlier.

"I know it's women seeking the right to vote, but that's about it," I admitted. Anne had asked me to a meeting in the neighborhood last month, but I begged off, claiming to be too busy. In reality, the thought of a room crowded with angry women held no appeal whatsoever. Had Anne attended without me? I honestly couldn't remember. I pulled up a chair and sat facing Fred.

"It's more than that. They've formed a national association," Fred said, emphasizing the word "national." I wracked my brain for details, attempting to carry on a meaningful conversation.

"Who exactly? Those women who published *The Revolution*?" Last year, Susan B. Anthony and Elizabeth Cady Stanton had founded a periodical with the motto "Men, their rights and nothing more; women, their rights and nothing less."

"Yes, Miss Anthony and Mrs. Stanton just created the National Women's Suffrage Association. They are seeking Congressional approval for all voting rights and support of other women's issues. We may see this in our lifetime. Or at least for Charlotte and Marion. Can you imagine? Our girls voting in national elections alongside their brothers?" The vehemence in his voice surprised me.

"That is good news. But forgive me for saying I'm puzzled by your enthusiasm for a woman's right to vote."

"And might I say," he responded sarcastically, "I'm surprised you're not more enthusiastic. As a woman and as a mother of two daughters, don't you want women to be represented equally in decisions that get made?" He looked astonished that I could be less than passionate about the subject. I shrugged my shoulders.

"If I'm honest, I have never given the idea much thought. I suppose it makes sense. Women having a say in the world and the direction it takes."

"Mary. Women make up at least fifty percent of the population, live longer and God knows, are more than capable of making sound decisions. My stepmother is a perfect example of a woman who knows her mind and speaks it openly." He frowned slightly, apparently picturing the outspoken Mary Ann, who had married his father when Fred was still a boy. "I did not always agree with her views, but I respected her right to share them and I respect yours." He reached for my hand. "All I'm saying is you owe it to yourself to understand what's going on in the world. Whatever you choose will be fine with me."

"You're right. I suppose I have been so busy with the children and running the household I have thought little about myself. As a woman, I mean. Perhaps the next time Anne attends a meeting, I'll join her.

What do you think?" Fred beamed as he folded the newspaper and placed it in front of me. As he did, he bent down to kiss my cheek.

"That sounds wonderful. Why don't you read the article while I get our young ones bundled up and out the door?" I watched him leave the room with a smile on my face. *The man never fails to surprise me.*

Chapter 34

Fall 1869

Between getting John ready to head off to Yale University, his father's alma mater, keeping up with the three younger children and Fred's ambitious work schedule, it seemed there were never enough hours in the day. And lately, we were receiving countless invitations to parties and evening receptions. While Fred appeared to be in his element, I struggled to connect with those I met. I stood on the sidelines most evenings, wishing to return home. Memories of last year's ill-fated luncheon continued to haunt me.

I was feeling blue in the days following John's departure. He was my first-born, my sweet, shy boy. *Where have the years gone?* Our lives were changing, and I found myself clinging to the past. "What I wouldn't give to be sitting around the campfire after an afternoon riding horseback in the Yosemite Valley," I said to Anne one afternoon.

She snorted in response. "You may try to fool yourself, but you can't fool me. Don't you remember how worried you were back then? About your finances and Fred's not being able to settle down and provide for your family? Be careful what you wish for." I laughed at that.

"You're right, of course. I need to count my blessings. And I will," I said, but feelings of sadness continued to plague me.

When Fred arrived home from work one evening, he found me in the parlor, an open book by my side and an empty glass in my hand. He rushed into the room.

"Mary, whatever are you doing? Have you forgotten we are due at the Knapps in less than an hour? Charlotte and Marion are still at the dinner table and who knows where Owen is, and good God woman, you're not ready." He regarded me critically. "You're still in your morning dress and—have you been drinking this evening?" He snatched the glass from my hand and sniffed it. "Really, Mary? Drinking port on an evening when we are going out? I'm surprised at you."

When I failed to respond, Fred sat next to me. "Whatever is going on with you? Lately you seem so detached. Are you feeling poorly? Could you be pregnant, perhaps?" he asked with a touch of wistfulness. I turned to look at him. "Mary, tell me. Whatever is the matter?" I let out a sigh and collapsed against him.

"Oh Fred," I said. "I'm just feeling so lost. John is all grown up. He's a college man and we see him so rarely. Owen will be gone before we know it, and the girls don't need me anymore. This morning I offered to help Marion fix her hair, and she told me she preferred Charlotte and you... well, you're so busy with your work and at night..." My voice drifted off and I fell back against the settee.

"At night? We are together, you and I, most every night. I don't understand what you—" I turned to face him.

"It's just that you're the most sought-after guest of honor at all the best homes. *Everyone* who is *anyone* wants to spend time with the celebrated *Frederick Law Olmsted*," I muttered, feeling aggrieved. Always reticent to acknowledge his success, Fred reddened and shook his head.

"Why yes, there are those who wish to be seen with me or throw my name about as if they know me, but you know how insignificant that is to me, don't you? All I care about is doing the best job I can and returning each night to be with my family. My ties to Central Park were tenuous, but it appears the current administration wants to parade me around and make me the public face of the park. Who am I to fight City Hall?" he asked with an attempt at humor. I nodded in agreement.

"I know and I'm proud they continue to value all you did to make Papa's Park a reality," I assured him.

"This bout of fame will be over in a flash, and when it is, I'll still be the man who puts his family first. If I don't have you and the children by my side, well, then it's all been for naught. And I promise to turn down more invitations than I accept. You have my word." He looked exhausted and his shoulders slumped as he watched me for some sign of understanding. I knew he needed my support. Throwing a pity party was not the answer. *I am made of sterner stuff.*

It was my turn to reach out and pull him close. I patted his back as if he were a child. "It's all right, Fred. We'll go tonight, but I insist we beg off invitations for the next few days. Let's take this weekend and spend it with the children. Maybe we can travel to New Haven and see John for a day. And on Sunday, let's plan a picnic in the park, just the two of us. What do you think?" I could feel his head moving against my shoulder and took it for a sign of agreement. I sat holding him close before he pulled away.

"I heard the most interesting rumor today," he said with a gleam in his bloodshot eyes. "You were right about my being the celebrity of late." I asked what he meant. "Well, I heard my old friend from Hartford, William Peet—do you remember me telling you about our antics as boys?"

"Yes. I remember you spent hours of time with him, camping and traipsing around the countryside. But what does this have to do with your current notoriety?"

Fred got to his feet and pulled me up alongside of him. He whispered in my ear. "Apparently my old friend has been bragging to anyone who will listen that he has spent more time sleeping next to me than anyone in the world. Except for you, of course." I giggled and kissed him on the cheek.

"That old rascal," I said with a smile. "Not that sleeping with you is not a delight, Mr. Olmsted, but that is a most pitiful claim to fame for a man of fifty, don't you agree?" Fred nodded and we prepared for yet another night on the town.

Chapter 35

Winter 1869-1870

We spent the holiday season with family and a few close friends. This required turning down countless invitations as it seemed everyone wanted to spend time with the Man Who Built Parks, the moniker recently assigned by the *New York Times*. We celebrated New Year's Eve quietly. After an afternoon of sledding and skating we had a family supper, followed by Fred reading *Robinson Crusoe* to Marion while I played cards with John, Owen and Charlotte.

On the first day of the new year, I sipped a tepid cup of tea while Fred sat nearby reading a stack of newspapers. I liked to tease him that reading days-old news was not the best use of his time, but today I was silent, troubled.

When was the last time I'd had my monthly? It couldn't have been that long, could it? Anne and I had laughed about the subject recently. She was a few years older and had already begun the change of life.

"I'll be good and fat in a year or two," Anne predicted. "I'll be some old dowager, you'll see." I had laughed along, knowing I was only a few years from the same condition. But how long had it been? September or October? I grew frantic as my mind raced towards the conclusion I had been avoiding for weeks now. It was something I knew well. My stomach had roiled against food in the mornings, and I had been drinking tea with honey and lemon to reduce the queasiness I experienced. Later in the day, I would be ravenous, eating all the food on my plate. I knew with a startling burst of clarity that I was pregnant for the seventh time. Sometime this summer, I would bring another baby into the world.

I was nearly forty years old, and Fred was close to fifty. Was it even possible? Or would this only end in heartbreak? *Don't think of the babies you've lost.* But I couldn't bear the thought of losing another child. I must have spoken this last thought out loud as Fred put down his newspaper and was watching me.

"Another child?" He looked concerned, and I held back my tears. I could not hide my feelings or condition much longer, as my body would betray me soon. It wouldn't be long before my day dresses grew tighter at the bust and waistline. I let out a sigh and smiled at Fred.

"I believe we will welcome another child later this year, Mr. Olmsted," I said. Fred's face registered his total surprise, followed by a look of joy. He got to his feet and rounded the table to me. He took my hands in his and bowed his head.

"My dear, I had lost hope this day would ever occur. Another child? We are blessed." He stopped and looked at me and his expression changed, perhaps registering the fear I was feeling. "Oh Mary, I know what you are thinking. Of the other babies, our sons, am I right? The doctor said there was no medical reason we shouldn't have another child, a healthy one. Look at Marion. The girl is thriving. Don't you see? There is no need to fear this baby will be anything other than healthy. A son, perhaps?" Fred's voice trailed off to a whisper, but I detected a note of hope, of wistfulness. I knew every man wanted a son of his own. Fred was a wonderful father to both John and Owen and never treated Charlotte any differently than he did his natural born daughter Marion. But a son of his own? I knew he longed for nothing more. Perhaps he would get his wish.

"Well, you know who will be more thrilled than anyone, don't you?" We both spoke at the same time, "Charlotte!" We laughed, and I started to relax.

"She will be overjoyed with another baby," Fred said with a smile. "I doubt she has ever forgiven Marion for growing too big to carry everywhere."

"You are so right, Fred. But let's wait before we share the news. For now, let's just keep this to ourselves, until we are certain I mean." Fred leaned in to kiss me gently.

"Of course, my love. I shall follow your lead. Now, is there anything I can get you? A nice cup of tea, perhaps? Your favorite shawl? Or maybe I should stoke the fire and warm up this drafty room? The wind is blowing madly today. You mustn't catch a chill." I agreed a cup of tea would be just the thing and leaned back against the cushions as I watched him exit the room, his uneven gait so familiar to me, and his hunched shoulders so dear. *How lucky I am that the man who builds parks is also a man who builds families.*

Chapter 36

Summer 1870

On a blisteringly hot July afternoon, I gave birth to my seventh child, a boy. While it thrilled us, there was an unspoken tension in the days that followed. We had already buried two sons, and although I tried to blame my apprehension on fatigue and the sleepless nights that go hand in hand with a newborn, I sensed it also worried Fred. For several weeks he came home every night and rushed to the bassinet. As soon as he could determine that Boy, as we called him, was alive and well, he seemed to relax. I had been attempting to keep the baby awake as long as possible to get him to sleep at night, but the newest member of the household refused to cooperate. He preferred sleeping during the day and remaining awake for all hours of the night.

When Boy was six weeks old, I decided it was time to broach the subject of a christening. That night, as Fred sat at the kitchen table eating the meal that I had kept warm for him, I began.

"Dear, are you still in favor of the name Henry after my late father?" Fred stared at me for a moment before turning his full attention to the plate in front of him. "Fred? What do you think?"

"Henry is a fine name, but what is the rush? The lad is still adjusting to his new home," he said. "Must he adjust to a new name as well?"

"Yes, but Marion was already christened at this age, and John and I, well, we had the older children christened by this time." Fred nodded and slumped back in his chair. I tried to reassure him.

"Fred, our son is hale and hearty and if you need a reminder, please join me in a few hours as he exercises those very healthy lungs of his. You can see for yourself."

"I realize he is doing well, Mary. I'm not an idiot," Fred said. I abandoned the pile of dishes I had been washing and crossed the room. I pulled out a chair and sat next to him, our knees touching.

"I would never accuse you of being an idiot, Fred. And I understand your apprehension. But *not* naming our son will not guarantee his health."

"I know that. It's just that, well, to be honest, I'm uncertain Henry is the right name."

"Oh, so that's the problem. You're not averse to naming our son *per se*, but the actual name is the issue. Hmmmm, well, I prefer Henry. I think it is an excellent choice."

"I suppose that everyone will call him Hank," Fred said. "Mark my words. Everything will be 'Hank this' and 'Hank that.'"

"I will forbid anyone from referring to young Henry as Hank. You mark *my* words."

"Everyone knows when you don't allow something, it just ceases to exist," he said with a chuckle. "So, it's decided then. We will christen our son Henry Perkins Olmsted. A fine name. You are right, as always. I'm sorry you married such a grump."

"Well, the next step after grump is curmudgeon and you are far too young for that moniker," I said. "Why don't you finish your supper and I'll meet you upstairs. I'm told the best chance to sleep as a *new* mother is when the baby does, so this old mother is going to try it out to see. Care to join me?" Fred pushed his plate aside and got to his feet.

"That sounds like an invitation if I ever heard one, and I accept. I'm most pleased to accompany you," he assured me and, taking my arm, we headed out of the kitchen. Unlike many nights when we rushed up the stairs for a few stolen moments of lovemaking, I was certain that the only thing either of us were looking forward to was a chaste kiss and a good night's sleep.

Chapter 37

Winter 1870-1871

I hid my face in my hands, trying hard to slow my breathing. Ever since Fred had arrived home an hour earlier, he had been in a rage, pacing back and forth, slamming doors and yelling when I attempted to calm him down. I rarely saw him raise his voice and knew whatever was troubling him had to be of huge significance. Something about Tammany Hall, the corrupt political machine that had overtaken New York City, and a statue in Central Park. After putting Henry to bed and instructing Marion to stay in her room, I returned to the parlor. I wanted to coax Fred into the kitchen where I had saved him a plate of food. He had missed eating with us nearly every night for the past two weeks, and his frazzled appearance was upsetting to behold. My offer of a hot meal fell on deaf ears.

"You don't understand, Mary. I am telling you this is a travesty. That they could honor a corrupt politician like William Tweed in such a way is inconceivable. Boss Tweed! Boss! More like Shyster or Crook Tweed. A statue! In one of my parks? My very first park? I had every desire to punch that henchman of his right in the face for suggesting it. A big ugly man he was. Peter Sweeny! Everyone knows he is called Sly Sweeny. And he had the nerve to waltz in to the Parks Commission and demand his boss be given his due. I had to drop everything and rush over in order to not inconvenience the newly appointed president of the Department of Public Works. And bow and scrape in front of him? I'll tell you this will not rest with me. If they erect a statue, why, I will knock it down. I swear I will."

I had to smile at that last threat of Fred's. That my slightly built husband could overpower a larger-than-life stone creation of Mr.

Tweed in the middle of Central Park was laughable. But knowing how upset he was, I changed my expression to one of warmth and concern.

"Well, surely they would need to vote on this," I said. Fred laughed bitterly.

"Would that be the same procedure that allowed the cutting of thousands of low-hanging branches? Tweed got it in his mind that branches less than thirty feet high needed to be destroyed. Increased air circulation! That man rose to power by trading jobs and favors for cash bribes and political favor. He hired thousands of his workers to chop down *my* trees in *my* park. Then he lines his pockets from the sweat of those men and everyone thinks, 'Oh, that Mr. Tweed. What a true humanitarian! Giving all those unemployed laborers a chance to earn an honest day's work and make that horrid park more enjoyable for all.' Why, I have half a mind to go into Andrew Green's office first thing in the morning and resign. I'll tell him that Olmsted, Vaux and Company will not be cogs in the blasted Tammany Hall machine. Surely, Cal will agree with me. And stuff him if he doesn't," Fred said.

Just last week, Fred had come home from a meeting with the board, furious over their latest decision. The Dairy, an area of the park set aside for mothers to bring their children to receive fresh milk, was going to become a restaurant. Fred had fumed at the idea that they would eliminate a much-needed public service in order to provide a money-making opportunity and a place where Tweed could entertain his cronies. Coming so quickly after last week's debacle, I predicted Fred would not get over this new proposal any time soon.

"I agree with you completely. But giving up your role as a consulting architect? Wouldn't that be something Tweed and his people would celebrate? You would be playing right into their hands. If honest men such as you desert the ship, would it not be even more vulnerable to the likes of Tweed and that Sweeny fellow?" Fred groaned and rubbed his hands over his face.

"Yes. You are right. Cooler heads shall prevail. I should take you up on your offer of a hot supper and try to get a decent night's sleep. We need to live in order to fight another day, yes?"

"Of course, Fred. You are right as always." I led him towards the kitchen. "We'll have a nice quiet supper and turn in early, shall we?"

Chapter 38

Summer 1871

After months of reckless behavior, the political powerhouse known as Tammany Hall was a thing of the past, following the arrest of its infamous leader, William "Boss" Tweed. Although he never attempted to take any credit for Tweed's downfall, Fred was satisfied with the role he had played. Knowledgeable about the power of the press, he had parlayed his years of newspaper and magazine work into a series of damning articles in the *New York Times*, all exposing the ring of corruption Tweed and his henchman Peter "Sly" Sweeny had built. After the arrest of his boss, Sweeny had fled and had not been heard from since. No statue had ever been erected bearing Tweed's likeness, and although Fred had confided, "it actually would have been very satisfying to get in line in order to swing a sledgehammer at the disgraceful structure," things in New York were returning to normal. A new Central Park Board was assembled, and they named Fred and Calvert consulting architects.

Although the Chicago proposal was still pending, plans for the park in Buffalo kept everyone busy. Although Cal continued to voice his concerns, Olmsted, Vaux and Company continued to grow and they hired additional staff to sort through proposals coming in from all over the world. Fred leased additional office space on the next block and spent a good deal of time shuttling back and forth between the two locations. He ignored my concerns about his staggering workload, but promised to spend only an hour or two at work on the weekends.

John was home for the summer, on a break from his studies at Yale, and more often than not it fell upon him to make the weekly trip to

Buffalo. He stayed for two or three nights and I grew used to wishing him safe travels and telling him, "See you when I see you." Charlotte and Owen were also home from their boarding schools in Boston and Plymouth, Massachusetts. Despite all the comings and goings, it had been a most enjoyable summer. Most nights, we gathered around the table to share what had happened that day. Although Fred liked to grumble his children were "eating him out of house and home," I knew how pleased he was to have everyone together and how much he enjoyed his seat at the head of the table.

Earlier in the month, Fred had traveled with John and Owen to Iowa to determine if a request to redesign the grounds of their Agriculture College was viable. They returned home after ten days, certain this job would be worthwhile. It would be delegated to John when they broke ground next May. I was thrilled at the progress John was making at the firm. His meticulous attention to detail made up for his shyness. The first opportunity I found to get him alone, we sat in the kitchen after the rest of the family had left the house and baby Henry was being looked over by our new governess, Miss Rutledge.

"John," I said. "This is a delicate matter, but I must enlist your aid in something important." He regarded me fondly, his hazel eyes so reminiscent of my late husband's.

"Mother," he said. "It's not like you to not speak your mind," he teased. "Whatever it is, believe me, I—"

"It's your father," I said. "He's looking unwell since you returned last week. He hasn't seemed like himself for some time now. Don't you agree?" John spoke slowly, seeming reluctant to share his thoughts.

"Well. the trip was tiring for all of us. And Father is a bit past his prime, but honestly, he can run rings around men half his age. Owen and I can barely keep up with him." He sat back and chuckled. "Those Iowan farmers hardly knew what hit them when Father showed up. Within minutes, he had them eating out of the palm of his hand." I let go of the table edge I had been gripping.

"But you don't think he's overdoing it. Working too hard?" John leaned forward.

"Believe me. After a couple of days to rest up, Father will be his old self again. With me taking on the Iowa project—"

"John, I must tell you how proud I am of you. Your father, your late father I mean, would be overjoyed at your success." John nodded, looking pleased. "Just don't ignore your studies," I said.

"I won't Mother. I am eager to show you all what I am capable of," he said, a touch of pride in his voice. "I'll be of even greater help to the company. It's a shame none of the Vaux sons have expressed any interest, but between me, Calvert and Father, we will be capable of running things, and maybe give your husband some well-deserved time off," he said with a smile.

"And don't forget your brother. Owen is getting ready to contribute his talents."

"Well, of course," John said. "And while we're at it, let's throw young Henry in the mix too."

"We should wait until your baby brother is out of diapers and sleeping through the night first. And darling, I shouldn't have to ask, but—" John cut me off as he rose and smiled down at me.

"This conversation is just between us, Mama. Of course." He kissed the top of my head and strode from the room. I watched him go. So tall and handsome. The tightness in my chest had faded, and I felt light, almost giddy with relief. I knew everything would work out fine.

Chapter 39

Spring 1872

Marion and I were sewing in the parlor one morning when Fred burst in. Waving a telegram, he hurried over to the sofa where we sat.

"Marion, my pet, won't you please excuse us? I need to talk to your mother about something, well, quite queer," he all but shouted. Marion left the room after bestowing a kiss on her father's cheek.

"What has got you so excited?" I asked. "Were you asked to design a park for Queen Victoria herself?" Fred sat, stopping to catch his breath.

"That would make sense as I am a landscape architect. A builder of parks, I am." Never one to boast of his accomplishments, it was rare to hear him talk like this.

"Then what, Fred? What has you all up in arms?"

"An invitation to design a park would make sense. But this," he crowed, waving the yellow telegram, "this takes the cake. They have asked me to run for vice president."

"Vice president of what?"

"Vice president of these United States of America, that's what!"

"Ugh. With that Grant fellow, I suppose?" I had never forgotten the well-known drinking and carousing habits of the former general Ulysses S. Grant. "Isn't he the presumed nominee of the Republican Party?"

"Well, that's where this gets even queerer. That fop Horace Greeley is likely to get the Liberal Republican nomination, but they have created a dissident faction to take votes from him. They are calling it the 'conscience ticket.' There was a meeting here in New York just last night. They chose," Fred squinted at the telegram, "William Groesbeck of Ohio as the presidential delegate. They want to add my name to the slate for vice president. It appears the vote was unanimous." Fred sat back, a grin spreading across his face.

"But, Fred. That is ludicrous. What do you know of running a country?" At his crestfallen look, I hurried on. "You have much experience with the Sanitary Commission during the war, and the Park Commission, but is politics the best place for you?" *And is Washington, D.C., the best place for our family?*

"It *is* a dirty business. Still, it is an honor. Absurd, but still an honor." He shook his head, and I imagined he was ruminating over the sound of a title like that. *Vice President Olmsted.*

"So, you won't accept the nomination? Can you even refuse such a thing?" Fred chuckled.

"Of course, I can refuse. This is America. They can't force a man to run for office against his will. I will respond via telegram to, er... Mr. Carl Shurz at once. I will advise him that while I am honored to be considered for such a prestigious role with the party, family and professional obligations prevent me from accepting. With much gratitude, etc., etc., very truly yours, and so on." With a groan, Fred put his hands on his knees and got slowly to his feet. He kissed the top of my head and as he left, turned to face me once more. With a twinkle in his eyes, he said, "Unless you're sure returning to our nation's capital isn't our next family adventure, that is."

I laughed at that. "Oh, I am quite certain. They'll just have to find someone else to run our country."

Chapter 40

Fall 1872

I sat in the kitchen sipping a cup of tea, thinking how tranquil our house was. An early riser, I enjoyed time alone when I first awoke, but it was already late morning and so silent. Henry was napping, Marion was at school, and the older children were back on their respective campuses. It would be only a few years before Marion was at boarding school and by then, John would have graduated and Charlotte and Owen would be in college. *How quickly the years are passing.* I knew Anne shared similar concerns about her own family and considered reaching out to see if she was available for a visit. But today of all days, it was probably not a good idea to spend time together. Things between us had grown strained as the partnership between our husbands reached its breaking point. At that very minute, it was likely that Olmsted, Vaux and Company was being disbanded for good.

Just last night, I asked Fred if he thought they could salvage their partnership, but he had shaken his head. "I'm certain it surprised many we lasted as long as we did. We're so different," he said. I nodded in agreement. Different? That was an understatement. Fred had been the visible face of the partnership since day one and frequently received the lion's share of the credit. It was his name everyone remembered and although Fred gave his partner the accolades due to him, Vaux clearly resented his outgoing partner's popularity. Even Anne complained that Cal's role as second-in-command was unfair and should not continue.

I had walked an uneasy path for years, torn between love and admiration for my husband and loyalty to my friend. I tried to minimize any bad feelings and frequently reminded Anne that "opposites attract" and that their success resulted from their different strengths and personalities. What mattered, I said, was that the partnership flourished. But that defense had grown thin.

Although both men bore the title "Landscape Architect and General Superintendent" for Central Park, their individual roles were very different. Fred continued to gain the support of the commission and was elected acting president and treasurer of the Department of Public Works. Vaux was now answering to his partner; whom he had always considered his equal. He refused to discuss his progress on his projects and seemed to take, according to Fred, an "unhealthy delight" in failing to report on his activities.

The last project they had worked on together was a bit of a departure for the two men. Despite their initial reluctance to do so, they had created a design for the grounds of the McLean Asylum for the Insane in Belmont, Massachusetts. It was unlike the public parks they had built their careers on, but the finished product was well received. However, there'd been so much disagreement on other jobs that year, they sat down one day and split up all the remaining work between them.

Although I feared the dissolution of the partnership could harm my friendship with Anne, I had encouraged Fred to make a clean break. Confident that Olmsted and Sons would be even more successful than Olmsted, Vaux and Company, I lobbied him to decide and end all the fighting. And today, the years of disagreements and bickering would finally end. The two men had agreed to sit down and "discuss" the dissolution of their partnership.

I spent the day tidying up, and I took Henry for a long walk, but my uneasiness made me jumpy and unable to concentrate on sewing or reading a book. I felt a sense of relief when I heard Fred's key turn in the lock early that evening.

At dinner, I watched him feign interest in both the food and the conversation. As soon as Henry finished his meal, I asked Miss Rutledge to get him ready for bed. The boy hugged his father, bringing a smile to Fred's face.

"Good night, dear boy," he said, and after a planting a quick kiss on the top of his little blond head, he watched as Henry and Miss Rutledge left the room. Once we were alone, I dove right in to what would be a hard conversation.

"Tell me, Fred. How did it go with Calvert?" Fred looked at me sadly, shaking his head before he spoke.

"I assume it went the only way it could. We have been together for fourteen years, Cal and I. It is the longest relationship I have had with anyone outside of my family."

Fred shared how they had sat with an attorney and drafted an agreement. Unfolding a piece of parchment from his pocket, he cleared his throat and read aloud.

"It is hereby mutually agreed between Frederick Law Olmsted and Calvert Vaux that the partnership of Olmsted and Vaux Landscape Architects shall close so far as new work is concerned, and that all engagements on joint account shall, as soon as practicable, be adjusted to this date."

"What happened next?" I asked. Fred wiped his eyes before responding.

"We signed the document and shook hands. We parted amicably, agreeing to work together if the right opportunity presents itself. Neither of us left the lawyer's office with a dry eye."

"It must have been painful," I said. "But this is the start of an exciting new chapter for all of us. Come now, it has been a long day and someone is waiting upstairs for his Papa to read him a bedtime story."

"You're right and I'm sorry for being such a sop," he said and leaned on me as he got to his feet. "I hope he will be content with a short story. I'm afraid I cannot entertain him for more than a moment. I'm craving my bed, and my wife beside me."

Hours later, I lay awake beside my sleeping husband. Despite my assurances, I worried about the future. Without Cal, would it fall to me and John to monitor Fred's tendency to take on too many ambitious projects? Would Cal's conservative approach put an end to his own career? And how would all of this affect my friendship with Anne? I finally fell into a fitful sleep as streaks of sunrise filtered through the window.

Chapter 41

Winter 1872-1873

John Senior took ill, and Fred left for Hartford soon after the start of the new year. Their relationship was close, but Fred had not seen his father in nearly two years. John did not like to travel, preferring to be home with his wife and their three children. Over the years, they had invited us to Hartford, but more often than not, we had to decline due to family obligations or, more recently, Fred's business trips. Fred packed hurriedly and returned midday on Monday, reporting all was well and that his father appeared to be fit and as sharp as ever.

"He wanted to discuss the terms of his will with me and his son Albert, and all seemed in order," Fred said. "As his sons, it will be our responsibility to see his wishes carried out properly."

"And Mary Ann? How is she doing?" I asked.

"She was her usual self," Fred said with a half-smile. "I imagine she was pleased Albert will look out for her when the time comes. Not that it will be anytime soon," he added. "Father is in possession of all of his faculties and gets around better than I," he finished, gesturing to his left leg.

Sadly, Fred's cheerful prediction was not to be. A couple of weeks later, John fell and suffered a broken hip. Fearing the worst, Fred traveled to Hartford, but finding his father in good spirits, returned to New York the next day. When Fred received a wire a few days later, he rushed back to Hartford and found his father feverish and in a great deal of pain. Shortly after midnight, surrounded by his two sons, his daughter and his wife, John drew his last breath and died without ever regaining consciousness.

The funeral was private and Fred persuaded me to stay home with Henry, who was getting over the flu. John and Owen traveled to Hartford and returned with their father a few days later. At first, it appeared Fred was taking the loss of his father fairly well, reasoning the man had lived to the ripe old age of eighty-two. Back at work, Fred spent a couple of days in his office, working until all hours. He then fell into a deep depression and began roaming the house at night and lying on the sofa during the day. I knew how debilitating the loss of a loved one could be, and gave him a wide berth to grieve as he saw fit.

Early one morning, I stood in the doorway watching Fred. He was lying prone on the sofa; the damp washcloth I had placed on his forehead an hour earlier lay abandoned on the rug. His eyes were closed and his breathing appeared steady, but I could sense that, despite all evidence to the contrary, he was not sleeping. He had not been eating and had lost weight in the two weeks since returning from Hartford. He was thin and haggard looking, but I was more concerned with his emotional wellbeing. John, Charlotte and Owen were away at school, leaving only Marion and Henry at home. Marion tiptoed around, trying not to bother her father, but Henry was not easily dissuaded. Several times a day, he would rush into the darkened parlor and ask for a story or beg his father to play a game. But even his adored son could not bring Fred out of the dark place he had gone. I tried to talk to him, remembering how patient Anne had been with me when I had been inconsolable.

"Fred, dear," I said as I knelt by his side. "You can talk to me, my darling. You are not in this alone."

"He was a good man and a kinder father never lived," Fred mumbled and I nodded and squeezed his hand.

"Of course he was. You are also a very good man and a wonderful father." *Please get up! I need you, but more importantly, your children need you!*

Fred remained silent and his eyes once again closed. I left the room, but returned later that day, believing Fred needed to be jolted out of his state of malaise. He had clients waiting on him, employees requiring direction, and a family who needed him. I bustled into the room, and with an attempt at cheerfulness, called out to him.

"Why Fred, it is as dark as a tomb in here. I'm going to switch on a lamp and light the gas fire. This room is so chilly this time of year, what with the north-facing windows and all." Getting no response, I busied myself lighting the gas lamp closest to the sofa and then crossed the room to light the fireplace. "Oh, that's so much better, don't you agree?" Fred seemed to realize he was no longer alone, but had not yet uttered a single word. I squeezed into a space at the end of the sofa and lifted his feet onto my lap.

"Did I tell you we heard from John? He's fine, adjusting to being back at school. His last semester at Yale. Can you believe he's turning twenty-one? What a fine young man we've raised, don't you agree?" But I still could not elicit a response. "He's quite interested in the offer you made him over the holidays. While I agree with you Owen appears to have more God-given talent of the two boys, I am certain John will do you proud as a first-rate head draftsman. Perhaps over his break, he could help down in Washington. Wouldn't that be great fun for John to visit the place where he spent a couple of his formative years? Fred?" He gazed blankly at me and I stamped my foot in frustration. "Fred, talk to me dammit! This has gone on long enough."

Fred roused himself into a sitting position and shuddered deeply. I waited it out for a minute or two. My patience finally paid off.

"Mary, I am sorry to be so unapproachable. It has not been my intention to saddle you with all the household responsibilities, you must believe me." I nodded, and he continued. "It's difficult to imagine a world where John Olmsted doesn't exist anymore. As a father, he was the best. But he was more to me. Everything I've been able to achieve I owe to him. He was the inspiration for all of my work. I'm afraid the value of any future success is gone for me." Rubbing his temples, he leaned back and closed his eyes. I stared at him, dumbfounded. Disbelief turned to anger, and I pushed his legs aside to extricate myself from the plush sofa. Standing tall, I spun around and faced him.

"Frederick Law Olmsted, how dare you say that? I have been at your side for nearly fifteen years. As your partner, I have listened to you, tried to counsel you, and helped every step of the way. I have entertained your colleagues and stood by you more nights than I care to count, laughing at your jokes, helping you remember the names of dozens of politicians and donors. I served meals to that horrible Mr. Green so often he acted like it was my job. I have moved our family to Washington and all the way to California to help you realize your dreams. I have borne you four children and buried two of them. I've kept your supper warm and never complained when you were too tired or too busy to pay attention to any of us. I stretched every dollar during some very lean times, so your children had a roof over their heads and food to eat. And now, you have the audacity to tell me you have no reason to go on? That future successes are meaningless? That you did it all for your *father*?" At this, I was practically sputtering my words. I finally stopped, knowing for certain that if I uttered another word, I would burst into tears. Fred was awestruck.

"Oh, my dear, you have misunderstood. You mean the world to me, you and the children. It was a complicated relationship between me and my father. I wanted him to be proud. He helped me out before I found my true calling. But it wasn't until I married you that everything fell into place. You *were* there, every step of the way. Together, we built all of this. My father watched me from afar, but you truly inspired me. I'm sorry. It came out wrong. I'm just feeling so lost." I watched him for a moment, then crouched down in front of him.

"Now it is your turn. It's up to you to inspire our children. You are no longer the son, but you must be father to our children and husband to me. We deserve no less than your very best."

Fred shakily got to his feet and pulling me up alongside of him, held me closely. The tears he had been holding in finally broke loose and he sobbed into my shoulder for several minutes. I patted his back and let him cry himself out. When he finished, I fumbled for a handkerchief and handed it to him. He mopped at his damp eyes and attempted a smile.

"It will all be fine, Mary, you'll see. John will join me on a full-time basis this year and before you know it Owen and young Henry too. We'll take Olmsted and Sons to new heights and I'll count on your counsel and support as we climb to the top."

I nodded, but drew back, wrinkling my nose. "One small request. Before you join us at the table, a bath is in order. Cleanliness is next to—" Fred kissed my cheek as he interrupted me.

"Yes, yes. It's to the tub for me, and then supper with my family. I am a lucky man." I watched as he limped out of the room. Checking on the joint of lamb that had been roasting for hours, I reassured myself that while Fred would no doubt continue to face some dark days dealing with the loss of both his father and his business partner, Cal, the worst of it was hopefully behind him.

Chapter 42

Summer 1873

After months of renovation, our new home in Manhattan was ready. It was a typical New York brownstone, large enough to accommodate the seven of us and live-in help with suitable office space for Olmsted and Sons. Only an hour after moving in, young Henry located the dumbwaiter which originated next to the dining room, and rose all the way to the top floor. The three-year-old decided immediately it would serve as his personal form of transportation and used it frequently, eschewing the stairs whenever possible.

I was thrilled with the size and layout of our new home and happy to have room for my upright piano, which had been in storage for years. Having learned to play as a child, the piano was one of my most valued possessions, inherited when my grandfather died. I began playing daily, singing in a voice Fred deemed both "sweet and true."

Also pulled from storage were dozens of books, which more than filled the built-in bookcases flanking the fireplace in the parlor. Both Fred and I were avid readers, and our collection of books reflected our eclectic tastes. There were novels, collections of poetry and memoirs, and books on government, politics, history, and religion.

The entire family congregated in the parlor every evening to play games, share stories, and listen to music. John taught his younger siblings the game of chess and we all enjoyed backgammon. They easily convinced me to play the piano most nights, and the girls sang along with me. Many nights, neighbors would stop by and it was common for one or more of the children to invite school friends.

Everyone was welcome in the happy home I had always dreamed of, overflowing with laughter and good cheer. I was in heaven.

One night after an evening with family and friends, Fred cleared his throat and spoke up.

"Something has been troubling me for a while now." I had just unlaced my boots, and I wiggled my toes contentedly.

"Oh Fred, is there anything as satisfying as freeing your feet after a day squeezed in a pair of tight shoes? Well, perhaps removing one's corset is even more—"

"Mary," Fred said as if I hadn't spoken at all. "I want to talk to you about Henry."

"Now Fred, we've already had this discussion. I am certain the lure of the dumbwaiter will fade soon. And besides, I can assure you it is structurally sound and poses no threat to him." I had been concerned about our son's interest in the contraption and had tested it out with large stacks of books. I estimated that my most recent experiment with roughly four dozen books totaled more than twice Henry's weight. "It's really—"

"It's not the blasted dumbwaiter," Fred said. "You are not listening to me," he complained. I took a deep breath and let it out slowly.

"Tell me, Fred. What is troubling you?"

"His name is what I'm concerned about." He leaned against the headboard, relieved to get this declaration off his chest. I stared at him, dumbfounded.

"What is wrong with his name? You agreed Henry Perkins Olmsted was an excellent choice. A name to grow into and a fitting tribute to my late father." Fred spoke quickly.

"It is a perfectly good name and I'm certain your father would be proud of our young man." Now I was growing exasperated.

"Yes, he would be very proud. Why on earth would we change it?"

"I never shared this before, but it has been my dream to have a son named after me. Isn't it every man's legacy to see his son carrying his name on to future generations?"

"You have three sons, all of whom will carry on the Olmsted name and pass it down. Why does one of them have to bear your entire name? Explain it to me, won't you?"

"Well, I have achieved a good deal of notoriety, I would say. My name is well known and since Olmsted and Sons is a family concern, I would like to see a son of mine receive the same level of recognition someday."

"But Fred, what about John and Owen? They are also your sons. How would they feel that you named your natural born son after yourself?, John is already working with you and before you know it, Owen will join the firm. It will be many years before Henry is ready."

"That is precisely my point. These parks will live on long after I'm gone. Wouldn't you rest easier knowing that another generation is watching over their care and growth? And besides, my own father named his second-born son after himself. Why wasn't I christened John Hull? And you and my brother wasted no time after marriage, siring a boy and naming him after his father. Shouldn't I be granted the same privilege?" I shook my head, still not convinced.

"You raise a good argument; I'll grant you that. But won't this be confusing?"

"Most times when I address any of the children, I invariably get their name wrong. I am constantly mixing up their names and just this evening, I called Owen by John's name and vice versa. I doubt it will be anything more than a quick grace period and Henry will be proud to answer to the name Fred."

"So now when I call 'Fred', must I specify which one? Will you be *Big* Fred or would you prefer *Old* Fred? Or maybe we can just refer to our son as Freddie." Fred groaned.

"You know I detest the name Freddie. Even in the schoolyard, none of my classmates would dare to bastardize my name that way. I will not have my son subjected to that form of torture." He brightened suddenly. "What about Rick? That is a suitable nickname, and it sounds nothing like the other children's names. What do you think?"

"I think I'll leave it up to you to break the news," I said briskly. "And of course, you must pay a visit to one of the attorneys you hobnob with. If we're going to do this, we will need to do it properly."

"Yes, of course, my dear," Fred said. "Whatever you say."

Chapter 43

Fall 1873

"Mother, what on earth are you doing?" Charlotte's voice was shrill and her sudden outburst startled me. I put down the gloves I was mending and watched her cross the room towards me.

"Why, I'm teaching pigs to fly, of course. What does it look like?" I stared at Charlotte. "Whatever is wrong with you? You've been out of sorts all morning." Charlotte had been packing her trunk to prepare for her return to Boston. "What has you so upset?" I was growing increasingly concerned about her mood swings, and we had been walking on eggshells around her all summer long. I had spoken to her several times about her unacceptable behavior.

Charlotte flounced onto the sofa, just far enough to be out of my reach. Despite the coolness of the day, there was a fine sheen of perspiration on her pale face. "You're mending that tattered pair of gloves for the millionth time. Why can't you buy a new pair?"

"That is what this is about? These gloves are perfectly fine, and I can get at least another year out of them. Why does it concern you so?" Charlotte jumped up and paced. At eighteen, she stood just an inch or two taller than me, but her thin build and ramrod-straight posture caused her to appear much taller.

"It's ridiculous. And it's an embarrassment how we go around in threadbare clothing from last season, when everyone knows..."

"I don't care for your tone." I said. "What does everyone know?"

"Well, it's Papa. It is common knowledge he is very successful and Cecily says—"

"That would be Cecily Morgan, I presume?"

"Yes, her father says Papa is well on his way to becoming one of the richest men in New York City. That he'll soon be one of the Upper Ten. That's the list of the 10,000 richest—"

"I know what the Upper Ten is. But how is that any of Cecily's or Mr. Morgan's concern?"

"Yesterday, she was showing off her new clothes for school. More dresses than you would find at Macy's department store." She continued, speaking rapidly. "She said she couldn't wait to see my new dresses, and I said I had bought nothing new. She expressed surprise, commenting how rich we were and how it was unreasonable for you to be so tight with the purse strings and how sad it was I was part of such a miserly family." Charlotte broke off and looked like she was about to cry. "I'm sorry, Mother. I don't think you're miserly, and I am fortunate to be part of our family. It's just when I came in here and saw you stitching on a pair of old gloves, it made me very sad." I smiled at her.

"It's all right, pet. I realize how painful it can be when well-meaning 'friends' comment about matters on which they have no true knowledge. Surely you know better than to let someone else's opinion hurt so much. Do you want to know what *is* real? Can I share with you the facts about our finances?" She nodded slowly.

"Yes, if you feel you should."

"It's true our family's fortunes are on the rise. But don't believe for one second that comment about your father becoming such a rich man. Yes, he is quite sought after and his reputation is well deserved. But don't you see how quickly all of this could disappear?" I swung my arm around to take in the large, well-appointed room. "Your father and I have seen some hard times. When we returned from California, we were all but destitute. Those swindlers from Mariposa hadn't paid his wages for months." Charlotte swallowed hard and looked crestfallen.

"Oh Mama, I did not understand things were that bad. You joked we would replace our ragamuffin clothes once we got back. You said that it was no use purchasing new clothing only to have them ruined by a long trip home." I chuckled at the memory.

"I also said there were no stores worth spending our hard-earned money at anywhere west of the Mississippi. Anyway, it has never been in my nature to spend money foolishly. Your great-grandfather Cyrus Perkins raised me to believe in a life of frugality and I've never forgotten that."

I patted her arm. "But your friend Cecily was right about the need for a new dress or two. What do you say we find Marion and the three of us spend a little of our family fortune on some new clothing at Macy's?" Charlotte's response was immediate. She hugged me and dashed from the room, calling over her shoulder.

"I'll tell Marion, but let's leave Rick home, can we? I'll ask Miss Rutledge to look after him." I nodded and followed her up the stairs. Perhaps I should add a pair of gloves to today's shopping list. Looking at the pair I was holding, I had to agree with Charlotte. They really were beyond repair.

Chapter 44

Spring 1874

Fred paced back and forth while I bustled about, helping him pack for a last-minute trip to Plymouth, Massachusetts, where sixteen-year-old Owen was attending boarding school. We had received word from the headmaster about Owen's "troubling behavior" and Fred determined it best to deal with the issue face-to-face. I thought this was just a case of Owen being Owen, but Fred wanted to nip the problem in the bud.

"He's just like my brother John," Fred said. "He looks like him, acts like him, and now it appears he has inherited his problems." I sighed wearily. We had been going over this since yesterday's telegram reporting Owen's unwillingness to take part in extracurricular activities like swimming and horseback riding. I had long ago recognized that he was growing up to be the spitting image of his father. The two shared an almost uncanny physical appearance and a winning disposition. Compared to his shy brother John and his moody sister Charlotte, Owen was a breath of fresh air.

"Do you remember the telegraph network Owen cobbled together last summer?" I smiled at the memory of his creation of a working system between our brownstone and four of his friend's homes, one nearly ten blocks away. Fred stared at me in amazement.

"Mary, that is precisely the issue. His head is in the clouds. The boy needs to toughen up—learn how to saddle and bridle a horse, how to build a fire, how to save a person from drowning…"

"He is a clever boy at the top of his class. Plus, he is sweet and kind. They have already accepted him at Yale, which will prepare him for a fulfilling career. If Olmsted and Sons isn't interested, perhaps he will need to take his talents elsewhere."

"I never said Owen wasn't any of those things. But I would not be doing him any favors by mollycoddling him. He needs to be ready for the real world."

"Owen might not be the outdoorsman you want him to be, but mark my words. With his sweetness and clever ways, he will eke out a successful life for himself."

"You're right, Mary. When I meet with the headmaster, I'll suggest that perhaps the importance the school places on physical prowess is unreasonable. Maybe I'll convince him to allow Owen an extra hour or two of tinkering instead of swimming laps or riding horses. What do you think?"

I agreed and headed to the kitchen to prepare some sandwiches for the trip. I added a package of Owen's favorite lemon wafers to the lunch sack. When I had last seen him, he had been so thin. I would remind Fred to take Owen out for a proper meal off campus before returning to New York. I smiled picturing the two of them together; father and son enjoying excellent food and pleasant conversation.

Chapter 45

Fall 1874

I looked up when I realized Marion was standing in the doorway. I set aside my dog-eared copy of Jules Verne's *Around the World in Eighty Days* and smiled at her.

"What are you doing up at this late hour? Some warm milk perhaps?" Marion shook her head as she crossed the room and perched next to me on the sofa. At thirteen she was solidly built, already taller than me and Charlotte. After a day spent sledding, skating or boating, she would often read in bed far into the night. Fred described her as "quite glorious, so mature and even-tempered." She appeared anxious as she fiddled with the gold band of her watch, a gift for her last birthday.

"Mother, I'm worried about Father. He works too hard for a man of fifty-two." I put an arm around her and pulled her close.

"Pet, what is worrying you exactly? That your father will get sick or that he's not capable of —"

"No, it's not that he's not capable. But he's tired most nights and when he's away? I'm afraid that without his family to eat supper with, he'll work all night long." I shook my head with a smile. Naturally, Fred was tired. He worked hard. Why was Marion making a mountain out of a molehill?

"Now you know your father. He enjoys his work and has his pick of the most prestigious jobs in the country. Surely you're not suggesting he give that up." Marion continued to fidget.

"But couldn't he slow down a bit? Maybe John can take over the overnight travel. And when Father does need to travel, maybe I could, um, accompany him." I looked at her in surprise.

"Travel with your father to job sites, stay in rooming houses and roadside inns?" I was aghast, knowing how decidedly unglamorous his travel arrangements frequently were. For every night in a five-star hotel in a city like Chicago, there were several more spent in guesthouses with shared bathroom facilities and not even a lock on the door. And the men her young and most impressionable daughter would be exposed to? Construction workers and laborers. No, she would never allow it.

"To what end, my girl? And what about school?" Marion shook her head in exasperation.

"I would still need to go to school, Mother. At least for the next few years. But during breaks, that would be all right, wouldn't it?"

"I still don't understand what you could do to help. You're too young to learn to draft and besides, you're a girl."

"You are not listening to me. Here at home, you have Rick and me. And Miss Rutledge and Sarah and now John. Charlotte and Owen are in and out. Don't you see? Father is all alone out there. He needs to be reminded of home. I could travel with him so he's not lonesome for us. I could remind him to eat and coax him to get a good night's sleep. I could take care of him, like you do when he's home."

I thought my heart would split in two. With tears in my eyes, I hugged her once more. *What an amazing young woman!*

"I'm so proud of you. Perhaps we can consider a family trip soon. The next time Papa has to be away for an extended amount of time, we could join him, you, me and Rick. And maybe we could consider allowing you to take a quick trip with him. When you're a bit..." Marion grinned happily.

"Thank you, Mother! You'll see. I'll be worth my weight in gold to Father. He'll never want to travel alone again." After a quick hug, she skipped across the room. "Good night, Mama," she called and disappeared up the stairs.

Well, I'll be. Our children are growing up to be such amazing young men and women. If it weren't for four-year-old Rick, I would consider the raising of children to be *a fait accompli*. Phileas Fogg and his travel adventures would have to wait, I decided, putting the book back on the shelf. For now, thoughts of my wonderful family were all I needed to stay entertained.

Chapter 46

Spring 1875

I sipped my tea and unfolded the letter I had just received from Fred. The ten-day trip that he, John and Marion had embarked upon was nearing an end. Things had gone well and everyone was looking forward to coming home. I read it once more.

> *My Dear Wife,*
>
> *It is cherry blossom time in our nation's capital. Spring is in the air, and I write to you from my room overlooking the Capitol building. It is a beautiful day and I miss you and young Rick terribly.*
>
> *It would appear my efforts at creating the Summerhouse were not in vain. When I first envisioned the spot that would be the sparkling gem of the Capitol grounds, I saw it as a place to relax after a long day of seeing the sights. I planned the location so one would first encounter it after entering the grounds off of Pennsylvania Avenue. It amazed me how well the actual structure satisfies the need I predicted. I confess I was the first visitor to sit and appreciate my hard work. If I'm being honest, this is possibly my favorite of all the projects I've had the good fortune to complete. You must accompany me on my next visit. There is to be a ribbon cutting ceremony planned for late summer. Perhaps then?*
>
> *John remains an indefatigable worker and can literally run circles around me. He is even more talented than he has let on, and I remain grateful his pipe dream of becoming an artist was just a passing phase. Our Maid Marion has been a delight, rising early to ensure I eat a proper breakfast (can you imagine that she is not in favor of pickles and black coffee?) and that I end work at a reasonable hour in order to have a bath before enjoying a good meal. She is*

already asking about the next time she can join me. She has completed all her school work and I am confident she will return to the classroom next week an even better-educated student.

So, my work here is just about complete. I supervised the planting of hundreds of oak trees and am pleased to report that the workers, although apparently unused to taking much direction from a gray-haired old gent with a bum leg, followed my instructions to the letter.

Let's pack a picnic upon my return for the two of us. We can visit the Ramble in Central Park and like a mad botanist, I can tinker with the plantings that abound in my wild garden. Of course, that tinkering will not begin until you are ready to nap following a meal and a glass of wine. I realize you always claim to be only resting your eyes, so I'll let you set the schedule.

We are leaving in just two days and will be in your hair and wreaking chaos on the household before you know it, and you'll wonder why you ever thought to miss us. I remain your loving husband,

Fred

P.S. Kiss our youngest for me and tell him that his Papa will be home soon to read to him and teach him more card games.

I set the letter aside and decided that a celebratory meal was in order. I would send word to Owen and Charlotte that we expected their presence at home this weekend and ask Sarah to prepare something special—maybe lamb with mint jelly? Or roasted sirloin with horseradish sauce? I would bake a selection of cakes and cookies, as all five children had inherited their father's penchant for sweets. I would ensure every one of them was well-satisfied.

Chapter 47

Winter 1875-1876

Beaming, I looked around the table, crowded with those I loved best in the world. After a couple of years of estrangement, Calvert Vaux and Fred had reunited once more. Anne and I took credit, both of us having lobbied for a reconciliation, if only for social get-togethers like this one. "You don't have to be joined at the hip professionally, for pity's sake. Just agree to break bread occasionally," I had begged Fred. "If not for you, think of me and the children."

The two men sat at one end of the table, gossiping and sharing stories. Even during the best of times, there had been an uneasy tension between them: Cal, the penny-pincher who saw precisely what was in front of him, and Fred, the spendthrift who envisioned much more. But today, all of that was forgotten. What remained were two old friends, both of whom had enjoyed much success over the past two years. Three of the Vaux children had joined us, and we watched happily as our families reconnected.

"I can't tell you how happy I was to hear Cal had agreed to join us," I said. Anne spoke up, her words somewhat slurred from the second glass of wine she'd consumed with dinner.

"If he hadn't agreed to come, I'd have left him to fend for himself with naught but a cold bowl of porridge," she crowed. "Would you look at how well the children are getting along?" I stifled a laugh as most of the "children" were adults or very close. The oldest of the young ones, thirteen-year-old Marion had taken Rick and little Helen Vaux off to play upstairs, grumbling that although Charlotte was studying to be a kindergarten teacher, *she* was the one watching the children. Charlotte remained at the table, chatting animatedly with her brothers and our guests.

Following a variety of canapes and hot cider, we had dined on roast turkey, mashed potatoes, a medley of root vegetables and my chestnut stuffing. Our stomachs were full and life, I reflected, was good. John had settled in to a career with his father, Owen was enjoying his studies at Yale and Charlotte would graduate in May and thankfully, her mood swings have lessened. Not a single outburst since she had arrived home on Tuesday afternoon! I was thankful for dear Marion, surely the one of our five children who would care for us in our dotage.

And darling Rick! The bright light of the family and the apple of his doting father's eye. Contrary to my prediction, he had yet to give up his penchant for hiding in the dumbwaiter when it was time for a bath. I pitied the poor teacher who would be responsible for him when he started school next fall.

And most of all, I was grateful for Fred, without whom none of this would be possible. As if he was thinking of me, Fred suddenly winked and blew me a kiss. I blushed and shook my head at him. *What a wonderful man!*

I removed the linen napkin spread across my lap and regretted once more giving in to the demands of the latest fashion. Missing the comforts of generously cut dresses, I smoothed my narrow, close-fitting skirt and groaned silently. I would wait a bit before urging everyone to enjoy a brisk walk to work up an appetite for the pies Anne had brought. I had previewed the selection of apple, pumpkin and minced meat, all of which I would serve with a dollop of clotted cream or, for the apple pie, a slice of sharp cheddar cheese. I fully planned to sample a small sliver of each, the stabbing stays in my corset be damned!

Chapter 48

We were getting a telephone today and workers had been milling about our home for hours. When Fred first told me about the latest invention of Alexander Graham Bell's, I had been mystified. He believed having a telephone would be a competitive advantage in his efforts to attract new clients. He tried to describe the contraption and how it worked, but the conversation had stalled when it was clear he was getting nowhere in explaining the technology to me.

"Repeating the same thing over and over, just in a louder voice, is *not* the way to teach something," I had fumed. Finally, Owen, home for the semester break, had taken over. He explained how the telephone was based on the discovery that musical notes could be sent down the same wire if they differed in pitch. Bell's experiments had proven that different tones would vary the strength of an electric current in a wire and he had built a device capable of turning those tones into varying electronic currents, and a receiver to reproduce the variations and turn them back into audible format at the other end.

That had been a month ago, and while the process still puzzled me, I was looking forward to having telephones installed in the parlor and Fred's office.

"I'll be able to call my cousin in Boston and Anne to invite her over for tea or ring Charlotte or Owen up at school," I had announced over breakfast. Marion had looked amused, reminding me I could only call another person if they, too, owned a phone. "Then who will I call?" I said. "No one I know has a telephone."

Rick had been racing around the house all morning, shouting out the first words ever spoken over a telephone. "Mr. Watson, come here. I want to speak to you." I missed the days the young spitfire napped and tried in vain to get him to be still.

Fred had been popping in and out during breaks from working downstairs, almost as excited as his six-year-old son. "I'll take him to the office with me," he said, and after a quick kiss, the two of them disappeared. I sagged against the sofa in relief.

I closed my eyes briefly and tried to relax. It had been a hectic year, and I was frequently overwhelmed by the fast-paced life everyone else seemed to take in stride. I had talked to Anne about my concerns just the other day. We had been out for a stroll through Central Park in the late afternoon sunshine with Rick and little Helen, when I suddenly began to hyperventilate. Close to fainting, I sank down onto the nearest park bench.

Anne hurried over, concern evident in her dear face.

"Mary, whatever is the matter? You're so pale and you're perspiring. Do try to slow your breathing. Talk to me, please," she said.

I took the proffered handkerchief and dabbed at my cheeks and forehead. *What on earth is the matter with me?* I had been feeling a bit off for weeks now, frequently waking in the night drenched in perspiration, needing to push aside my bedclothes and change nightgowns. I alternated between feeling ravenous and pushing my food around with great disinterest. The last time I had felt like this, I had been in the early stages of pregnancy with Rick. *Pregnant?* No, that was impossible. Well, not impossible, I realized, my cheeks flaming with embarrassment. Despite our ages; I was forty-six and Fred was fifty-four, marital relations between us continued frequently. But pregnant? No, that just couldn't be.

Anne was watching me, a curious smile on her lips.

"You might be going through the change. You're just a few years younger than me and if you recall, I complained of similar symptoms myself." I nodded.

"I imagine you're right. We've just been so busy. Fred is working harder than ever and even when he's not traveling, it's rare that he joins us for supper. John is just as bad, to be honest. He continues to live with us, but it's rare I spend more than a few minutes talking to him. And Owen and Charlotte are always on the go when they are home from school, friends of theirs milling about. I sometimes feel Marion and I exist only to serve refreshments to our many guests."

Anne frowned. "But you love that, I know you do."

"I'm tired," I admitted. "I have a loving husband, dear children, and a beautiful home. It's the life I've always dreamed of, and yet I sometimes find it hard to enjoy, you know?" My eyes had filled with tears and I dabbed at them with a damp handkerchief.

"You know what they say. 'Be careful what you wish for,'" Anne responded gently. "'You just might get it.' But let's address the issue at hand, shall we? You are no doubt starting to go through the change. It's a blessing, all things considered. No more monthly courses, no cramps and no mess. It's actually a relief."

"But what about...?" I looked away, embarrassed by what I had been about to ask. Anne looked at me knowingly.

"About the bedroom? Is that where your concerns lay?" I nodded, my cheeks flaming red. Anne chuckled and patted my hand.

"While I am certain Cal and I are not as active as you and Fred appear to be, I am every inch the woman as I ever was, and Cal remains my ardent, albeit infrequent lover." I smiled gratefully, struggling to wipe the image of Cal Vaux in the throes of passion from my brain. "I can make a few suggestions to ease some symptoms. Things my mother and older sister shared with me."

"You're the closest thing I have to a sister, Anne. What would I do without you?"

Anne stood and grasping my arm, pulled me up. "That is something you'll never have to find out. First thing tomorrow, I'll bring a selection of herbs. We'll brew the worst-tasting drink you have ever had to force down, but it will help. We'll have you as right as rain in no time, I promise."

That had been two days ago and now, as I watched the telephone installers finish up their work, I sighed gratefully. True to her word, Anne had prepared a large pitcher of tea, using a selection of herbs and plants and instructed me to drink a mug full several times a day.

Last night, I had slept through the night for the first time in ages and my daytime symptoms seemed to lessen. I still felt overwhelmed, but without the panic I had experienced. I sat back, wondering who I should call first once the telephone was ready to use. I would convince Anne to get on the waiting list and install one soon. Other than my family, there was no one on earth I would rather converse with.

Chapter 49

Fall 1876

"Why does Tom trade his trinkets for a Bible, Mama?" Rick's high-pitched voice jolted me upright. While reading aloud, I had dozed off.

"What did you say, pet?"

"Mama," Rick scolded. "You can't nap now. You must read. I asked you why Tom wanted the Bible." I struggled to remember the plot. *Bible?* I had been paying no attention to the words as I read Rick's favorite book, *The Adventures of Tom Sawyer*. It was written by Samuel Clemens, an author acquaintance of Fred's. But he had a pen name. Stealing a look at the cover, I read the name "Mark Twain." *Of course. I knew that!* I had been so forgetful lately. Fred had been working in Buffalo and had been away overnight frequently, often for days at a time. Rick had been sick with a terrible cold, and he passed it back and forth between Marion and me. I was thoroughly exhausted, having not had a full night's sleep in weeks.

Although Fred grumbled about the amount of social commentary in the story of two boys, Tom Sawyer and Huckleberry Finn, enjoying adventures along the Mississippi River, it was the book Rick requested most often. I had lost track of how many times I had read it cover to cover.

Oh, wait. *The Bible, of course.* "Don't you remember? Tom knows the Bible will impress Judge Thatcher. Do you know who that is?"

Rick turned to face his mother. "Of course," he told me with practiced exaggeration. "He's Becky's father and Tom likes Becky. She's his girlfriend," he said in a singsong voice.

"So that's why Tom wants to win over the Judge. So he'll get permission to court her."

"Did Papa have a Bible to give to your father?" asked Rick innocently. Oh, how to explain all this to a six-year-old?

"No, that wasn't how it happened with your father and I. You remember I was married to Papa's brother John, don't you? Surely you know that's why —" Rick cut me off excitedly.

"Why John and Charlotte and Owen have a different father than me and Marion," he said. "But their father died and Father married you so you could have Marion and me," he concluded proudly.

"Yes, that's correct. Aren't we a lucky family?" But Rick had heard enough and wanted to get back to the book.

"Read," he said and settled into my lap. Now, where had I left off?

"Tom suddenly had the grand idea he would appear at his own funeral," I read.

"What's a funeral?" asked Rick. I sighed and shifted his weight from my left leg, which had gone to sleep, and groaned inwardly. It was going to be another long day.

Chapter 50

Spring 1877

It was past midnight, but I would not fall asleep anytime soon. The letter I had received earlier lay discarded beside me. Having set it aside when it first arrived, I had forgotten about it until I was in bed, after Rick had fallen asleep. About to dive into a collection of short stories by one of my favorite French authors, Guy de Maupassant, I went in search of the letter, locating it on a table by the front door. I brought it back to the bedroom and had read with interest. It was from an old friend from school, Lillian Remington Steele. Lillian had lived in England since she married Alexander Steele after graduation and although I had seen her only a handful of times since, she wrote regularly. Her letters were full of gossip and references to people and places I was not familiar with, but Lillian had a way with words and I looked forward to receiving them. She described a life of luxury and fabulous-sounding dinner parties. Childless, the Steeles seemed to spend most of their time traveling through Europe attending one extravagant event after the next. I always felt a tad envious after reading of their adventures; my own life seemed so drab in comparison. Not that I would trade Fred and the children for anything, of course. Still, travel sounded like a wonderful idea, especially with Fred currently touring the parks of England. Maybe the next time he takes off for Europe, I would join him.

I had skimmed through the first couple of pages written in Lillian's spidery signature hand. She ended the letter in her usual manner, "With Much Love from Your Oldest and Dearest, Lil", but had added a postscript. I had read on, but stopped when I saw my husband's name. What had Fred to do with Lillian's life? As far as I knew, the two had met on precisely three occasions over the past twenty-five years, the last time nearly two years ago here in New York. I read more slowly, growing more horrified with each word.

Fred is looking well these days. I have seen him out and about a few times this past week, always in the company of that friend of his, a Miss Wormeley? Katherine, I believe they call her. The two of them have been thicker than thieves at dinner parties and this lovely supper club that recently opened. The foie gras they serve is simply divine! I have to say that while pleased to see him looking so gay, I must admit to more than a few pangs of jealousy. The last time we traveled to New York, we spent a few hours in your lovely home, and Alex still raves about that leg of lamb you served, but we were unsuccessful in reciprocating your hospitality. Despite offers to host you at the restaurant next to our hotel, you turned us down, stating Fred was loath to spend yet another evening on the town. Well, he is singing a different tune these days, especially with "Miss W" on his arm and hanging on his every word. Perhaps—and I can suggest this only as your oldest and dearest friend—you should plan to accompany your husband the next time he travels abroad. I am certain he will share the details of these innocent assignations when he returns after completing the important business that drew him away.
XOXO L

Stunned, I re-read the postscript several times. Disbelief turned to shock and then anger. *What exactly was Fred up to?* While our relationship lacked a certain level of ardor of late, Fred remained loving and affectionate. Had he grown so bored to seek affection in the arms of another woman? Or was Lillian misrepresenting the simple truth that Miss Wormeley was merely a place filler, a name on a seating chart to balance the guest list? That was certainly the case. Fred had been forced into accompanying the woman in order to satisfy the wishes of their hostesses.

But that didn't explain why he would accept all those invitations. He always intimated that he preferred a solitary meal convenient to his lodgings and the opportunity to retire early with a good book and a single glass of port to help him sleep. Elegant parties and supper clubs were not high on his list of preferred activities. Here in New York, we kept our social calendar light, preferring to spend evenings at home with Rick and whichever of his siblings were available. Why, the very night before Fred had traveled to Liverpool just two weeks earlier, we had attended a dinner at the home of the head of the Parks Commission. Fred had grumbled about the "obligation," as he called it, and insisted that we make our apologies early and return home soon after dessert, prior to the inevitable port and cigar portion of the evening. This was in glaring opposition to the *bon vivant* "man-about-town" Lillian described. There had to be some explanation.

But, try as I might, I could think of no reasonable way to defend Fred's actions. I knew Lillian to be a tad flighty and even thoughtless, but cruel? Never! There was not a mean bone in the woman's body. And to what end would Lillian invent such a story, so full of vicious innuendo? To upset me? To cause the first of many sleepless nights that would continue until Fred explained this totally out-of-character behavior? No, there had to be more than a shred of truth to what she had written. But that put the onus on Fred. My husband of nearly twenty years!

And just what did I know of this "other" woman exactly? This Miss Katherine Wormeley? She and Fred had a long-standing friendship, that much was certain. I remembered first hearing about a British nurse Fred had met during his stint at the Sanitary Commission shortly after we married. He had described her as earnest and hard-working, and totally committed to the cause, but had he ever referred to her in a physical sense? He had admired her, but did he ever hint at more? That he desired her in a way that should be reserved for his wife? Miss Wormeley and I were roughly the same age and after the war she had parlayed her notable connections into a plum assignment as lead nurse at the Army Hospital near Newport, Rhode Island. After several years, she began a brand-new career in publishing, as not only an editor and author of some acclaim, but as a sought-after translator of well-known French authors. I recalled with fresh anger how irksome had been the knowledge the illustrious Miss Wormeley had recommended Louisa May Alcott's novel as a Christmas gift. Just who was this woman to presume she knew me or what I might enjoy? A spinster who understood precisely what the greatest writers of our time really meant to say? A home-wrecker with a long-held obsession with Fred? And were those illicit thoughts returned?

This can't be happening. I turned off the oil lamp and angrily punched my pillow. I tried to think calmly. Rick would be awake in a few hours, and I had agreed to take him to the park while Miss Rutledge enjoyed a much-deserved day off. Perhaps I could persuade him to accompany me to seek counsel from Anne? Surely she could offer her fresh perspective to this mess. I sat up quickly and unearthed the letter which lay crumpled in my tangled bedclothes. In the dark, I tried to smooth the pages in order to share them the next day. Anne would know what I should do. I finally let flow the tears I had been holding back and cried silently into my pillow.

Chapter 51

Just as I hoped, the day after receiving the news my husband was keeping time with Miss Wormeley, I addressed the issue with Anne. And as I knew she would, she offered wise counsel, declaring her vehement support of Fred.

"Mary, you know how much your husband loves you. How can you imagine anything untoward would occur across the sea? You must give him the opportunity to explain himself." I had agreed and tried to put the whole matter out of my mind. I would speak with him when he arrived home and not give it a second's thought until then.

A few days later, Anne showed up unannounced at my door. It was pouring rain, and I ushered her in quickly. After taking her cloak and getting her settled by the fire, I hurried off to prepare a pot of tea.

Minutes later, I bustled into the room, carrying a tray. "Just the thing for a day such as this," I said and poured us each a cup. After offering milk and sugar and a couple of chocolate biscuits, I sat back. She'd hardly said a word and looked positively miserable. *What on earth was wrong?*

"Anne," I began. "What brings you out on such a wretched day? Please tell me why you look so forlorn." She cleared her throat and spoke hesitantly.

"I was wrong, Mary. I gave you poor advice," she said.

"What on earth are you referring to? What sort of poor advice?" Surely this had to be more than just a recommendation of a butcher or a greengrocer. This was serious. My heart beat fast and I felt bile rise in my throat. Was it Fred? As if she heard my unspoken thoughts, Anne nodded.

"It's about Fred. I'm so sorry, Mary. I was wrong—what I told you. About believing in him." I thought I would be sick, but I tried to steady myself.

"Why shouldn't I believe in him?"

"I received a letter from Cal's younger sister. Do you remember Barbara? She lives in London with her family, twin girls who are just the…" She must have noticed the frantic look in my eyes as she hurried on. "Barbara wrote to tell me how she was recently the guest at a dinner party hosted by an old friend of the family. She was seated across from Fred, who had arrived with Miss Wormeley." Although I expected this, I felt a sharp pain at the sound of the woman's name.

"Well, I surmised as much from Lillian's letter. It is no surprise Fred accompanied her to a party or two recently. What is—" Anne cut me off.

"I'm sorry, but I can no longer vouch for your husband's innocence in this affair."

"Affair?" I slammed my teacup down as heat rose to my face. "What is leading you to believe there is something illicit going on?"

"I am trying to tell you what I know. Please do not presume to shoot the messenger." I sat back and attempted a sip of tea, but found it hard to swallow. I nodded slowly.

"Yes, I understand. Please continue." Anne squared her shoulders.

"Barbara talked with Miss Wormeley after dinner. While the men gathered with their port and cigars, the ladies enjoyed an apéritif and listened to a pianist brought in to entertain them. Barbara shared that her older brother was Fred's former partner back in the States. Miss Wormeley commented proudly how she had encouraged her *dear friend* Fred to sever ties with Cal, that he was holding Fred back from reaching his full potential." At that Anne's eyes flashed with barely contained anger. "The cheek of that woman! I can't imagine who she imagines herself to be. She has never even met Cal. And to tell his own sister of her mistaken belief that he has made little contribution after all these years!" I took another deep breath and let it out slowly. Surely there was more.

"Was there anything else? Did she tell you more?" Anne nodded sadly. I held my breath and waited anxiously.

"Yes, Miss Wormeley hinted that she had Fred's ear on all professional matters. That she had been negotiating commissions on his behalf all over Europe and that Fred would look for housing in England to be closer to his work. With his children grown and out of the house, Fred would have few real ties to New York any longer." She shook her head at that. "I'm so sorry. I hate to be the one who…" She stopped as we stared at each other. Finally, I broke the silence.

"And what was said of me? Was there any reference made to his wife?"

"No, your name didn't come up in their conversation. I guess that is to be of some comfort to you? That you weren't mentioned directly?" I dabbed at my eyes and sank back in my seat. *Oh, Fred. What have you done?* Anne looked miserable, and I wanted to reassure her she had done the right thing in telling me.

"Thank you for telling me. It must have been overwhelming to have to share this with me. It would seem Fred has much to tell me." Anne nodded mutely as I hurried on. "Did I tell you he sent a telegram just yesterday? He'll be setting sail from Liverpool on the *Persia* tomorrow and will be here by the end of the month. Rick is so excited his Papa will be home once again."

I would need to hear Fred out, but was a reasonable explanation even possible?

Chapter 52

I had been sitting at the kitchen table staring at a cold cup of tea for nearly an hour. Rick was in his room reading, following a supper of oatcakes slathered in butter and honey. I had nibbled at a dry oatcake, but had little success swallowing solid food. I had been subsisting on tea and a generous glass of port to help me sleep, ever since hearing the news of my husband's betrayal some ten days earlier. My dress hung loose and the extra weight I carried since giving birth to Rick six years earlier had vanished. At one time, I might have been delighted with the change in my appearance. Knowing Fred would be home any day, I had considered bathing in the bath salts he liked or styling my hair, but failed to do either.

When Fred, John, Owen, Charlotte and Marion came trooping into the house an hour later, there was much laughter and whoops of joy. Rick came down to see what all the fuss was about. I was reserved, despite hugs and kisses from Fred and both daughters, neither of whom I had seen since the holidays. John bent over and whispered in my ear.

"I wanted to surprise you, Mama," he said. "When Papa notified me that his ship would dock tonight, I asked Owen and the girls to meet me at the harbor. I almost gave it away this morning as I left for work and you asked me if I would be home for supper." I spoke slowly, almost mechanically in response.

"You said you had plans. You said not to wait for you. Rick and I have eaten, I'm afraid." Fred overheard the last part and patted me gently on the shoulder.

"Don't worry, Mary. What does everyone think about going out to dinner this evening?" John and Owen voiced approval of their father's plan, and left the room with their youngest brother to help him get ready. The girls hurried after them, leaving me alone with Fred. I hadn't spoken to him yet or even made eye contact. He looked closely at me. "Mary, what do you think? Shall we head out for a meal and a glass of wine or beer?"

I bit back the first response that came to me. I wanted to shout, "Since when are you in the habit of going out on the town after a voyage like the one you just took?" He was usually reticent to spend an evening anywhere but in his own parlor after an extended trip. "Who are you and what have you done with my husband?" I wanted to scream. "Is this dalliance with your precious Miss Wormeley responsible for the newfound spring in your step?" Or maybe it is the desire to avoid an evening alone with me that is causing his desire to go out for the evening? Looking at him now, his blue eyes sparkling happily, I wanted to say these things, to ask these questions. But hearing the boys clattering down the stairs, I took a deep breath.

"Sounds delightful. Let me get my cloak and we'll be off."

***

Hours later, I sat and tugged at my boots. Despite my weight loss, my feet were swollen, and the leather clung to them. When Fred saw what I was attempting, he hurried towards me. "Let me help you, my dear," he offered gently, then looked shocked when I angrily pulled away.

"I'm capable of removing my own footwear," I said, continuing with the task at hand. Fred stood a few feet away, a puzzled look on his weary face.

"What is it, Mary?" he asked. "You've barely spoken a word all evening, and you hardly touched your meal. Even with these old eyes of mine, it is easy to see you have lost weight. What are you not telling me?" I removed the second boot and flung it across the room.

"I talk too much, I talk too little. I put on weight and I take it off. It appears I am unlikely to satisfy your many expectations." He shook his head as if he could not believe what he was hearing.

"I love the sound of your voice and I don't recall ever suggesting that you talk too much. And as far as your weight, I love you whether you are as plump as a partridge or slender as a reed. I always think you are beautiful." I nearly snorted, biting back an angry retort that would have shown my hand to him. I had decided that I would hold off this discussion tonight. I wanted to be well rested before I brought up the subject of his dalliances and our future together.

I grabbed a pillow and a blanket and pushed both into Fred's arms. "You should sleep on the sofa in your office. I'm coming down with something and it would be dreadful if you were to take ill right after returning home from your trip." He gripped the bedding tightly, apparently waiting for me to say more. "Go," I said more gently. "Save yourself. I'll be fine after a good night's sleep." He nodded, and I watched him leave the room, closing the door softly behind him. I threw myself down on the bed and tried not to cry. *What would happen tomorrow?* Would Fred admit to having romantic feelings for another woman? Express his desire to move to Europe and leave me behind? And then, the question that nearly broke my heart to even consider: *how can I live without him?*

Chapter 53

I wasted no time in confronting Fred the next morning. I had lain awake for hours, stopping myself several times from taking the stairs to his office. I had finally fallen asleep close to dawn and missed seeing the older children off. Now it was near nine, and I was clearing Rick's breakfast plate when Fred showed up, looking rumpled and exhausted. I was certain the lumpy sofa in his office was to blame and felt a perverse sense of delight. Rick was excited to see his Papa, but I had arranged for Miss Rutledge to keep him occupied, so he headed with her to the park after extracting a promise from his father for a game of cards when he returned.

Fred watched him go with a wistful smile. "Is it me, or has that boy grown a foot since I've been gone?" I nodded curtly.

"Yes, Fred. Rick is sprouting up nicely. I believe he'll grow to be taller than either John or Owen." *Or you.* "But I don't wish to speak of our children this morning."

Fred watched me as he poured himself a cup of coffee and pulled out a chair. He sank down and patted the chair next to him. "Come join me, won't you?"

I ignored him and instead positioned myself directly across the table from him. I sat staring at him for a moment and Fred grew flustered. He cleared his throat and leaned forward. "Well, Mary, you have me in suspense. What is on your mind this fine spring day?" I gripped the table to steady myself. Suddenly nervous, I drew in a deep breath, before letting it out slowly.

"So, what is the n-news from London?" I asked. At his look of confusion, I hurried on. "London, you know. The capital city of England. Gay nightlife? Dinner parties and elegant supper clubs? Such an exciting place, so far removed from this oh-so-drab existence. Enlighten me, won't you? It is so rare an occasion I can spend time with a dashing man-about-town such as yourself." Fred's look of confusion turned to a tentative smile, then he laughed out loud.

"You are pulling my leg. For a moment there, you had me—" He stopped, alarmed by the look of fury on my face. He appeared to wilt right in front of me as I continued to glare at him. "My dear, whatever are you…" I couldn't hold back any longer. My words came out in a strangled whisper.

"How could you, Fred? How could you betray me like this? What have I done to be treated so poorly?" Fred's look of concern grew to one of puzzled confusion.

"My love, I have no clue to what you are referring. Betray you? Please tell me what you are talking about."

"I am referring to your assignation with a certain woman during your travels. Surely you recall being paired with Miss Wormeley, don't you? Dinner parties, smart suppers, and those interesting conversations about your future in Europe. Ringing any bells?" Fred still looked confused.

"While it's true Kath—er, Miss Wormeley and I sat together a handful of times at those dinner parties I detest, I would hardly refer to what we had as an assignation. Who is filling your head with such nonsense?" I shook my head crossly.

"Don't dare to make me the object of any inquisition. What is going on with you and that woman!"

"Nothing Mary, that's what I am trying to tell you. A couple of well-meaning hostesses couldn't bear the thought of an empty seat at the table. That is the extent of it, I assure you."

"Then why does she presume to plan the next phase of your life for you? Apparently, Miss Wormeley is scouring the English countryside for a cozy cottage for the two of you. No ties to New York any longer. Why not start a new life with a new woman?" Sputtering with barely controlled anger, I burst into tears.

"What's to become of me and Rick? Will I need to make a home with John if he is to marry? How could you do this to m-m-me?" Fred looked flabbergasted. He crossed over to where I sat. Grabbing my hands in his, he pulled me closer.

"Mary, that is utter nonsense. A country cottage? A life removed from you and the children? That is total fabrication. You must believe me."

"Then your Miss Wormeley must be misinformed, as she appears to be dreaming of a life with you. One funded by all the projects she has mined on your behalf."

"It is true claims for my services have stretched across the pond." Fred shook his head in amazement. "But honestly, there have only been a few actual projects that have gone beyond a casual conversation. And that is one of the exciting bits of news I wanted to share. I longed to tell everyone last night, but I thought it fair I have the conversation with you first." I looked at him curiously.

"What news? You planned this trip to seek inspiration for the projects here in the States. You said nothing of wanting to drum up business in Europe."

"I needed inspiration, but I had agreed to talk to some city planners who were meeting in London. The country is seeking to unify their many parks and create a network. They sought my advice and may wish to bring me on as a paid consultant for a couple of years." At my look of shock, he went on. "It would be a part-time commitment, allowing me to set my own timetable. And besides a healthy monthly stipend, there would be a housing allowance. I mentioned the possibility of this to Katherine, and perhaps that is why she took it upon herself to search for a home for me, you and Rick." I must have looked surprised as he hurried to assure me. "If I decide this will be a prudent course of action after conferring with my partner," he said with a finger pointed in my direction, "we would require a proper home to hang our hats while abroad." I breathed normally again, and tears of relief spilled forth. Fred wiped a tear making its way down my cheek and I grasped his hand.

"So, Fred. I need to hear you say it. Is there nothing untoward about your relationship with Miss Wormeley?"

"Nothing, Mary. You are my wife and mother of my children. I love you. I cherish you and I respect you. You have my word." I was once again crying in earnest. I fell back into Fred's arms, allowing the rough tweed of his jacket to sop up my tears. "If you need further proof, I can arrange a meeting between the two of you." I pulled away, a look of horror across my face.

"No, your word is good enough for me," I said, shuddering inwardly at the idea of a face-to-face with that woman. While I trusted my husband, I had no such feelings for Miss Wormeley. I would keep my husband close and my enemy far, far away.

Chapter 54

Fall 1878

"You are a beautiful bride," I said to Charlotte, who had been fussing with her veil for the past ten minutes. We were in a tiny anteroom off the main chapel of Trinity Church in Boston. Charlotte was marrying Dr. John Bryant, whom she had met through friends the previous year. They were off on a trip to Europe the following day, before settling into a home in Cohasset on Boston's South Shore. Fred and I were well-pleased with our future son-in-law and hoped his calm influence would steady our moody daughter. Charlotte had frequently grown distraught over the smallest of details concerning the wedding reception celebration and the itinerary of her honeymoon trip.

"Just think how exciting it will be to travel to Europe. I made a list of the places your late father and I visited there. Of course, you were too young to remember being—" Charlotte yanked the veil off of her head and flung it across the room.

"Mother, if you bring up that garden in Paris where I took my first steps or that café in Brussels when you first realized you were pregnant with Owen, I will scream. For the thousandth time, I am telling you I don't care about those trips. Or your memories. John and I will create our own special memories." I sighed in relief. Although hurt by her rude behavior, I was glad Charlotte was finally looking forward to something. I picked up the veil, smoothing it as I returned to Charlotte. Timidly handing it to her, I told myself all brides were nervous on their wedding day and it was natural to express any pent-up feelings to—or at—those closest to you. Poor Marion had already run from the room in the aftermath of Charlotte's outburst fifteen minutes ago.

"Of course you will. Shall we take a last look in the mirror and go find your father? He is looking forward to walking you down the aisle and giving your hand to your lovely doctor." Silence. "What do you say, my dear?" I held my breath, hoping there would be no more ugly flare-ups, and let out a sigh of relief when Charlotte fitted the veil on her carefully coifed brown hair. With one last look in the mirror, she took my arm, and we left the room.

"I'm so glad we found this new gown," she said as we caught sight of Fred waiting in the narthex with Marion. "The gown you wore when you married Father is just so dated," she said, wrinkling her nose. *Of course it was dated. I wore it over twenty-five years ago!* If Charlotte didn't want to wear my wedding dress, that was fine with me.

"It's perfect," I said after we reached Fred and Marion. John materialized out of nowhere and to the sounds of a large pipe organ playing Mendelssohn's Wedding March, my son escorted me to my seat in the front row.

***

Everyone agreed the marriage of Dr. John Bryant of Boston and Miss Charlotte Olmsted of New York City was the highlight of the fall social season in Boston. I had pulled out all the stops, as Charlotte was the first of our five children to get married, and to a doctor no less, from a well-established family. I had been determined to pull off the classiest of events. After an initial reaction to the size of the guest list and a question about how much this would cost, Fred wisely kept his thoughts to himself on the menu, the flowers and the gowns for the bride, Marion and me. We held the reception for nearly two hundred guests at the Parker House hotel overlooking the Boston Common.

Our guests dined on filet of beef and smoked haddock along with the hotel's signature Parker House rolls and mulled wine. The wedding cake was an arrangement of two dozen Boston Cream pies, a confection of yellow sponge cake with custard cream, topped with a thick layer of chocolate fudge fondant. The dessert, created in the Parker House kitchen, got rave reviews and I had enjoyed a generous slice, despite an acute case of nerves and the constricting stays of my corset. After a dance with his daughter, Fred had whisked me onto the dance floor. I was nearly breathless with excitement. Waltzing with my husband was an experience I had only enjoyed a handful of times in nearly twenty years of marriage.

As we prepared to leave for home the next day, after seeing the newlyweds off at the pier, I remarked to Fred that I had enjoyed the dance we shared.

"We should dance more often, Mr. Olmsted," I said with a smile. Fred nodded enthusiastically.

"If not for this bum leg of mine, I would enjoy it even more, Mrs. Olmsted," he said.

"When do you suppose we might have the opportunity again?" I wondered aloud. Fred shook his head.

"Well, if you are waiting for any of our other children to marry soon, I would advise you not to hold your breath."

"You don't think John will find a suitable mate?" Fred studied me before he answered.

"Honestly, Mary, I must confess I do not. He is a fine lad and a wonderful son. And a top-notch draftsman. Olmsted and Sons is a much stronger company with John by my side." I beamed with pride, but my smile turned into a frown as he continued. "But socially? I fear our son will be a bach for life. He's so shy. Have you ever seen him so much as look at a girl? Charlotte's friends have been parading about in front of him for years in vain. I'm telling you—"

"He's just a late bloomer," I said. "He's—"

"He's twenty-five, Mary. Why, at his age I had already, well, gotten out there, you know?" His voice trailed off at the sight of me glaring at him. Yes, I knew well what a ladies' man he had been. He'd had the reputation of being a bit of a dandy, leaving behind a trail of broken hearts. I smiled slowly. I couldn't honestly blame him or judge him harshly. I'd had a few beaux myself before meeting and marrying for the first time at twenty-two. *People who live in glass houses...*

"Mark my words, Fred. John will meet the right woman and fall madly in love. And, even if he is not heading to the altar, Owen may be the next to leave the nest." Fred agreed happily. Owen was a charmer and, despite a delicate constitution, would have his pick of women when he was ready to settle down.

"Quite the catch, our Owen," Fred said and began buckling our trunks for the trip back to New York. I omitted any mention of *Maid Marion's* chances for finding a suitable mate. At the tender age of seventeen, surely it would be several years before she would be in the market for a husband.

Chapter 55

Spring 1879

"When I return from the Falls, we will visit Charlotte and John, I promise you," Fred assured me. He had submitted a bid to design the State Reservation at Niagara Falls and was leaving for a preliminary visit. "I really wish you could join me this week." I did, too, but Rick had caught a cold and was coughing and sneezing, leaving me no choice but to stay home with him.

"If this looks like promising, perhaps I can join you next time," I said.

"We will need to squeeze in a trip before the first of the next generation arrives. Can you believe Charlotte is having a baby? It seems like just yesterday she was a little tot herself." I had to agree the years had flown by. We would celebrate our twentieth wedding anniversary this summer, and the birth of our first grandchild.

Despite all this joy, I had a concern. I had hoped marriage would help to steady Charlotte, but lately she seemed to fly off the handle at the slightest provocation. Just last month while I was visiting, I had dropped a china saucer. Before I grabbed the broom, Charlotte had taken the remaining eleven saucers and smashed them on the floor. While I stood open-mouthed in shock, Charlotte rushed from the room and seconds later a door slammed upstairs. Shocked, I cleaned up the mess, trying to recall my first pregnancy. I had been a newlywed, but I was certain I had not exhibited such fits as hers. I finished sweeping and dumped the broken dishes into the trash bin. I could have suggested Charlotte order replacements from Macy's right away, but had postponed offering any unsolicited motherly advice. So, I made a cup of tea and waited in the parlor for Charlotte to join me. After an hour, she did. We discussed baby names, and we never mentioned the subject of the saucers again.

***

When Fred arrived home later in the week, I tearfully reported that despite Rick being in the pink of good health once more, we needed to postpone a visit to see Charlotte.

"John called last night and was adamant. He told me in no uncertain terms it was not a good time and that Charlotte needed to rest."

"Well, he is a doctor..."

"And I'm her mother, I know her better than anyone. And how does he presume to refer to us as 'company'? He is her husband, but we're her family."

"Why, of course we are. And John knows that. He is a good man," Fred said. "He wants what is best for her. Perhaps this is as good a time as any to tell you about my latest project. I think you'll approve." I groaned inwardly but turned to face him.

"As long as it requires no overnight travel, I'll be happy."

"No, this would involve some travel for certain. In fact, I'll be gone for a good part of the summer." I stared at him in horror.

"With our anniversary coming up and the new baby? And you promised to teach Rick to sail. We joined the New York Yacht Club for that very reason. Frankly Fred, I'm shocked you would even..." Fred cut me off with a wide grin.

"It's Boston, Mary! I ran into some old school chums while I was returning home from the falls. They want me to build a park in the center of Boston. They plan to call it the Arnold Arboretum, after the family—"

"So you'll be nearby when Charlotte has her baby. But what about—"

"You'll be with me, my love. I told them that besides the design fee and a weekly stipend, I would need proper lodging for my family." I drew in a deep breath and spoke almost in a whisper.

"Do you mean it, Fred? We'll join you in Boston for the summer? Rick and Marion too?"

"Well, of course, silly woman. You'll want to be near Charlotte to help with the baby. It will be a grand adventure for all of us. I hear they even have a harbor where a certain young man could learn to sail," he said with a wink. "John can run things here and can make the trip to Niagara as needed. Owen will be home from Yale with the entire summer to pitch in. And Marion can join us or rotate between here and Boston if she chooses. It will be grand," Fred said. I threw my arms around him.

"That is the nicest anniversary present you could have ever given me. All I want in this world is to spend my days with you and the children."

"And you shall, my wife. All your days, I promise," Fred said as we stood together, locked in an embrace.

Chapter 56

Summer 1879

"He looks just like his papa," Fred crowed as he lit John Bryant's cigar.

"He does," the new father boasted as he puffed away. "He is a chip off the old block."

I watched the two men as they congratulated themselves on the birth of the as-of-yet unnamed baby boy who had arrived a few minutes after midnight. It had been a relatively easy delivery for Charlotte, with the help of a midwife and that of her husband. She had now been sleeping for several hours and, after watching her for the better part of the night, I had left the bedroom in search of Fred. The baby boy who appeared hale and hearty, had been bathed and swaddled and held first by his father and then by me, while Charlotte slumbered on. I had an almost palpable desire to wake her and place the baby in her arms, but John had asked me to let her sleep.

"There will be plenty of time for Charlotte to bond with her son," he said. "The poor girl needs her rest." Hearing Fred conversing in the parlor with John a few minutes later, I reluctantly placed the infant in his bassinet with a kiss on his nearly translucent forehead and left the room.

"Will you name him John Junior then?" Fred asked. *Not another John!* I was trying to decide if I should just bite my tongue when the new father spoke up.

"I was named for my father and answered to Johnnie until he died when I was entering college. I wouldn't do that to my son," Bryant said with a shudder. "And besides, Charlotte wants to get to know the child before we decide on a name." *What crazy notion was this? To wait to see what name would suit the child? Why not wait until he is old enough to choose his own name?* But the real reason for my annoyance was the lack of interest Charlotte was showing for her baby. It had started months ago with her unwillingness to express any excitement for the nursery or the dozens of booties and layette sets Marion and I had been working on. *What kind of mother would she be?* Lost in thought, I realized my name was being called.

"I'm sorry, I was lost in thought. What were you discussing?" Despite only having had a few hours of sleep, Fred's blue eyes twinkled gaily.

"Why the young lad's name, of course," he said. "I'm thinking Charles, but John is lobbying for Benjamin. What do you think, Grandmama?" My response was quick and certain as I looked up at the two men.

"What I think is we should allow Charlotte to meet her son before suggesting any names. Perhaps she'll choose a name like Will or Carl." Fred and John shook their heads almost in unison, signifying their disagreement.

"Let's discuss this over a drop of brandy," Fred said, and they headed towards the kitchen to fetch a bottle and a couple of glasses. I watched them go, then headed up the stairs towards the birthing room. *Men!* Charlotte would wake soon, and I would bring her son to her. She'd have no choice but to hold him in her arms and properly meet her baby. Surely she would rise to the occasion.

Chapter 57

Winter 1879-1880

I was deep in concentration, sketching away with a lead pencil, leaning over a drafting table. I started when Marion hurried in and then noticed Rick standing in the doorway of his father's office watching me.

"Mother, what are you doing? And Rick, I asked you to fetch her, not stand there like a fool," Marion complained loudly. Before Rick had a chance to defend himself, I stood and stretched.

"I had no idea how hard this would be on my back. Hunched over plans like that? Why, your father is always—"

"The soup has already been served, Mother. Didn't you hear the bell? We've been waiting for you and now our dinner will be ruined," Marion fretted.

"Marion, you are making a big fuss over nothing. I got to looking over these plans and time just slipped away. It as if I just came down here and before you know it, it's time to eat." I smiled at my children and crossed the room to join them. "Let's head upstairs, shall we? No sense upsetting Sarah." I took Rick's hand and started towards the staircase, turning when I realized Marion wasn't joining us. "Well pet, are you coming? What, do I have a smudge of dirt on my face or something?" She had been staring at me so oddly. Marion shook her head and headed towards us, closing the office door behind her.

"No, Mother, I'm just curious when Papa is planning on changing the name of the business to Olmsted and Family. 'Sons' doesn't seem to cover the actual distribution of work anymore." I let out a nervous laugh and hurried up the stairs.

"I don't know what you are going on about. Unless you have the desire to join your brothers, I think the name Olmsted and Sons is appropriate. Now, what sort of soup do you suppose is on today's menu? I hope it's not that cabbage soup we had last week. I much prefer something a bit heartier. Perhaps a nice corn chowder?" With my children following behind, I entered the dining room. "Looks like tomato," I said, catching sight of the three bowls full of a reddish liquid. I sat down at the head of the table as they pulled out chairs on either side of me. Rick immediately spooned the lukewarm broth into his mouth. I was about to encourage him to not slurp so loudly, but Marion, who was ignoring the bowl in front of her, began speaking.

"I am just saying you do a lot of work for Papa and I want to ensure you are being given your due." She frowned as she tasted her first spoonful. "It's gone cold," she muttered and reached for a piece of bread. Buttering it slowly, she continued, affecting an air of nonchalance. "It is only fair women are afforded the same accolades as men. Don't you agree?" I was surprised at the direction the conversation was taking.

"I'm hardly a suffragette, but yes, I agree women should receive equal praise for their accomplishments. At least, in theory, that is."

"In theory? Well, how about when, let's say, the woman in question is the wife of a man who designs parks for cities and private estates around the country?" I regarded her coolly.

"That's you, Mama," Rick said. "You're the wife of Papa, the park builder." Marion gave her nine-year-old brother a withering look, which he ignored, alternately lapping up his soup and dunking large chunks of bread.

"You're a genius," she said with a ghost of a smile. "But back to our woman. I'm just saying she should get credit for the work she does. Recognition for her contributions."

"Oh, psshaw. That is the silliest thing I have ever heard. All I do is suggest a tweak here and there. I have an eye for detail. Your father has always said so."

"It was *your* idea to add a cucumber magnolia tree for the Arnold Arboretum, and *you're* the one who came up with the plan to use

Roxbury puddingstone for the 99 Steps in Franklin Park. These are way beyond little tweaks, Mother."

"Marion is right, my dear." Everyone turned to see Fred standing in the doorway, an amused look on his face. I smiled at him.

"I thought you wouldn't be back until much later. I'll ring Sarah to bring you a bowl. We're having the most delicious soup." Fred smiled and pulled out a chair.

"Ahhh, tomato. Well, that bodes well," he said with a smile. "That cabbage soup last week left everyone in a foul mood. No rush. And anyway, I'm more interested in the conversation than the soup. I would like to hear more from you, Marion. What about the contributions your mother makes?" Marion turned beet red and took a large gulp from her water glass, in an obvious attempt to buy herself time to formulate a response.

"Well, uh, I just meant that, well Mother has been spending increasing amounts of time in the office lately. It would appear, well, what I mean to say is she should be, um…" She stopped and took another large gulp of water. I turned to Fred, who was watching our daughter closely. *He's enjoying this.* Marion swallowed and began dabbing at her mouth with a large linen napkin. "I'm sorry, Papa," she said in a voice barely above a whisper. "You work very hard and you deserve the praise you get; I'm just saying Mama also deserves a share." I was about to intercede when Rick hopped up from the table.

"I'm bored with this conversation," he said. "I'm going to see if I can find Miss Rutledge to read with me or help me practice my math." He raced out of the room, nearly upturning his chair in order to leave quickly. Fred chuckled briefly before turning serious.

"And Mary, what are your thoughts on the subject? Do you believe I am taking advantage of your talents?"

"No, Fred, never. You are always grateful for the minor changes I've suggested. And you know how happy I am to help. With John spending so much time in Boston and Owen back at Yale, I know how stretched thin you have been. Why ever since last summer, when you asked me for my thoughts on the Arboretum project, I've been so exhilarated. You have no idea how — well, of course you have an idea.

No one knows better than you how satisfying it is to transform a space into something so special. It's like magic."

"I do know, and I am delighted to work with you, to collaborate. You see things I miss. You know instinctively what to do with an unused section of land or how to turn a row of hedges into a work of art. You have talent, Mary. I'm so proud of you." I felt my heart soar at his words. His approval was all I needed.

"I cannot wait to show you what I've been working on. Would you want to come with me and take a look?" Fred pushed back his chair and walked towards me.

"It would delight me. Let's go take a peek, shall we?" He extended his arm, and taking it I turned to face Marion. "Be a love, will you pet? Go ask Sarah to heat up more soup for us. I'm bound to be famished when we return." Marion watched us leave, dejectedly spooning at her cold soup. I smiled when I overheard her mumble, "what a pair."

Indeed, we are quite a pair.

Chapter 58

It was late afternoon, and the bedroom had long gone dark. The solitary candle lighting the writing area did little to dispel the shadows looming from all four corners of the room. I shivered slightly and blew on my fingers. I needed to light a fire in the hearth or retreat downstairs if I intended to warm up. I had just finished writing a letter to my school chum Lillian.

I looked up when Fred came rushing in. He glanced around quickly and seemed surprised to find me alone in the dark.

"What the devil, Mary?" he said. "Do we not pay enough to keep the lights burning in here?" Without waiting for a reply, he hurried on. "I imagine you are wondering what has me so excited. Go on, ask me." I studied his flushed face and labored breathing. Noting his wide smile, I pushed back the fear of bad news.

"Do not leave your poor wife in suspense, I can tell you have something good to share."

"Well, being free of the Central Park project has opened up a whole world of possibilities for me." He shook his head in wonder, as if he had severed ties with the Central Park Commission just days ago instead of several months before. "That summer in Boston really got me thinking. Since most of our projects are up and down the East Coast, it doesn't matter where we live, does it?" Noting my shocked expression, he hurried on. "I understand you have no desire to return to D.C.," he said with a teasing lilt in his tone, "so why not consider Boston?" Perched on the foot of the bed, he leaned forward and grasped my hands in his. "Your poor hands are like ice," he scolded.

"Exactly how long have you been sitting up here, writing a letter to *Mrs. Steele*," he asked, after sneaking a peek at the envelope on the desk.

"Not all that long," I said, snatching my hands away and shoving them in the pockets of my full skirt. "And anyway, you're changing the subject. Why would I be in favor of a move to Boston? How would that be better than our life here in New York? Boston is growing at a fast rate, as you've said many times. There would be the same amount of noise and pollution and besides, we know no one there. Except for Charlotte, John and the boys, that is." It would be nice to live closer and help out more with the growing Bryant family, but what about Rick? "And Rick would have to change schools. Marion has her circle of friends, and Owen is due to graduate soon. Would you suggest that we mail him our new address and request he join us someday? And John? Would you leave him here on his own?" Fred gazed at me in amazement.

"I would think, after more than twenty years of marriage, you would know me better than that. First off, I daresay Boston will never grow to be the size of New York, and besides, I am not proposing we move into the heart of the city. I hear wonderful things about Brookline and Wellesley. The point is, we would be closer to Charlotte, and be able to take in the advantages of city life but have more room to spread out. A yard for Rick to tear around in? Maybe get him the dog he has been begging for? All that is possible with a move like this."

"A yard sounds nice. But do we have to move all that way just to gain a yard? Why not Long Island? Surely we could get something out there at a reasonable price." But I still wouldn't know a soul. And what of Anne? She had been my best friend and close confidante for the past twenty years. I was accustomed to having her nearby and seeing her regularly. Fred's nose wrinkled in distaste at the thought of relocating to Long Island.

"You're missing the whole point," he said, affecting a tone of exaggerated patience. "I'm not suggesting we uproot our family just for the sake of moving. I'm telling you, my work is frequently focused in Greater Boston. Now that the Arnold Arboretum is complete, the city fathers want me to get back to work. They want me to design a series of interconnected parks from Boston Common to Franklin Park. From a bird's-eye perspective, it will look like an emerald necklace when I'm done. Great splotches of green living space dotting the gray cityscape." Fred closed his eyes briefly, as if picturing the vivid image he was painting in his mind. He opened them to find me staring at him in amazement.

"Well, you have obviously given the matter some thought. You're suggesting a move given your work and the icing on the cake is being closer to Charlotte and the boys. And am I to assume you have already sought counsel from both John and Owen?" Fred hung his head sheepishly, but the sparkle in his eyes gave him away.

"Yes, I have, and both see it as a smart and strategic move. Owen is always so agreeable, and John was positively giddy about the idea." I swatted playfully at him. The thought of my deadly serious son appearing *giddy* about anything brought a smile to my face. Smart, loving and thoughtful? Yes. But giddy? Never. Not my John.

Chapter 59

Summer 1881

Our decision to move to Brookline, an upscale community just outside of Boston, had been a good one. We found a family to rent the brownstone in New York and moved when Rick finished school in June. I was thrilled, finding Brookline so refined after years spent living in a loud and bustling city like New York. The new house was not as big as the one we had lived in for years, but had a large yard and was next to a lovely park. I spent a great deal of time outdoors, enjoying the sunshine and the clean air. The availability of fresh seafood was a bonus and seafood chowder, shrimp and scallops were on our menu several times a week. I was in heaven!

It was wonderful living close to Charlotte and her growing family. She and her husband were expecting another child this January, and Marion and I would surely be called on to help. Charlotte had recently been confined to bed rest due to complications resulting from a third pregnancy in as many years of marriage. I tried to remain positive about her mental health, but found her remarkably distant these days, especially regarding her two sons. In all the time I spent in their home, I had never seen her hug or cuddle the little fellows. She spoke of them infrequently and expressed only a mild interest in their well-being. What a far cry from the 'little mother' who had delighted in the care of her younger siblings and the Vaux children. What had happened to that happy little girl? I prayed daily Charlotte would give birth to a healthy baby and finally find joy in raising a family.

The doorbell interrupted my thoughts. I pulled the door open and found a young man holding a telegraph. As soon as he saw me, he thrust it in my hand and before I could ask him to hold on so I could fetch him a couple of coins for his trouble; he hurried down the steps towards the road.

"Thank you," I called out and stuffing the envelope into my skirt pocket, walked towards the kitchen running the entire length of the house. Rick had already left on an outing, but Fred was enjoying a morning cigar and a second cup of coffee as he perused a stack of newspapers.

"Who was that?" he asked.

"A young man delivering a telegram," I pulled it from my pocket and handed it to Fred. "You've got your reading glasses on." Fred ripped open the envelope and started reading, while I gathered up the dishes and headed to the sink. At Fred's startled cry, I nearly dropped Rick's empty juice glass. I hurried back to the table where he sat looking pale and shocked. "What is it? What's the matter?"

"You should sit. It's bad news, I'm afraid." I pulled out a chair and collapsed into it.

"Tell me. Is it Charlotte? Did something happen to her or one of the boys?"

"No, Mary. I'm afraid it's Owen."

"Owen? What's happened?" Fred cleared his throat and read the telegram aloud. It was from our son, who had traveled west after graduation from Yale. He had convinced us a summer traveling through the largely unsettled Western states was the only graduation present he wanted. Still hoping he would toughen up a bit, Fred had relented and agreed to fund the trip, provided Owen return in the fall and join the family business. Owen had settled on a ranch in Montana last month and, according to his letters home, had been enjoying himself immensely. He had found a job as a ranch hand. "Of all things," I had sputtered to Fred. But, according to today's telegram, he had taken ill and could not return home by himself.

"Concerned over state of well-being. Stop. Unable to find proper medical care here. Stop. Too weak to travel home. Stop. Pray for me. Stop. Your loving son, Owen."

I burst into tears, sagging against Fred, who held me until my sobs subsided.

"What will we do? Should we look at a train schedule? How can we..." But Fred had already formulated a plan.

"We'll send John. He can leave today, meet up with Owen, get him stabilized and bring him home. It will all be fine. We'll be together and soon," he said.

***

John had set off for Montana that afternoon by train and after several days of arduous travel, reunited with his younger brother. Quickly realizing Owen's medical condition was dire, he located a hospital over one hundred miles away. After being treated for fever, difficulty breathing and extreme dehydration, they cleared Owen for travel and John called to say he had booked tickets for their return to Boston. A long and tortuous week followed, watching the door and the clock and waiting for a call from John. Everything would be all right. My sons were on their way home and we would get Owen the best medical care possible.

A few days later, John called us from the train station in Buffalo. I had a hard time understanding him and handed the phone to Fred.

"What is it, John?" Fred asked, then listened with a look on his face that grew from concern to deep sorrow. "I see. Get here as soon as you can. And John? Godspeed, my son." Frantic, I grabbed at his arm when he ended the call.

"What's happening? Tell me," I cried and waited as Fred placed the phone down. He turned, and I knew what he was going to say, even before he spoke.

"Just before the train pulled in to the station, Owen stopped breathing. The conductor called ahead and a pair of doctors met the train, but it was too late. I'm sorry, my love. They pronounced him dead. Complications from tuberculosis."

I stared at Fred, not believing what I had heard.

"No, that can't be. They cleared him for travel. John assured us."

"Our boy was very sick. There was nothing any of us could have done," Fred said, his voice breaking.

"But he is only twenty-four," I argued weakly, letting the tears I had been holding back overtake me. I sobbed in great gasps, unable to come to grips with the loss of dear Owen, our charming, witty son so like his late father in appearance, temperament and sadly, physical health. Taken from us decades too soon.

The rest of the day passed in a blur. The house filled with neighbors and friends, and donations of casseroles and cakes covered every surface of the kitchen. I was numb with grief and refused offers of food and drink. *Who could eat at a time like this?* I grieved for my boy and mourned his loss, unable to rid my brain of the images of all the things he would miss. He would never marry or have children, never join his father in the family business, never amble through the kitchen, snatching cookies still warm from the oven. Never tease me about my desire to fatten him up or my wish for him to meet a nice girl. In my mind, he would always be my charming son, poised on the brink of becoming an adult. *You think once they make it past infancy, they'll be safe. But they're not, they're never safe enough.*

After the funeral, the fog engulfing me lifted slowly, and I became aware of the needs of my family. I watched John attempt to keep young Rick busy, reading with him and playing cards for hours during a few days of persistent rain. Charlotte's pregnancy had her confined to her bed, and her husband John had sent their regrets and a lovely floral arrangement. Fred went back to work, but anyone could see he was just going through the motions of being busy, shuffling papers and sketching designs. He canceled his appointments and spent hours at his desk, staring at nothing and speaking very little. I longed to go to him and have him hold me and tell me we would get through this, but I resisted. The last thing I wanted was hollow promises. Owen's was the only voice I longed to hear, and the silence surrounding me was comforting. If I couldn't hear what I wanted, I would hear nothing at all.

Owen's death was hardest on Marion. She had taken to her bed, and like me, refused all offers of food and comfort. They had been so close as children, always concocting stories and pranks to play on their older siblings. It was weeks before she joined us at mealtimes and even longer before she could mention his name.

Anne was in England during this time, and I had only a telegraph from her expressing her shock and grief. She and her family were with Cal's mother, following the death of his father. Burying a third son was even more challenging without the presence of my dearest friend. All I had ever dreamed of was a happy, healthy family, but maybe some dreams were not meant to come true.

Chapter 60

Winter 1881-1882

Losing Owen left me nearly paralyzed with grief, and it was only on the days I spent with our grandsons was life worth living. All summer and into the fall, I traveled weekly to Charlotte's. I saw little evidence that she was excited about the upcoming birth, but hoped a new baby would bring her closer to her family. Fred and John had continued to throw themselves into their work and while I understood that was how men often dealt with tragedy, I longed to have Fred comfort me and hold me when I wept. Marion, always a quiet girl, grew even more silent, and only the antics of young Rick brought any joy into our home.

When we got the call that Charlotte had given birth to a third son, Fred and I rushed to the hospital in Boston. We could hear a loud commotion even before we reached Charlotte's room. We found her screaming at a nurse and refusing to hold her baby. Her husband, who had briefly left to go check on a patient of his, rushed back in at the same time. He shook his head sadly when Fred demanded to know what was going on. After requesting the nurse return the infant to the nursery, John lead us to the hallway, speaking in low, measured tones.

"I'm sorry. She's not herself," he said. "As a doctor, I can't say exactly why but, as her husband, I can tell you she is refusing to eat, won't talk to anyone and wants nothing to do with the baby." We stood silently before returning to the room. Despite my best efforts, alternating between wheedling, begging and demanding Charlotte settle down and hold her son, she refused, screaming at me to leave. I finally did, clinging to Fred and leaving John to comfort his wife. A week later, mother and son were discharged from the hospital and returned home. Charlotte took to her bed, wanting nothing to do with her children.

The weeks passed and Charlotte's condition deteriorated further. I continued to visit weekly, but she usually refused to see me. I spent afternoons holding the baby and reading to my grandsons, returning home in tears. When it became clear she was not recovering, John had Charlotte committed to an asylum. He told friends and family that she needed a rest to build up her strength, but admitted to Fred and me it was unlikely she would ever recover.

"I've seen no one in such a state," he confessed in a whisper. "I've called in favors from physicians at all the top hospitals. There is no apparent medical reason for her distress, but I fear she is irrevocably broken."

"Please don't give up on her," I begged. "I am praying for all of you." If ever there was a need for a Christmas miracle, surely this was it. I wasn't sure how much more grief we could take.

***

On Christmas Day, I sat staring at the snow melting on the lawn. We had passed the presents around and the dishes put away and I sat alone in the parlor. The highlight of the morning had been when our son-in-law brought his sons to visit. I held the baby while Fred and Marion helped the two little one unwrap their gifts. Claiming there was not enough room in their carriage for everything, John had instructed his sons to pick one present each and promised to return soon for the other gifts. When I pressed him for a day to pay a visit, he had hemmed and hawed and promised to get back to me. His widowed mother had recently moved in, and I assumed I would not be welcome to visit as often. Do the Bryants fault me for passing on whatever traits had sent Charlotte to an institution? *Am I to blame?*

Dinner had been a solemn affair and despite the delicious meal, no one seemed to have much of an appetite. It was an unseasonably warm day and Fred had coaxed Rick into joining him for a stroll in the neighboring park, giving me a chance to rest. John had headed down to the first floor office to work and Marion had gone to her room, claiming a headache. I tried to summon the strength to go lie down, for I was as wrung out as a dishcloth. My mind was a blur of emotions, all sad. Charlotte, my spirited daughter, was confined to a mental institution. Fred and I had buried three sons, and our daughter had given birth to three sons of her own. I vowed to do whatever I needed in order to be in their lives. *That* would be my resolution for the new year.

I looked around the gaily decorated room, failing to muster even a glimmer of joy. As I considered the daunting task of removing all the garland and baubles, I wondered why I had even bothered. I closed my eyes and prayed that the new year would provide some measure of relief for my family.

Chapter 61

Summer 1882

"I don't understand this sudden need of yours to go to Europe," Fred said. I shook my head as I crossed the room to sit by him. We had been having this argument for the past few days and while I tried to be patient, I felt that Fred would never understand my point of view.

"I need some time away, as does Marion. We have all suffered terribly. And before you say it, I know you are feeling the loss of dear Owen as much as anyone. And worrying about Charlotte, confined to an asylum. It is a nightmare I fear we will never awake from. But you and John have your work. It consumes you, so don't try to deny it. It's not a criticism, it's just the way it is. The way it has always been for you. Rick's far too young to realize what is going on. He's never experienced loss before. But Marion is grieving. She thought her brother hung the moon and stars in the sky and she looked up to Charlotte, her big sister. She and I need this," I said, my voice a whisper. I rested my head against Fred's chest, exhausted with the effort of trying to convince him of my need to get away.

"I understand loss. And believe me, I support whatever will help. But why Europe? How about a trip to the coast of Maine? I could arrange lodging in Deer Isle. Or Newport, Rhode Island? You love it there. The sea breeze, the salty air? You could eat your favorite lobster three meals a day."

"Europe is where John is. I have not been to his grave in Nice. I need to talk to my hus—John. He needs to know Owen is gone and Charlotte is… well, missing. I have to tell him and I want you to understand." Fred gazed at me, his eyes kind and his tone gentle.

"I understand. But can you put it off for a bit? Later this spring, I should be able to clear my calendar and escort you. It would be a splendid holiday for us."

"I'm comfortable making my way around Europe, Fred. Have you forgotten that I traipsed around over there for months after I lost John? And I had three little ones to boot. Why, Owen was just..." My eyes filled with fresh tears. "Just barely crawling." I mopped at my eyes with a damp handkerchief. "Marion and I depart on Tuesday. Will you see us off at the pier or should we say our goodbyes here at the house?" Fred shook his head, resigned to my plans.

"Of course I will bring you and Marion to the harbor. You can count on me." As he left the room, I squeezed his hand.

"Thank you, my dear," I said, fighting back another wave of tears.

***

Despite relatively rough seas, we had a pleasant voyage. During the two-week trip from Boston to Le Havre we spent most afternoons up on the main deck, walking round and round, enjoying the sunshine and the salt air. Unsure if it was the change in scenery or the passing of time, I found a renewed interest in food and we often lingered after supper, enjoying a second cup of coffee and a slice of cake or a glass of port. The other passengers assigned to our table were lively, and I was particularly drawn to two of the women. They were spinster sisters around my age from Haverhill, Massachusetts. The very first night, they had introduced themselves.

"I'm Lucretia Ford," the more outgoing of the pair had announced, "and this is my sister, Barbara." I greeted them with a smile.

"Hello, I'm Mary Olmsted and this is my daughter, Marion. We live in Brookline."

I detected a gleam in Lucretia's eyes.

"Olmsted?" she asked. "Would you be any relation to that fellow who has been building parks all over the country?"

"Why, yes," I said with a smile. "I'm Mrs. Frederick Law Olmsted." The men at the table looked up in interest. One of them spoke up.

"Is he here?" he asked. "Is Mr. Olmsted on board this ship?"

"No, I'm sorry. He and my son are too busy with the projects they are juggling. It's only my daughter and I."

"What is the purpose of your visit to Europe?" Barbara asked. "Are you visiting family?" I felt my throat tighten up. How do I admit I am going to the grave of my late husband to tell him the sad news that his son is dead, and they committed his daughter to an asylum? I was grateful when Marion spoke up.

"My mother and I are planning on touring France and visiting with family," she said. "And what about you, Miss Ford? Are you and your sister planning on an extended stay on the Continent?" The two women chattered away excitedly of their plans to visit Paris, followed by a week or two in the south of France. They had never been abroad and had many questions about the customs and the language. The two men lost interest in the conversation and announced they were off to the smoking lounge, leaving their wives with us. The six of us scooted our chairs closer and began a spirited discussion on the various sights that made France such a wonderful place to visit. I grew even more convinced that this trip had been an excellent idea and started to relax.

Chapter 62

It was soon clear that the Ford sisters did not share our level of energy nor our desire to see as much as possible during the time abroad. Before we arrived in France, the four of us agreed to meet up in two weeks in Paris. Departing Le Havre the day after we arrived, Marion and I traveled by train arriving the next day in Paris. We had reserved rooms at a quaint inn in the Opera House neighborhood on the right bank of the Seine.

"Lucretia and Barbara are probably still making their way off the ship," joked Marion as we sat in the courtyard our first morning, enjoying café au lait and freshly baked croissants. I smiled in response.

"The old dears are no doubt having the trip of a lifetime," I said. "And it will *take* a lifetime at the rate they move," I sat back and smiled at my daughter. Marion appeared much older than her twenty-one years, given her broad frame and serious nature. It was wonderful to see a smile on her face. "I do hope they stick with their plan to visit when they arrive in the city."

Marion nodded and with a mouthful of flaky pastry asked, "Where should we start?"

I had been planning this trip in my mind for years, never certain when or with whom I would return to Paris. I unearthed a dog-eared notebook from my bag, flipping through the pages. Other than a planned overnight trip to John's grave in Nice at the end of the week, there was no actual structure to our days. We could spend as much time as we wished visiting art galleries and museums and sightseeing in this most beautiful of cities.

The next several days were a blur of monuments, gardens and palaces. We spent an entire day viewing paintings by a talented array of artists, including Claude Monet and Paul Gaugin.

"Remember how much Charlotte and I loved looking at all your art books, Mama?" asked Marion as we sat on a bench studying Monet's *Poppies*. A lump formed in my throat at the sound of her name and nodded mutely, unable to speak for a moment. Marion seemed to sense this and reached for my hand. We sat quietly until I could speak.

"I do want to talk about her," I said, watching for Marion's reaction. "It's just so hard to picture her locked away and those little boys. Those motherless babies. I never could have imagined things turning out like this, not for a single moment. She loved children. She wanted to be a teacher. How —" Marion spoke suddenly, her words rushing out as if she had been holding them in for some time.

"I should be there for them. When we get back to Boston, I'm going to approach John about moving in with him and the boys. Why should they hire a governess when they can have dear old Auntie Marion?" She sat back, waiting for my response, which came quickly.

"That is a lovely and very generous offer, my pet. But what of your life? Is that what you want for yourself? Taking care of your sister's children? Don't you want a family of your own someday?" Marion spoke slowly, choosing her words with care.

"Marriage and a family? I don't think that's in the cards for me. I never have." I was quick to protest.

"Are you thinking of your father? How he used to call you Maid Marion? He was just being silly darling. No one thinks you should end up an —"

"Old maid? But that's the future I see. Caring for you and Papa? Helping my brothers? Taking care of Charlotte's boys? Why, with all of you needing me so much, how could I create a family of my own? I already have one!" Marion's eyes were bright with unshed tears, but her smile was happy as she stood. "C'mon Mama. I believe there are several creperies we have yet to visit and time is a wastin'."

The silence between us was comfortable as we strode purposefully through the fog. We stopped before a small café and Marion went inside to place our order. I found an open table on the brick patio and sank gratefully onto one of the small metal chairs. Fred would love the perfectly imperfect design of the park across the way. Not a straight line in sight!

"You must plan to return in a few years, madame," an older gentleman advised from his own chair, just a few feet away. His English was heavily accented, and I looked up in surprise.

"I'm sorry. Were you addressing me?"

"Why yes, begging your pardon. I don't mean to interrupt your solitude," he said.

"I was just thinking about my husband," I said. "And how much he loves it here. Perhaps I shall return someday with him."

"Paris is a lovely city, but like all lovely cities, it is constantly changing and shifting," he said.

"I suppose that's true." He seemed harmless, maybe just lonely. "I'm expecting my daughter. And here she is," I announced as Marion approached carrying a tray of coffee and a plate of crepes.

"Ah bonjour, mademoiselle," the man spoke up, standing and pulling Marion's chair out for her.

"Mother?" Marion asked. "Who is your friend?" The man beamed and introduced himself.

"I am Jean Eiffel," he said. "I was just telling your mother she needs to return to Paris in a few years." Marion looked confused.

"And why is that?" she asked, and Jean spoke quickly, excited to share his story.

"My brother Gustave is an engineer. He is designing an iron tower 1,000 feet high right here in the city. The Paris Exposition is in the final planning stages and my brother's tower will be the centerpiece. The crown jewel. You must come back and see it for yourself." He sat back, pleased. The whole thing sounded like a pipe dream, but far be it from me to burst his bubble.

"That sounds delightful, Monsieur Eiffel. We will await the news of this tower from back home. I wish your brother well in his em, ambitious endeavors," I said. Jean smiled happily and announced his departure. "Enjoy your afternoon," he said as he collected his newspaper and valise.

We watched him go and tucked into our plate of golden crepes topped with fresh strawberries and cream.

"Can you imagine? A tower 1,000 feet tall?" Marion spoke between mouthfuls. I chuckled in response.

"It appears your father has a *doppelgänger* here in Paris. Monsieur Eiffel sounds like a man with an imagination as big as his own!"

Chapter 63

"I understand if you wish to stay here at the hotel, my pet. It will be a long carriage ride across the city to the gravesite, and I'm uncertain how long I will stay." We were enjoying a second cup of coffee in the hotel's breakfast room, and I smiled as the waiter approached with a pot. "No more for me, thank you. Marion? More coffee?" She declined, and he strode away. I pushed past the stress I felt as I steeled myself for what would undoubtedly be an emotional day. We had arrived in Nice last night via the Calais-Nice Express, a day-long train ride from Paris.

"Really, dear." I said. "This might be an excellent opportunity to catch up on your postcard writing." Marion had been sending postcards to everyone she knew since we arrived in France nearly two weeks ago. She frowned and shook her head.

"Of course I'll accompany you, Mother. He's my uncle, after all. Papa's brother and Owen's father," she said, her voice breaking. She wiped at her eyes, looking miserable. I teared up in response. Marion and Owen had been so close. It should come as no surprise she would want to go to visit John's grave.

"Maybe I'll be able to find that wonderful patisserie I used to frequent," I said with a wink. "Quite literally, the best — "

"I'm not a little girl, Mother. You need not bribe me with eclairs and puff pastry."

"Oh, no, darling. I may make you watch as I work my way through the wonderful selection. Let's get started. With or without the croissants, it's going to be a long day."

After a lengthy ride through Nice, we arrived at the cemetery. Our driver agreed to wait for us. He was an affable young man who seemed to comprehend my blend of rusty French and English. He lit a cigarette and leaned back against the carriage.

"Oui, madame, mademoiselle," he said with a smile. "Take your time. I have nowhere else to be on this magnificent day." It *was* a beautiful day. I took Marion's arm, and we set off.

"Au revoir," I called over my shoulder as we entered through the cemetery's gate.

"Which way?" Marion asked, and I stopped short. *I had no idea.* It had been twenty-five years since John had died, and the only time I had been here was the day he was buried. I hadn't even seen the gravestone, but had received confirmation of its installation several months following his death. I turned to Marion, confused and starting to feel anxious.

"I'm not sure. I don't recall it being so large. Maybe we can find someone to ask." We began the arduous process of crisscrossing the multi-acre cemetery in search of a staff member. As we studied the gravestones for names, we commented on what we read.

"Leopold lived to eighty-seven," I remarked in awe. I turned to Marion, who was kneeling in front of a tiny headstone.

"Poor Antoinette," said Marion. "Only twenty-one and mother of three. And wife to Jacques. Just think, Mother. A girl my age, already married with three children. And now gone. That's so sad, don't you think?" I nodded, trying to erase the image of Charlotte, a mother of three, confined to an asylum. *There was so much sorrow in the world.* But today the sun was shining, I had my dear girl with me and I was going to visit my late husband. Miraculously, just a few minutes later, we stood in front of a large gravestone.

Dr. John Hull Olmsted
Born 1825
Died 1857
Loving husband to Mary
Beloved father to John, Charlotte and Owen
Rest in Peace

We stood silently, reading the inscription, and I did not break down as I had feared. Sensing my desire for privacy, Marion hugged me gently and headed down the hill towards a small pond.

"I'll go watch the ducks. You and Uncle John have a great deal to catch up on." As I watched her go, I dug in my satchel for the small blanket borrowed from the hotel. I placed it on the ground at the side of John's grave, sat down and made myself comfortable.

"You always were a wonderful listener. And I have much to tell you," I began. For the next hour, I talked to John. I told him how, as he had hoped, Fred and I had made a wonderful life together. "He's such an amazing man. You would be so proud of all he has accomplished. And young John. The two of them are changing the landscape of our country," I boasted, feeling my heart would burst with pride. I told him about Marion and young Rick, about our stay in California, our move to Boston and all the projects Fred had completed over the years.

I drew in a deep breath. "But there is more, my dear. Everything has not been milk and honey. We lost darling Owen last year. We miss him so much. He was your son in every fiber of his being. You would have loved..." I broke down and let the tears flow freely. After a few minutes, I dabbed at my eyes with a handkerchief and tried to continue. "I'm sorry to tell you Charlotte is doing poorly. She has always been high-strung, but we hoped marriage and motherhood would suit her. She married several years ago, a doctor just like you, and he's called John as well. He's a wonderful man, but none of it suits her. They have three handsome sons, but she's currently in an institution. She's quite mad. I—at first, I thought she had a case of the baby blues. But it kept getting worse. I don't understand any of this." I wiped away fresh tears and hung my head sadly. "I wanted to tell you, to let you know about our family. I don't want you to worry." I sat quietly for several minutes, picturing my handsome, charming first husband. Losing him had been devastating, but I had moved on and found a life filled with passion and purpose. With Fred by my side every step of the way. *When God closes a door, he opens a window.* After a few more minutes, I struggled to my feet.

"Goodbye, my darling. Until we meet again. *À bientôt!*" I kissed my fingertips and lightly touched the headstone. Please, my love, will you take care of my three sons until Fred and I can join you someday? Tucking the blanket under my arm, I made my way down the hill to where Marion was waiting.

Chapter 64

Fall 1882

We returned home to a record-breaking heatwave. It seemed the citizens of Boston wanted to do little more than soak for hours at a time in the nearest lake, pond or, for the lucky ones, ocean. Rick begged daily to go to the lake in the middle of Boston Common with his pals and, after sending Marion along to chaperone the first couple of times, I let him go. The boy was an excellent swimmer and despite a devilish sense of humor, he was level-headed and responsible for a lad of twelve.

Marion had offered to help John Bryant with the children and when he finally consented, she had packed and left for Cohasset. She called every few days, sounding happy to be of help in the bustling household. Fred took a few days off from his own hectic schedule and it delighted me to have his company. With John spending most of his time in Buffalo, the big house seemed empty. When the heat broke, we enjoyed late afternoon bicycle rides through the Common. All in all, it had been a pleasant summer.

Rick started school in September and a couple of days later, Fred set off for a hastily scheduled business trip. His plan was to visit a private estate in the Catskills, followed by a meeting with town officials from Albany to review final plans for the park that would break ground shortly. His last stop would be Rochester, NY to check on the progress being made with Seneca Park. He returned home after six days of travel in an absolutely foul mood. He turned down my offer of a warmed up meal and a glass of port, choosing instead to pace angrily the length of the front porch, muttering under his breath. He wouldn't tell me what was wrong and, growing weary of being ignored, I went inside. In the kitchen, I put water on to boil for tea. I hoped he would join me once he shook off that nasty mood.

I heard him walking down the hall just moments later. "There's the almond shortbread you love," I said. He agreed, and we sat together at the table. The trip had been a disaster, according to Fred. The Whittemore family had balked at the upfront consulting fee that Fred had instituted last year, compensating him for his time and travel. Despite confirming prior to his visit, the question of payment had surfaced early in the meeting and when it became clear that they had no plans to pay him, Fred had stormed out of their home. Now, days later, he was still upset.

"Like a streetwalker, Mary. It was humiliating, I tell you. Having to grovel for a piddling sum before they had their way with me. Never again, I can assure you of that. I will not step foot into another meeting until I have cash in hand. Can you imagine?" I had been the one to suggest the new procedure once Fred let it slip that a park in Waterbury, Connecticut, had been designed using the plan he had described months earlier to the city officials. They had turned down his proposal, but ended up with a final design suspiciously close to the one he had proposed. I nodded vigorously in his defense.

"Of course, Fred. I'm glad you left them with nothing. They'll come around. You're the one everyone wants. I'll wager you'll hear from them within a fortnight." Fred frowned.

"Perhaps. But wait until I tell you what happened in Albany." I sat back and listened patiently as he continued to complain about his week. Travel delays, a lost room reservation for his first night's lodging, being forced to wait for all the attendees to go over his final plans in Albany, and a less than satisfactory visit to Rochester. "Those dunderheads," he fumed. "Any schoolboy knows the difference between a poplar and an elm. I swear Mary, I have half a mind to cancel all new projects and clear the decks of half the ones pending. The level of incompetence I am forced to deal with is simply astounding."

It was a perfect opportunity to suggest Fred cut back on his demanding schedule. "Perhaps it is time to slow things down a bit."

The minute the words were out of my mouth, I regretted them. Fred was now frowning and looked as if he was ready to bolt from the room. "I'm not suggesting you quit. But maybe John and that lovely Mr. Eliot could be put to greater use." Fred slumped forward in his chair. He ran his fingers through his snow white hair, which had grown long. He had recently grown a beard in an effort to not be confused with Benjamin Butler, the current governor of Massachusetts, who he was often mistaken for when closely shaven.

"We should plan a trip to see Marion and the young ones," he said with a hint of a smile. I was about to remind him if his schedule was not as busy, we could travel even more frequently to Cohasset but held my tongue. If I kept silent and let him think about this for a day or two, it was likely he would arrive to a similar conclusion. Patience, I determined and not for the first time, was a virtue.

Chapter 65

Winter 1882-1883

I cleared my throat and sipped at a glass of water. Being interviewed for *Woman's Home Companion*, my favorite magazine, had sounded exciting when the idea had been proposed, but the reality was something else. Miss Diane Robinson, the reporter who had contacted me, was interested in my perspective on Fred, the Man Who Built Parks. I watched nervously as the young woman scribbled my latest response. *How old is she?* Younger than Charlotte, possibly the same age as Marion? *Please don't ask about Charlotte. Or Owen.* Talking about such sensitive topics to a total stranger was out of the question. Fred had helped me to prepare and had instructed me to lay my cards on the table prior to the start of the interview.

"You won't be comfortable talking about Owen's death or Charlotte's hospitalization," Fred had reasoned. "But reporters love these kinds of stories, so nip it in the bud right away. Tell her neither subject is up for discussion." His advice was sound, based upon his years as a reporter, but felt awkward bringing up topics that were a no-no. Wouldn't it be just as likely that the follow-up questions would be almost as awkward? Why didn't I want to talk about my children? What was I trying to hide? I was probably worrying for no good reason. John Bryant had never gone public with news of Charlotte's illness, and what good Christian woman would bring up a recently deceased son?

So far, the questions had been like those Fred had predicted and helped me plan responses to.

What is it like to live with a creative genius? Fred had thought the opening question might be something along those lines, although he never would have referred to himself as a genius. My initial thought was that he put on his pants one leg at a time just like everyone else, but decided that could be misconstrued as denigrating his talent. So, I went with a description of how Fred saw the world and that he found inspiration everywhere. How he disliked straight edges and flowers, preferring natural curves and greenery in his designs.

What was my favorite of his many completed projects? The iconic Central Park was the answer to be expected, but I had decided to name Mont Royal in Montreal as my most favorite. It had been thrilling to visit Canada with Fred during the work on the park. The young woman was hanging on my every word.

How difficult is it to withstand his long absences? I had answered that my days were so busy that I scarcely noticed when he was gone, and then I giggled self-consciously. "But of course, I note his absence at the supper table and at night, next to me in our bed." *Stop gushing like a ninny!* Miss Robinson leaned forward and patted my hand gently.

"That's off the record, of course," she said with a smile, continuing to scribble away on her pad.

Then I realized Miss Robinson had stopped writing and was watching me with interest.

"I'm sorry. My mind was a million miles away. Did you have another question for me?"

"Yes, if you don't mind. I'd like to learn more about your family. How many children do you and Mr. Olmsted have?" *I've given birth seven times. And I have buried three sons.* But that wasn't the right answer. Not really.

"John Charles is our oldest. He lives here with us and is a graduate of Yale University. He is a lead designer for Olmsted and Sons. We're very proud of him." Realizing that more was expected of me, I hurried on. "And our daughter Charlotte is a mother of three sons. She and her husband Dr. John Bryant reside in Cohasset." I paused and sat back, relieved.

"Oh, how lovely," Miss Robinson crooned. "Three grandchildren! You must visit with them all the time." I nodded with a smile.

"And our daughter Marion is with us when she's not with her nephews. She's a lovely girl, always helping, tending to her little brother. That would be Rick. Frederick Law Olmsted, Junior. He's only twelve. Such a little scamp he is." I glanced at the young woman who had again stopped writing and was looking at her folder. Background notes, she had told me when she first sat down. Was she checking up on Owen, the missing son? Miss Robinson looked up and met my gaze. She was clearly intelligent. And kind as well. If she had found any reference to Owen, she was clearly not planning on pursuing that particular thread, I predicted with relief.

"So, what sorts of things do you do as a family? What would represent a perfect day for the Olmsteds? Our readers are dying to know," the reporter said.

"Oh my, we love to be out of doors, of course. Picnics in the park, long walks, sailing, bicycling and horseback riding. When it's not desirable to be outside, we read or play cards. We have lots of big family meals. When everyone is around the table, that's when I'm at my happiest. Even if we are just having tea and toast, it's always enjoyable." My eyes welled up at the sound of my words. Since Owen's death, family suppers had been glum and if not for the antics of young Rick, mealtimes could be downright somber. Miss Robinson looked concerned.

"Oh you poor dear," she murmured. "Are you all right? Do you need a moment?" *Yes, I do.*

"No, I'm fine. Right as rain. What else are your readers interested in?"

"Knowing more about you, Mrs. Olmsted. So much has been written about your husband, but we know so little about Mary Perkins Olmsted." I chuckled nervously.

"There's not very much to tell, I'm afraid. I'm a mother and wife with little time to think about myself. I'm sure your readers will understand that. It is my duty to manage a proper home for my family, isn't that so? A haven of comfort and quiet, sheltered from the harsh realities of the working world." Had I laid it on a bit too thick?

"Well yes, that's true. But with three grown children and a husband who travels much of the time, certainly you have been able to develop some interests of your own."

"Well, I write a lot of letters. We have family and friends all over the world and I enjoy keeping up with them." I was warming to the idea that I had a life of my own, insubstantial as it was. "And I enjoy reading. Why, I can sit down with a good book in the morning and before I know it, Fred is home for supper." Miss Robinson perked up at that and leaned forward with a curious smile.

"Well, that brings up a couple more questions. Have you read any of the titles translated by the American woman, Katherine Wormeley?" I felt my face flush. Thoughts of Fred carrying on with that woman, living the life of a gay bachelor. "She was a close friend of your husband, isn't that correct?" I sniffed and shook my head.

"They worked together decades ago, during the war. You said you had another question?"

"Did I hear that you and your first husband lived abroad for years? France, wasn't it?" *John!* Were Fred and I that naïve to expect that no questions would be asked about him? I paused a moment before plunging in.

"We were a couple of vagabonds," I said with a careless wave of my hand. "We loved picking up at a moment's notice and going wherever we liked." Always in search of a cure for John, rarely having more money in our pockets than the cost of next weeks' lodging.

"And aren't your two oldest children actually Mr. Olmsted's stepchildren?"

I sat up straight and addressed the reporter directly. "Mr. Olmsted and I raised our children together. We are one family and I'm afraid that's all I have for you today."

"I just have a couple more questions. Do you feel that your contributions to your husband's work go unnoticed, Mrs. Olmsted?" I almost snorted in disbelief.

"Oh, what nonsense. You sound like Marion. Going on about my rights as a woman. I help my husband with a design here or there. I'm more like a sounding board, if I'm being honest." Miss Robinson smiled knowingly.

"My sources tell me you are far too modest, Mrs. Olmsted." I shook my head and frowned.

"I'm afraid I've said all I have to say on the topic, Miss Robinson."

"Well, thank you for your time. And don't forget that one of our photographers will contact you later this week. Our readers will enjoy seeing lots of photographs of you and Mr. Olmsted with your family," she said with a smile. I groaned silently. Getting my picture taken ranked right up there on the list of things I could not abide, along with visits to the dentist or spring cleaning.

"Oh yes, of course," I said with forced gaiety. "I'll look forward to his call. Goodbye now," I called out as she shut the door behind her. That could have gone much worse, I told myself.

Chapter 66

Spring 1883

I looked up from my sewing to find Fred and John huddled together in the doorway. They seemed happy, and I was eager to hear why.

"Don't keep me in suspense. What are you so excited about this morning?" Fred hurried into the room, with John following closely behind. Fred sat next to me and John perched on the arm of a nearby chair. I put my sewing aside and asked again what was causing them to be so excited. Something was up.

Fred spoke, then turned to his son. "You tell your mother, John. It's you who came up with the solution." John reddened and nodded deferentially at Fred.

"But Father, it was your idea that started the ball rolling," he said.

"The two of you are wearing me out," I said with a sigh. I removed the spectacles that I had started wearing and rubbed the bridge of my nose. "What has you going on like a couple of stuttering schoolboys?" Fred beamed proudly at his son.

"You should be proud of John," he said. "Thanks to his genius and vision, I'm pleased to announce that the house will soon be ours." I'm certain I looked as perplexed as I felt.

"The what? I do not understand…"

"The farmhouse here in Brookline, Mother. The Clark sisters agreed to my plan. Our plan," John added quickly.

"Don't be so modest, John. It was your plan through and through. I charged in like a bull in a china shop and queered the whole deal before it began, but it was your creative solution that brought it to fruition. Well done, my son," Fred told him as he walked over to the liquor cabinet. "This calls for a toast." I looked at John, still perched on the arm of the chair.

"Will you please tell me what is going on? I remember hearing about a property your father had his eye on, but dear me, I don't remember any of the details." John slid into the space his father had just vacated and told me what had transpired.

Weeks earlier, Fred had stumbled across a picturesque property owned by the Clark family. Deciding it was the perfect place to both live and run his business, Fred had contacted their attorney with a generous offer to purchase both the house and the land. He was eager to make the move and expand his business operations. But the current inhabitants, the elderly Clark sisters, had lived on the property their entire lives and rejected Fred's offer.

John had gone back to the attorney with a revised plan. He and Fred would build a spacious cottage on the grounds for the sisters to live in rent-free for the rest of their lives (which at their advanced ages did not appear to be all that long) and the purchase price, in the form of a mortgage, would provide them a monthly income to cover their expenses, allowing them to live out their lives in comfort.

"They are thrilled, Mother. It's a great deal for them and we'll have the chance to modernize the old farmhouse to accommodate our family and the new offices of Olmsted and Sons."

"And what of the main house?" I asked. I hoped it would be larger than our current home, with plenty of space for entertaining and sufficient bedrooms for John, Rick, and Marion, and ample quarters for the servants. Rick was old enough that we had not hired a new governess when Miss Rutledge left to take care of her ailing mother, but we employed both a cook and a maid who would under no circumstances be willing to share a room.

Fred promised to give me a tour of the farmhouse and assured me they would consult me every step of the way as they converted the property. Satisfied our family would be well taken care of, I went back to my sewing. We had moved more times than I cared to count over the past twenty-five years and I had succeeded in quickly turning each place into a comfortable home. This move would be no different.

Chapter 67

Fall 1883

After months of renovation, our home was ready. John had been living there for weeks, overseeing every detail of the work and camping out on an abandoned horsehair sofa. Both women loved their new cottage and, buoyed by the funds coming in each month, had embarked upon an around-the-world cruise. They had already set off on their trip, promising to return in the new year.

I wanted to call our new home Fairsted, "a beautiful place," and Fred agreed. The neighborhood was resplendent with rolling hills and twisting country roads. The seventy-year-old clapboard farmhouse featured dark red paint with green trim. They had transformed two acres into a miniature park featuring a craggy set of steps up to the main house and a fieldstone arch creating a grotto. Rhododendrons, dogwood, cotoneasters and vines were brought in and the overall effect was a perfect example of Fred's design aesthetic, which he described as wild and slightly ordered, a sort of organized chaos.

As soon as the paint was dry, we moved in and soon were ready to welcome the friends and business associates who dropped in. I kept busy planning an open house scheduled for early in the new year.

Fred had kept to his promise to scale back at work and to become more involved in the community, had gotten himself elected to the Saturday Club. Begun in Boston in 1856, the club's stated purpose was 'informal social exchange between intellectual and accomplished men.' Always insecure of his own incomplete formal education, Fred was proud to have been selected and took his role as a member seriously.

One night, while he was getting dressed to attend a monthly meeting of the club, I approached him with a frown on my face.

"I want to ask your opinion on the guest list for the open house." Realizing he was struggling with his tie and paying no attention to me, I dropped my pad on the bedside table and went over to help. "Stop twisting and stand still, would you please?" I took over the process and when finished, adjusted his black suit jacket. "There, now, you look quite smart. If I can get your attention for just one moment, please…" But Fred was gathering up his hat and a pair of gloves and stopped me.

"Mary, I need to get to my meeting. I'm already late. Can't this wait until the morning?" I groaned under my breath. Fred had been putting me off for the last couple of days. I felt confident completing the arrangements for the open house, but knew Fred had his own opinions. I decided to humor him, knowing how important the club was.

"Of course, darling. I would hate for you to keep Mr. Emerson or Mr. Longfellow waiting." I loved to tease Fred about hobnobbing with the founding members of the Saturday Club.

Fred crossed the room to where I stood and smiled before putting his arms around me and hugging me closely. Pulling back after kissing me soundly, he stood with his hands on my shoulders, regarding me with mock severity.

"Ralph Emerson has been dead and buried for over a year, as has Henry Longfellow. And I don't think either gentleman would have deigned to wait on the likes of me. Perhaps I should attempt to recruit my old friend Sam Clemens to the club. How do you think the members would feel about welcoming the man who imagined the adventures of Tom Sawyer and Huck Finn to our esteemed ranks?"

I grabbed my list and started scribbling madly.

"Yes, you see? That's why I need your input. I would have forgotten to invite Sam and his wife to the party. Do you think they'll come from Hartford?"

"Yes, I'm certain we can expect them. And now, I'm off to rub shoulders with the greatest minds in Boston." And with a wave of his hat, he left the room.

Of course he would fit right in. He was the smartest man I knew. And a darned good kisser to boot.

Chapter 68

Spring 1884

I sat behind the desk dominating Fred's personal office space. As was becoming increasingly common, Fred sat in the chair across from me, the one reserved for guests or one of the young apprentices. More and more, Fred relied on my memory and head for figures as Olmsted and Sons took on additional clients. I managed the day-to-day operations, although I was careful to include Fred as much as possible, because I relied on his judgement and hoped to break him out of the doldrums. Only occasionally could I coax him into a jolly frame of mind. Since Owen's death, Fred had become reserved, with very little of the old spark in his blue eyes. When Rick was home from school, he was usually successful in making his father smile. One night, Fred laughed aloud at his son's silly antics and I realized it was a sound I hadn't heard in months.

John was becoming the face of the company, travelling most weeks to meet potential clients and to check up on ongoing projects, the largest of which were Belle Isle in Detroit; Providence, Rhode Island, and the Lawrenceville School in New Jersey. John did not appear to mind the travel, although he reported with a touch of rancor how prospective clients frequently expressed their disappointment in not being able to meet his more charismatic father.

"I am the runner-up prize, apparently," he had admitted the other day.

But despite Fred's taciturn demeanor, his work did not appear to suffer. He was currently involved in the most challenging project we had ever undertaken, right here in Boston. After years of delays, Fred was designing an interconnected park system, reminiscent of the one he had done in Buffalo. Besides creating new parks, he needed to cobble together existing ones, including a wet lands preserve and an arboretum, an earlier project of his. The properties would be joined by ribbons of green space, generously proportioned parkways and waterways. "Nothing else compares to the Boston work," Fred repeated daily.

Today, we were discussing the status of the individual projects that would form Boston's 'Emerald Necklace'.

"What is the latest on the West Roxbury property?" I asked.

"There has been no further word on the funding. I guess old Ben Franklin will never see his bequest to the city of Boston actually utilized for a park," Fred said with a chuckle. He had given up hope that the money Franklin had left to the city where he was born could offset the park's burgeoning budget. "But you can bet the name Franklin Park will stick either way," he said with a smirk.

"And is the construction on track?" I asked with a touch of impatience. We had a long list of projects and we expected a new client within the hour.

"Yes, dear. Well, more or less. We divided the five hundred acres into two parcels. The larger will be remarkably simple. We will continue planting hemlocks and other old-growth trees and leave the hills intact, just as nature intended," Fred responded. He preferred to leave well enough alone, especially with an attractive tract of land like this one.

"And the smaller parcel is being transformed into a recreational space with, let's see…" I consulted my notes, "a three-hundred-foot-long raised terrace."

"Yes," Fred said, and for a moment, I was looking into the sparkling blue eyes of the man I had fallen in love with nearly half my lifetime ago. He continued on with much excitement. "I told Rick that he can assist me with the planning of the locker room."

"Isn't it enough to build a terrace where onlookers can watch the tennis matches and baseball games? Is a locker room really necessary?" I shook my head in amazement. A recent article in the *New York Herald* had referred to Fred as a most "unpractical man" because of his penchant for form over function. But if it put a smile on his dear face, even if only for a moment, then it was probably worth the extra time and cost. Fred had already moved on and quickly provided new cost estimates for the large glacial kettle hole pond planned for Jamaica Plain and the Back Bay Fens.

"We must table discussion of the adjustments to Commonwealth Avenue and the Common and the Public Garden," he concluded, stuffing his notes into his battered leather briefcase. "I fear the town fathers were nearly apoplectic when the early cost estimates were identified." He stood suddenly and pulled on his overcoat. "I am due at the City Hall for a budget meeting in less than an hour and, if memory serves, you will meet with that young man from Springfield shortly." He hurried over to where I stood, pulled me into his arms and held me tightly.

"I owe all of this to you, my love," he said and kissed my cheek.

I watched him shuffle out the door, his limp more pronounced than ever on this damp day. Despite occasional memory lapses and his persistent melancholy on the loss of dear Owen, at nearly sixty-two years old, Fred possessed the stamina and work ethic of a man half his age.

Chapter 69

Summer 1885

Over the past several months, Fred had been part of a team of architects and engineers charged with returning Niagara Falls back to its former glory. Once the number one tourist destination in America, the area had become overrun with amusement parks, sideshows and industry, with pulp mills lining the banks of the Niagara River. The recent election of Grover Cleveland to the governor's seat was a real boon to the movement to improve the area and the state not only passed legislation to preserve the falls, but set aside money to allow the state to buy back the surrounding land from private parties. An initial visit to the falls confirmed Fred's belief that they would need to do more than just tear down the mills and remove the carny-style attractions. He immediately started a petition drive to turn the falls back to a more natural state.

When he returned from his first visit, he had complained that, far from being accessible to the locals and visiting tourists, only the most affluent could enjoy the falls. Getting an unobstructed view of the falls was challenging, and the best views were to be had from standing on private property. Cunning landowners charged exorbitant fees to those willing and able to pay for the privilege.

"I overheard a man complaining he had paid over ten dollars a head for his family of five to enjoy the view. It's an outrage," Fred had fumed.

"That's more than a month's wages for most men," I had agreed. "Do whatever you need to make it a national treasure again." The next day Fred contacted the head of the five-person commission assembled to spearhead the project in order to confirm his interest. They informed him there "may be a problem." He reported back to me that although he was a "natural choice to design the landscape of the grounds," one member of the commission claimed that the choice of Frederick Law Olmsted was "particularly offensive" to him.

"That dunderhead Andrew Green," Fred had roared when he found out they might not choose him because of the "tiresome bean-counter" he had reported to during the Central Park years. "He doesn't have a creative bone in his body. Why he couldn't…." I tuned him out at that point, ruminating about all those meals served to the unwelcome guest years earlier. What a colossal waste of my time and energy!

But only a few days later, they announced that Fred was the top pick of the remaining four members and to placate Green, who had lobbied to hire Fred's former partner Calvert Vaux instead, it was agreed Fred and Vaux would work together on the project. Fred seemed pleased to work once more with Vaux, and it thrilled me to parlay this opportunity into more time with Anne. Since we had moved to Boston, we found our regularly scheduled phone calls were no substitute for being together.

***

At the stroke of midnight on July 15th, with the ceremonial cutting of a ribbon, Niagara Falls officially re-opened to the public. Fred and I were there to celebrate with the thousands of tourists eager to view the iconic falls. The evening was a true celebration, and I sipped wine and watched dozens of state officials congratulate Fred, replete with handshaking and backslapping. I scanned the crowd for Anne. We had arrived together a couple of hours earlier in a horse-drawn carriage that transported us from our hotel, but had gotten separated. As had been the case throughout his long partnership with Cal, Fred had been receiving the lion's share of the accolades, due in part to his gregarious nature and outgoing personality. Tonight he was in rare form, even for him, I noted as I watched him being repeatedly recognized for his work. He was smiling and beaming with pride, and

I had never been prouder. But I strongly felt the absence of Anne and Cal Vaux, especially as the crowds thinned. Everyone had gotten their fill of the iconic landmark, even Fred who had first visited the falls as a young boy. I stood on tiptoe to whisper in his ear.

"Where do you suppose Anne and Cal disappeared to?" I asked.

"Well, I hope they didn't get swindled into taking one of those barrel rides over the falls," Fred said, failing to bring a smile to my face. "Oh now Mary, I am only having a laugh here. You know Cal. Early to bed, early to rise. I'm certain they are back at the hotel, sleeping soundly. We should do the same," he said, taking my arm as we made our way through the remaining groups of visitors.

Chapter 70

The next morning, I entered the hotel dining room alone. Fred had slept in, nursing a headache caused, no doubt, by the prodigious amount of alcohol he had consumed last night.

"A table for one," I said to the hostess who lead me into the room. Just then, I spotted Anne sitting alone at a table for two. "Actually, I would like to join my friend, if I might," I asked, gesturing in Anne's direction. Certain she had seen me, I was perplexed at the lack of a greeting when we approached the table. "Good morning," I said in a sing-song voice. "Aren't we the early birds?" Receiving only a mumbled "good morning" in return, I sat down and faced my old friend. I surveyed her choice of buttered toast and a cup of tepid-looking tea with surprise.

"Well, I could eat a full English," I said, referring to the traditional platter of eggs, beans, sausages and grilled tomatoes Anne frequently prepared for her British-born husband. I motioned for the waitress. "But since we are in New York, I would love a couple of soft-boiled eggs, an order of rye toast and some crisp bacon. And orange juice and a pot of strong coffee too. Oh, and oatmeal. I think that will be all." I waited until the waitress left us before turning back to my friend. "Anne?" I asked gently. "Can't I talk you into joining me? They say breakfast is the most important meal..." I stopped when Anne suddenly pounded the table angrily, causing her lukewarm tea to spill. "Why whatever—"

"So, I should be more like you then, is that it? You're all bright and cheery this morning and ready for a full breakfast and suddenly, I have to comply to suit you?" Her face was red, and she was positively spitting out her words. I leaned in and tried to take her hand, but Anne snatched it away from me. Her anger somewhat dissipated, she sank back into the plush banquette and stared coldly at me. I gratefully accepted the glass of juice the waitress placed in front of me. I drank a couple of sips and patted my lips with a large linen napkin. My appetite gone, I considered retracting my order when Anne spoke up.

"I'm sorry for my outburst. It's not you I should direct my anger at," she said. "It is, of course—" She stopped and looked down at her lap.

"It's Fred?" I asked. "Is that who you are upset with?" Anne looked miserable as she nodded slowly.

"If I'm being honest, it's just as much Cal's fault. He allows himself to play second fiddle. Always accommodating the great Frederick Law Olmsted, always standing in his shadow." She watched silently as a heaping platter overfilled with steaming food was placed in front of me.

"An extra plate, please," I asked the waitress who grabbed one from a nearby table and placed it in front of Anne. "There's no way I can eat all this," I announced to no one in particular. "Anne, won't you be a dear and help me to not let this delicious-looking food go to waste?" Without waiting for an answer, I scooped half of the eggs and bacon on to Anne's plate along with a couple of pieces of toast. "Now where is that oatmeal?" I asked, then beamed as our waitress carried over two small bowls of steaming porridge. "Thank you so much," I said, before I turned to Anne, who was staring blankly at the food. "Let's eat up now, shall we?" I dug into my meal and after a moment, Anne joined me and we sat in silence for several moments as we ate. When I realized I couldn't eat another bite, I pushed my plate away and reached for the thermos of coffee. Pouring us both a cup, I sat back and sipped slowly.

"Now do you want to tell me what has you so cranky this fine day?"

Anne pushed her empty plate away and took a long drink of her coffee. "Bloody Brits and their damn tea," she groused good-naturedly. "All I needed was a cup of American coffee. Thank you, and not just for the breakfast, although I must say it was divine."

I watched her closely. *What is wrong with her?* She had been a little cool to my overtures last night when we met in the hotel lobby, but I had attributed it to opening night jitters.

"Anne," I persisted. "What is going on? Are the children...?"

"No, the children are fine. Everyone is fine. Well, except for me, that is. I'm not so fine. You can't say you didn't ask for this," she began and shared how difficult things had been for Cal these last years. She described how they had moved to a smaller house to save money and how job opportunities for Cal had all but dried up. "He wants us to move to England. 'Home to England,' as he put it. 'It's not my bloody home', I told him. He's too proud to ask Fred for help, and when this Niagara project landed in his lap, I was over the moon. At last we can get out of the debt we're in. Pay our bills, buy gifts for the grandchildren. Like normal people, like you. How is Charlotte by the way, speaking of grandchildren?"

"No change," I said. "But we're not talking about me and my problems right now."

"Well, to be frank, the commission for this job is to be paid in installments and Cal was too embarrassed to ask for an advance. We had barely enough money to pay our rent this month, let alone take a trip up here. Then Cal found out they would cover our lodging, so we agreed to come. I asked at the reception desk if breakfast was included and was told no, it was extra. Then I saw the prices on the menu and..." She shrugged sadly.

"And I come in all Miss Mary Sunshine and order enough food for an army," I said. "That was the last thing you needed this morning."

"No," Anne said, "it was actually the only thing I needed. I missed my friend."

"And I missed you. Now how about we order another pot of coffee and start figuring out how we can get our stubborn mule husbands working together again?" Throw some work Cal's way *and* lessen the workload that was crippling my husband. That would be wonderful for all concerned.

Anne positively beamed. "That sounds splendid. Anything to keep me from having to move 'back home' to jolly old England." So we drank coffee and plotted out a scenario guaranteed to please everyone and to allow our husbands to think it was all their idea.

Chapter 71

Spring 1886

I looked up in surprise as Fred hurried into the room where I had been writing a letter to my cousin Louisa.

"What has you in such a tizzy?" I asked as I watched him pace. "Is everything all right?"

"Yes, Mary. But I need your counsel on a business matter. A pressing one." I studied him closely. He was red in the face and—were those tears in his eyes?

"Tell me, please. What is it?"

"I just received a letter from Leland Stanford, a senator from California. Do you remember me telling you about him? He's very progressive and his focus has been on the importance of education. Do you remember?" If I could even recall even a small percentage of the people Fred had met over the years, it would be nothing short of a miracle. I gave him a weak nod.

"Um, of course I do. But why is Senator Stanford contacting you?" Fred cleared his throat and appeared to skim the letter he was holding.

"It would seem the senator and his wife, a lovely woman as I recall. She—"

"Fred, what is he asking of you?"

"He and Mrs. Stanford want to build a new university in Palo Alto. He is asking me to design the grounds." Although I thought all of his projects were spectacular, I had a particular interest in institutions of higher learning where the future leaders of the country were educated. How I had enjoyed strolling the grounds of Yale University with both John and Owen.

"A new university! That sounds wonderful. You'll say yes, won't you?" Fred's expression had turned glum. "Isn't this the work you wish to be doing? None of the politics and shenanigans of the publicly funded projects? No obstructionist committees and city councils?" Fred nodded slowly.

"Yes, it's just that the Stanfords are building this school as a tribute. In memory of their son, Leland Junior."

"In memory of?" I repeated slowly. Fred looked away, unable to meet my gaze.

"The Stanfords lost their son recently. Typhoid fever. He was not quite sixteen years old." My eyes filled with tears.

"Those poor people," I said. Who knew better than us just how devastating it was to lose a child? "Was it their only child?" I asked, then immediately regretted it. Well-meaning friends and relatives had tried to comfort me when the babies had died, and again when we lost Owen. "At least you have other children," they would say as if living children were a consolation prize.

"Yes, and they want to build the Leland Stanford, Jr. University in his honor. I assume they will want a memorial statue in the boy's honor in a prominent position on the grounds." He frowned, and I recalled how much he disliked statues.

"Well, of course they will. But that won't deter you from coming up with a world-class design, now will it?" Fred's smile did not quite reach his eyes.

"If the Stanfords wish to erect a statue, then who am I to deny them?" I hugged him then, my cheek against his scratchy tweed jacket, grateful to have him beside me.

"I miss Owen. Every single day. I panic as I try to imagine how his voice sounded. What he would say about something or other. It's only been five years. How hard will it be in another five or ten years? Will I be able to remember him at all?" I broke down, crying in earnest. "My Owen. So sweet and kind. How could he have been taken from us so soon?" Fred held me close and patted my back gently.

"Oh, Mary, there are no answers for that question. Life is full of mystery and wonder. Perhaps there is a plan somewhere. Maybe we are not supposed to know exactly what is in store for us." Only partially mollified, I pulled away and dabbed at my eyes.

"Even more reason for relaxing your hard and fast rule about allowing statues," I said. "There's more than one way to mourn the loss of a loved one, so we need to be more accepting about whatever keeps memories alive for us."

I decided to locate the family photo albums in storage since our move to Brookline. Tonight, after supper, we would relive memories of our family, looking at photographs and swapping stories. And tomorrow, I would write a letter to Mrs. Leland Stanford, expressing my condolences and sharing memories of my own son. We are not meant to be alone in our grief. Sharing our feelings about the loss of those we love keeps them alive, if only in our hearts.

Chapter 72

Fall 1886

Our son-in-law repeatedly rejected my offers to visit or help with the children. While I understood his anguish over his wife's continued hospitalization, his reluctance mystified me to welcome me into his home. Did my grandsons remember me or realize how much Fred and I loved them? I sent letters and gifts and bided my time in the hope John might reach out soon. It had been easier during the several months when Marion was living with the Bryants, but in the years since then communication between us had all but broken down.

With Rick away at school much of the year, I spent more time working with Fred in the office. It was a welcome distraction, and I enjoyed completing design plans, overseeing the drawings created by the team of young draftsmen and even, much to my surprise, conducting meetings and corresponding with many of the clients. Apparently, I had a real knack for calming those who were upset and convincing those who were uncertain. Clients for the larger projects, such as Senator Stanford out in California still required personal visits by Fred or John, but I had, according to both Fred and John, proven indispensable on several small- and mid-sized commissions. It had started earlier in the year when a Mr. William Brennan had shown up, claiming to have an appointment with Fred.

"But he's in New York this week," I had said. "There must be a mix-up." Brennan had insisted this was a long-standing appointment, and it appeared he fully expected me to produce Fred out of thin air. Knowing John was due back at the office within the hour, I decided to stall our unexpected guest.

I invited him to join me for tea and almond cake while we waited. After enjoying several slices of cake and slurping a third cup of sweet, milky tea, Mr. Brennan, a pleasant fellow, appeared relaxed. He got to talking about his plans for the sixteen-acre parcel of land he had purchased in nearby Jamaica Plain. As I listened, it became obvious that he had major misgivings about not only the overall design Fred had proposed last month but also the budget and the timeline. One by one, I addressed each of his concerns and listened carefully to his responses. Allowing him to talk through the issues seemed to calm him, and although I didn't alter a single detail, he appeared satisfied and committed to the plan.

Later in the day, John called his father, and I overheard him telling Fred how I had saved the day.

"You should have seen her, Father. Mother was so confident and reassuring. She had Brennan eating out of her hand. He had been ready to cancel the entire project, but after devouring her cake and listening to her, he left a retainer of $1,000. Yes, $1,000. I'm telling you, she's our secret weapon." He listened for a moment, before nodding eagerly. "Yes, I'm proud of her too. Let me get her on the phone for you." I scurried away from the door so as not to be caught snooping. John found me over by the window, casually staring out at the yard. "Father's on the phone, Mama. He wants to talk with you about today." I pretended to be uncertain what he would want to talk with me about, but hurried to the phone, eager to hear the praise that was forthcoming.

Since then, I spent a few hours in the office each day, answering the phone, taking messages for Fred and John and greeting the occasional visitor. Telling myself it was just clerical work, I filed order forms and tracked expenses incurred on each of the projects. I was amazed that although Olmsted and Sons had nearly fifty projects on the books at any one time — ranging from initial requests, proposals in process, proposals pending a final decision, active projects and completed work requiring minor follow up — there was no process in place for tracking expenses and attaching bills and invoices to each one in order to include these expenses on the customer's final bill. I quickly realized how easy it would be to lose track of those expenses and the impact on the company's profit margins. I created a new procedure to track and code expenditures and spent hours explaining it to Fred, John, and the draftsmen. At first dismissing it as one of "Mother's bright ideas," both Fred and John came to realize how they had missed this critical step and quickly came on board.

"Your mother is a genius," Fred crowed at supper one night. He had just received a check from a former client who had not balked at receiving a bill for ancillary expenses nearly a year after paying what he had believed to be the final bill. "One thousand, eight hundred dollars," Fred exclaimed as he raised a glass of sparkling wine in my direction. "Your mother found $1,800 in a pile of papers shoved in a drawer," he told John, Marion and Rick. I blushed and smiled happily.

"One thousand, eight hundred and forty-seven dollars," I corrected him primly and everyone roared with laughter. Maybe that visiting reporter from the *Woman's Home Companion* was correct. I had worth beyond raising children and running a household. I was a good listener, fairly creative and extremely organized. Olmsted and Sons was lucky to have me!

Chapter 73

Summer 1887

I set down my pen and took a gulp of tea, long gone cold. With a shudder, I sighed and gently massaged my temples. It had been a very unproductive day, the kind I rarely experienced. I had grown accustomed to finishing most, if not all, of the items on my to-do list, but today the list had grown in size. New requests for proposals had arrived in the mail and while that normally pleased me, today I groaned, reflecting on the task of creating new folders for each and sending out invoices to compensate Fred, John or one of the apprentices for their time preparing an initial proposal and a sample design. The project on my mind today was the Stanford estate. Senator Stanford and his wife regularly changed their minds on critical design elements and costs were skyrocketing.

I looked up to find Marion entering the office carrying a tray laden with a fresh pot of tea, two cups and a plate of chocolate biscuits.

"Oh, you are a sight for sore eyes," I said and cleared a space on the edge of the desk. But Marion headed for the sofa at the far end of the room. With a flourish, she deposited the tray on a small table and motioned me to join her.

"Come, Mama," she said. "You have been slaving at that desk and never came up for dinner. It's time we had a proper visit. It's like we never talk anymore." I looked at my daughter. At twenty-six, Marion was past the age by which most girls married, or at least had a steady fellow. Perhaps Fred's half-joking prediction Marion would be an old maid was accurate. I pushed my chair back and got to my feet.

"You're right as usual, pet. I have been trying to work through a trying situation and have not reached a solution." I sat down and hugged her close. "Have I told you recently how much I appreciate you?" Marion leaned forward and poured two cups of tea.

"Yes, Mother," she sighed. "You and Father and John appreciate me. You tell me all the time. Anyway, do you recall that curious gentleman we met in Paris?" I chuckled.

"The one with the brother who planned to build a tower?"

"He did it," Marion said. "It's in today's *Gazette*."

"What on earth?" Marion handed me the newspaper, and I quickly skimmed the article. Gustave Eiffel had seen his dream come true in the form of a 1,000-foot iron lattice tower in the middle of Paris. "Will wonders never cease?" I asked Marion with a smile. "I can't wait to tell your father." I studied her closely. My cheerful girl seemed sad this afternoon.

"If you don't mind my saying so, you seem down in the dumps. If so, after a cup of tea and a couple of these delightful biscuits, you'll be right as rain. At least that's what my grandmother always..." I stopped as Marion burst into tears. I set my cup down, and pulled Marion in for another hug, and this time, I didn't release her as quickly.

"Whatever is the matter?" I murmured in her ear. "You can tell me anything." Marion pulled away and let out a sigh as she reached for her tea. Taking a large gulp, she smiled briefly and settled back into the contours of the sofa.

"I feel life is passing me by. No, don't—" she began when I frowned and tried to speak. "You're about to tell me I live in a lovely home, I've had an excellent education and am a talented photographer and I am well-traveled and possess a keen intellect." I looked sheepish and nodded. *That was all true.* "So don't you see? It is because of all those attributes I find myself at a loss. How do I make the most of my education and clever mind? I travel on the rare occasion with my older brother, who by the way is as dull as dishwater. I long to try new foods and experience different cultures when we leave Boston, but John is content with a ham sandwich in his room and turning in with a book to read or a report to write before it is even dark out." I smiled at the image of my son, who relied on the familiar whenever possible, and Marion continued.

"Enough about John. I shouldn't have even brought him up. Who am I to complain about his lack of desire for adventure when I am an old maid, with nary a prospect of my own? I am the proverbial pot, calling the kettle black. Do you understand what I'm trying to tell you, Mother?" My mind was working overtime as I tried to identify some options for her. At twenty-six, I was already married with two children and a third on the way.

"What about an extended visit to Cohasset? Perhaps John Bryant would appreciate help with the boys. You are their aunt," I finished weakly as I saw Marion's frown.

"As far as I can tell, his mother and their full-time governess can handle the boy's care. But seriously, Mother? I come to you and tell you how unhappy I am, always looking after everyone else's needs and you create a situation where I would have four more family members to help? *That* is your brilliant solution?"

"I didn't say it was brilliant, Marion. And please stop being so melodramatic. I want to help you identify a proper solution. Assisting the Bryants was just a thought." I waited for Marion to nod before continuing. "What about looking for employment as a governess? That would..." I stopped as Marion frowned again. "All right, still helping others out, I see. So teaching?" Marion shook her head again. I took another sip of tea and bit into a biscuit to buy some time. What on earth was Marion experienced to do?

"What about travel? Not with your brother, but perhaps a change of scenery is in order. I can speak with my cousin or maybe an old friend from school? Some of them live in exciting places. Wouldn't Europe be lovely this spring?" Marion looked doubtful.

"I not sure if a visit with an older woman would really be what I had in mind," she said slowly. I was losing my patience.

"You don't want to look into employment as a governess or a teacher. You don't want to consider an extended trip abroad as a lady of leisure. How about selling gloves at Macy's or serving tea in a café? Would that be what you're looking for?"

"Actually, a part-time job might work out well," she said. "Provided it is in New York."

"New York? Why would you want to live in New York?" I asked. "What's there that you can't find in Boston?"

"It's just, well, New York is where everything is happening, with the movement, I mean," Marion responded. I was now even more confused.

"What movement are you referring to, pet? You're not making sense."

"Honestly, Mother. I wonder if you even listen to me half the time. The women's movement, of course. Suffrage? Women's right to vote? It's positively criminal we make up more than half of the country, yet we are still disenfranchised." I remembered Marion mentioning how women should be able to vote, but working to make it so? Is that how she wished to spend her time?

"Well, you've captured my attention. Tell me what you would do in New York to benefit the suffrage movement?" Marion's eyes grew wide.

"Oh Mama, so many things. I love to paint and take photographs. Susan tells me these skills can help spread the message. They need signs and—"

"Susan? Do you mean Susan B. Anthony?" Marion flushed and shook her head.

"Oh, no. I can only hope to meet Miss Anthony someday. I'm referring to Susan Stanton. She is a niece of Elizabeth Cady Stanton. She and Miss Anthony were the women who—"

"I am aware of Miss Stanton. So how and when did you meet her niece exactly?"

"It was at Cecily's house last fall. Cecily Davenport, remember her? It was the first time we met. I've run into her several times since then. She thinks I would be a significant addition to the group in New York."

"Is this a paid position?" I asked, causing Marion to look sheepish.

"No, it would be as a volunteer. That's why I might look into a waitressing job or a clerk's position in one of the department stores."

"Where would you live? Not alone. Why that's unheard of, a girl in your—"

"A woman, Mother. I'm a woman now. And there is a rooming house nearby the headquarters where several of the other volunteers stay. The rooms are clean and cheap, too." Marion's face was now flushed with excitement. "What do you think? Can you help me to tell Father?"

I sat back and sighed. Half an hour ago, my biggest concern was the inflated budget of the Stanford estate. Now I was apparently the mother of a budding suffragette who wanted to live in New York City. I closed my eyes for a moment, then smiled at Marion, determined to match her enthusiasm.

"Of course, I will. But I want to meet this Susan Stanton and go to New York to evaluate the rooming house." I was suddenly crushed in a tight embrace, Marion looking happier than I had seen her in years. Perhaps it was time to let this little chick of ours leave the nest.

Chapter 74

Spring 1888

I accompanied Fred to Asheville, North Carolina, in late April on an extended business trip. We arrived the night before Fred was to meet with George Washington Vanderbilt. The twenty-five-year-old was the grandson of Cornelius Vanderbilt, who had amassed a fortune in the railroad and shipping industries. The young man had inherited much of his family's fortune and was reported to be worth thirteen million dollars. Fred had left our hotel hours ago, and I was about to venture downstairs to the dining room, feeling a bit peckish and hoping for a cup of tea and a sandwich. Just as I finished adjusting my hat, Fred burst into the room.

"You'll never believe this, Mary. Not in a million years," Fred called out as he prepared to unpack his valise, bulging with files and papers.

"What I can't believe is you failed to kiss me after leaving me alone all day," I said with a pout. He took the opportunity to kiss me soundly. "That's better. Now exactly what won't I believe?"

"Vanderbilt is hiring me for the project," Fred announced. "He said I came highly recommended, and we shook hands."

"Congratulations! So, what is he like?" I asked. Fred looked thoughtful.

"Young, of course. A most serious man, bookish and refined. Delicate, though. Nothing like his grandfather, the late Commodore Cornelius Vanderbilt." Although he had never met Cornelius Vanderbilt, Fred was involved in projects for other members of the Vanderbilt family in Lenox, Massachusetts, and on Lake Champlain in

Vermont. I was interested in knowing what was so special about this particular member of the Vanderbilt clan.

"This is good news, but what has you in such a state of excitement?" Fred looked up from the stack of papers he was trying to organize.

"The scope of the project, for starters. George has been buying up thousands of acres of land all around Asheville. He goes through a broker, using a variety of pseudonyms. If word got out that a Vanderbilt was interested…"

"Yes, of course. Prices would skyrocket. But what else besides the size is so interesting?"

"Well, I imagine it's the land itself. It shocked me to see trees cut down with no rhyme or reason. Enormous areas of burned wasteland serving as a cafeteria for hogs. It was on par with the original site of Central Park before I transformed it. It will be my privilege to restore much of the land to forest. I want to experiment with managing forestry on a grand scale and this is the ideal opportunity."

"Is that what young Mr. Vanderbilt wants?" I asked. Who would buy up that much land only to release it to the wild? Fred chuckled in response.

"He's not sure what he wants. Besides me, that is. And that is the real reason for my joy. The young Mr. Vanderbilt is leaving the entire project in my hands. I'm to oversee the choice of an architect for the grand home he envisions, and I have full control of the land. I mentioned the idea of managed forestry and reserving some acreage for gardens and perhaps a small deer park and he told me to get started right away. I asked for a retainer of $15,000 and I had the check in my hand before I left." I was awestruck. Although Olmsted and Sons was the most sought-after firm in the country, a retainer that large? How could Fred manage a project of this scope from Boston?

"I know what you're thinking, Mary, and I have thought of what I would do if chosen for a project like this. Asheville is already well-known nationally as an ideal spot for rest cures and the train we took runs regularly. Not too long of a trip either." I sat down on the edge of the bed with a long sigh. A twenty-four-hour train ride had seemed an eternity only yesterday, and now Fred was crowing over the relative brevity of the very same trip.

"So," he said, "I requested lodging for me and my men, and George is arranging for rooms here at the hotel for as long as the project runs. I'll look to bring on additional draftsmen and surveyors, and we'll hire dozens, probably hundreds of local workers. If John does not want to manage the project, I may ask William Elliot to step up. What do you think?" I was warming up to the idea of traveling here with Fred. The climate was so temperate. No more snowy Boston winters?

"What? Mr. Elliot? Why yes, I think he would do nicely. But ask John first. When he turns you down, which I am certain he will, you can ask Mr. Elliot." I took his arm possessively. "Meanwhile, why don't you take me for an early supper to celebrate?" Fred happily agreed and off we went.

Chapter 75

Spring 1889

"I have said goodbye to more friends this year than in all of my prior years combined," Fred said, his voice hoarse and barely audible. He had been laid up for the past week, barely eating and not talking to anyone except for Rick and me. I squeezed his hand and smiled at him.

"That is a testament to the number of men who have called you friend, my love. You have been a confidante, a role model, an ally and a mentor to so many," I reminded him. "The friendships you made as a boy in Hartford, as a student at Yale and as a farmer on Staten Island are still as solid today as ever. That alone speaks volumes." Fred continued to look morose.

"How do I say goodbye to Henry Bellows or William Van Buren or, just last week, George Geddes? I am but a common man, being asked to complete herculean tasks. I feel bereft and alone." I bridled, but held my tongue. Laying into Fred would do no good with him utterly despondent.

"But you're *not* alone. You have me, your wife of thirty years. You have John and dear Marion and darling Rick," I chided him gently. "And our grandsons as well. I think a visit to the Bryant household is in order when you're well enough to travel. How does that sound?" Fred gave a mirthless chuckle and shook his head.

"Oh yes, just what the boys want is an old fool like me, decrepit and good for nothing to come calling. And as for our children, John is running the firm and Rick will be right by his side soon. They don't need me. Marion's got her hands full with her petitions and rallies in New York. What does she need of a washed-up old sod like me?" I was losing patience, so I attempted counting to ten. Before I could finish, Fred spoke again. "I ask you, Mary. What is the point? What is the meaning of it all?" he asked in a whisper. "Children are meant to live past their parents, yet we have buried three sons and what of Charlotte? What is to become of her, shut away in that asylum? She's as lost to us as dear Owen is." Fred broke into sobs — huge, rattling ones that seemed to come from deep within him. I hugged him and he cried into my shoulder for several minutes, before regaining his composure. He pulled away and dried his eyes with a handkerchief from the pocket of his bathrobe. He blew his nose loudly, before reclining once more on the sofa.

I looked closely at him and for the first time in a long while, tried to imagine my life without him. This dear man, whose bearded face had weathered and whose slight frame had filled out in the last couple of years. He had married me solely out of an obligation to his late brother, but had surely come to love me as deeply as I loved him. A marriage born of obligation and duty had developed into a deep and abiding love and years of shared passion. I attempted a smile and nudged him to open his eyes again. I spoke firmly but — I hoped — lovingly.

"My darling. Instead of focusing on all we have lost, and I'll grant you, we've suffered more than our share, shouldn't we concentrate on all we have been given?" It appeared I had his attention, so I hurried on. "A wonderful marriage with more love and kindness than I ever imagined. Strong and talented children who are each following their passions in their own way. You are the most sought-after man in the country. Every city official and estate owner with half a brain wants to work with you, and millions of people have had their lives greatly enhanced by your designs. You've provided the opportunity to explore nature and enjoy the outdoors with your walkways, paths and gardens. And let's not forget the thousands of acres transformed back into green forestland thanks to your efforts." I paused, waiting for a response, some sign that he had heard me. "Fred? Please tell me what you are thinking, would you?" Fred sat up and after gently kissing my cheek, whispered in my ear.

"You forgot to mention that I walk on water, dear wife. How could you neglect that most remarkable of my talents?" He watched me with a smile spreading across his face, his blue eyes beginning to sparkle. "I need a good night's sleep in our bed and tomorrow I'll be in a better frame of mind. I promise. This sofa was never intended to serve as my bed despite my efforts over the last few nights to make it so." He pushed himself up, still shaky. "What do you say? Will you help your old fool of a husband to bed?"

"Of course, my dear. Whatever you say." I switched off the gas lamp and, arm in arm, we headed towards the stairs.

Chapter 76

Summer 1890

Early in June, Fred had been summoned to meet with officials in Chicago to develop plans for the World's Columbian Exposition of 1893. Bringing together people from all different countries to share ideas in commerce, industry, technology and entertainment inspired him. Fred would lead a group of artists and architects to create a world-class venue for the event. He had left the very next day.

A few days later, he called to fill me in on his progress. He chose a 600-acre swampy parcel known as Jackson Park for its proximity to the city and to Lake Michigan. The project would be especially challenging as the structures were designed to be temporary, only standing for six months. Unlike most of Fred's earlier designs, the grounds would play second fiddle to these temporary buildings, and needed to be designed for their intended afterlife as a public park.

"Tell me more about the design, Fred. You must have something spectacular in mind." He chuckled before he continued.

"I envision a chain of interconnected lagoons and a circular road system with a bridge and a long pier extending into Lake Michigan." Fred told me about the exhibition buildings, which would be accessible by both land and water, and a great courtyard serving as the entry point for fair attendees.

"Mary, I tell you. I project the attendance for this event will topple all the previous fairs combined. We could reach 150,000 visitors daily for six months. The budget is not to be believed. Olmsted and Sons will be paid over $25,000. Can you imagine?"

"That is wonderful, Fred. I'm so proud of you." *The man behind the next World's Fair is my amazing husband!*

"Well, don't be too proud just yet. Years of hard work are in order before we can celebrate. But when it's done, I plan to take the lot of you with me, including our grandsons. We'll make it a family adventure to never forget," he boasted. *Family.* I thought of Charlotte and the hole her absence left in my heart.

"Something to look forward to, my dear." I dug in my pocket for a handkerchief and dried the tears from my cheeks. The silence on the other end of the phone had me wondering if we had lost the connection. Then I heard him.

"I'm thinking of our girl, too," Fred admitted with a catch in his voice. "And Owen. How on earth can we have lost so much and still have much to be grateful for?" I nodded, though of course he could not see me. Even with a thousand miles separating us, I felt so close to this wonderful man. We spoke the same language, Fred and I.

"This call is costing you a fortune, my dear. We'll talk more when you get home," I said, and he agreed.

"I'll be home soon," he promised, and we said goodbye. I couldn't wait to share the exciting news with the children.

Chapter 77

Spring 1891

I found a wallpaper pattern advertised in the Sears and Roebuck catalog and impulsively ordered enough for our dining room. Hoping to surprise Fred, I hid the rolls in a spare closet until he went out of town for several days. I arranged for the installation of the paper and had been excited for him to see it. Despite Fred's talent for making something beautiful out of something quite plain, he rarely showed much interest in the furnishings of his own home. He generally allowed me full control of the houses we lived in. But, in a rare moment of discontent, Fred had returned home from his trip and immediately pronounced the design of the wallpaper to be downright gaudy, more befitting a bordello than a proper household. Stung by his reaction, I angrily demanded to know when he had last visited a bordello. He ignored me and started to leave the room, as if he could not stand to be surrounded by such vulgar furnishings for another minute.

"Perhaps I should have sought the opinion of a true harbinger of taste. I'm certain Miss Wormeley would have loved to choose what should adorn the walls of our dining room," I called out. Having hoped to get a reaction, I was not surprised when he marched over to where I stood.

"What on earth are you going on about, woman?" Fred had bellowed. "I have not spoken to Miss Wormeley in eons. How in blazes do you manage to bring her into our home of all places?"

"How dare you waltz in here and question my decisions? I'll have you know this is *my* home and I won't be second-guessed by you or anyone else. If you don't like it, I suggest you find another place to eat your bloody supper," I shouted, right before I rushed out of the room.

The next day, Fred experienced flu-like symptoms. Always a bit of a hypochondriac, he had summoned the doctor to make a house call. Despite the doctor's opinion that it was a mild case of the flu, Fred got it into his head that it was the house making him sick, specifically the new wallpaper. The doctor was barely out the door when he turned on me.

"I am telling you woman, it's the blasted wallpaper. Everyone knows mass-produced wallpaper contains high levels of arsenic. It's downright toxic." He was as mad as I had ever seen him. He was practically sputtering as he paced back and forth in front of the desk where I was working. I sighed impatiently. Ignoring him hadn't helped calm him down, but neither had agreeing with him, offering encouraging smiles or tut-tutting between his outbursts.

I pooh-poohed the idea and wondered aloud what he had against my lovely wallpaper. He responded by asking me exactly what there was to like about deadly fumes emanating from our walls and in the very room where we took our meals as a family. Just before he stormed out of the room, he all but accused me of wishing to kill him. I watched him go, deciding to ignore him, and we avoided each other for the rest of the day.

Laughing together over one of Rick's jokes at dinner thawed the ice between us and things returned to normal. Fred's health improved and the wallpaper incident was all but forgotten.

One morning a couple of weeks later, I thought back to our first year of marriage. That summer had been dreadful. All three children were sick, we were crammed in a too-small home, getting ready to move, and Fred was ill-prepared to transition from his life as a carefree bachelor to a married father of three. Despite all of that stress, I recalled him telling his father we had a good deal of happiness 'between the drips'. I had not made too much of the comment at the time, but now I pondered it more carefully. Is that what marriage was all about? Periods of happiness and contentment between the drips of illness and disagreements? If so, they should give new brides umbrellas as wedding gifts. Something to ward off all those dreadful drips, I thought with a smile.

As I gathered up the files I had been working on and placed them in their proper drawers, I overheard Fred coughing in the next room. Regardless of the exact cause, he had been suffering with aches and pains beyond the normal signs of aging. At nearly seventy, he would benefit from slowing down a bit. Working six days a week, seven if I let him, was too much. It was time to convince him to stop and smell the roses a bit more often. If he had forgotten how, I would be glad to remind him.

Chapter 78

It was a gorgeous sunny day, and I had an idea to cure the cabin fever I had been experiencing. I called our son-in-law, John. When we talked a couple of weeks ago, he had suggested we visit when Fred was better. I was almost giddy with relief when John agreed a visit was long overdue and that today being a Saturday would be perfect.

"We'll see you in a few hours then," I said and hung up the phone. "We're going to Cohasset," I called out to Fred. "No dawdling," I warned as he looked at me over his newspaper. He smiled happily and stood, pulling on his jacket.

"Whatever you say, Mrs. Olmsted. I'm sure Rick will want to join us." I hurried around the house, gathering up the stash of gifts I had been accumulating and calling to Sarah to pack a basket of food. It had been several months since I had laid eyes on the boys. I was determined to not waste a single moment. Rick agreed to the trip and the three of us arrived at the Bryant's home late morning. John greeted us warmly.

"Mother was so sorry, but she cannot join us today. She had made plans to visit her sister in Cambridge," he said, and I felt relief. I had always wondered how much of a role the elder Mrs. Bryant played in essentially freezing us out since moving in with her son and taking over the role of lady of the house.

"Please give her my best, won't you?" I asked John with a smile. "And now, where are those precious little ones?"

"Miss Hughes is getting them all spiffed up. They'll be down in a minute. Please come in and have a seat." We followed him into the spacious parlor. Fred sank gratefully in an overstuffed chair. But I was too excited to sit still.

"Run to the carriage," I instructed Rick. "And gather up as many of the presents as you can. Quickly now." John shook his head as he watched him leave.

"He's grown so since I saw him last," he said in wonder. "He's nearly as tall as you are, Fred." Fred started to comment, but I spoke first.

"Let's not let so much time go by next time," I begged and John reddened. "We just want to be part of your lives."

"I know," John said sadly. "Believe me, I want that as well." We all looked up as Rick, his arms full of gaily wrapped gifts, strode into the room, followed closely by a trio of tow-headed boys. Rick dropped the presents on the carpet and the boys made to attack the pile, but stopped short when their father called out to them.

"No opening presents until you have greeted your grandparents properly," he ordered, and I was pleased to see how polite and well-behaved they were. One by one, they came over and hugged me and shook Fred's hand. Such handsome boys! William, the oldest, was going to be twelve this summer. Charles was ten-and-a-half and the youngest, Samuel, was nine. They stood straight and tall, and I had to resist the urge to gather them up and run away with them. *Three sons. My dear Charlotte's three sons.*

"That's some handshake you have there, young man," Fred said to Samuel with a twinkle in his eye. "Go on now. Join your brothers and be sure to get all the gifts with your name on them." Samuel smiled, and I felt my heart leap. *He looks just like Owen.* I watched the boys unwrapping their gifts. Blocks, marbles and spinning tops received high praise, but it was the box of linking logs that really got their full attention. They immediately set out to construct a tower, shouting out orders to each other and totally engrossed in their efforts.

"Well done, Mrs. Olmsted," Fred beamed. I smiled at him, before turning my attention back to the boys. I could watch them play all day.

"I'm afraid I haven't prepared much in the way of a midday meal, Mary," said John. "Mother oversees all that, and our housekeeper is off today. I'm not sure..." I brushed off his concerns.

"We're family, John. There is no need to stand on ceremony with us. And we all but forced ourselves on you at the last minute. Rick," I called out, and he stood and headed for the door.

"I'm imagine you need me to fetch the food hamper," he said good-naturedly and soon returned with a wicker basket. I shooed him and John away, promising dinner would be ready shortly and set to work. Checking the Bryant's paltry larder, I was glad to have packed as much as I had. I laid out a couple of platters of cold, sliced meats and cheeses, a basket of rolls and an assortment of pickles, chutneys, relishes and dark, grainy mustard. I was soon ready to call the family in to eat. I sat back and listened to the lively chatter. A happy family. This is all I wanted in life. I caught Fred's eye across the table. He winked, and I knew he was thinking the same thing.

After dinner, I left the dirty dishes at John's insistence and we headed to the park across the street. Rick tossed a ball back and forth with the three boys. They played for a while, chattering about baseball, recently declared the national sport of the United States. They all seemed knowledgeable about the game.

"I want to join one of the leagues that are forming," an earnest Charles said to his Uncle Rick. His older brother scorned that idea.

"You're not nearly good enough," William said, but Rick came to his defense.

"Keep practicing, Charles. You're the best ten-year-old player I've ever seen," he said, and Charles beamed at him.

Samuel had stopped playing to sit on the bench, holding fast to my hand.

"I want to be a doctor like Papa," he said.

"That's a wonderful idea," I said.

When we returned to the Bryant home, John had cleaned up and put away all the leftovers. He had set out a pitcher of lemonade and a plate of sugar cookies, which the boys happily devoured. Sam chose several books from the well-stocked library and I read aloud to the boys, while the men enjoyed a glass of port. By late afternoon, I decided we should get on the road. Not wanting to overstay our welcome, I promised we would return soon. Hugs and kisses followed, and I thought my heart would burst with happiness.

"You'll tell Charlotte we were here then, won't you?" I asked, trying not to cry. John glanced worriedly at Fred, who took my arm, leading me out to our waiting carriage. It wasn't until we were out of sight of the Bryant house that Fred told me John had confessed that despite the best medical care money could buy, Charlotte's mental illness had escalated to where she barely recognized her husband during his weekly visits. And she had not asked about her sons in months.

"For years, John held onto the belief that she was suffering from nervous exhaustion," Fred said sadly. "And hoped she could recover. But he has realized she is beyond help at this point. All he can do is to ensure she is well cared for and safe from harm."

I buried my head in his chest and sobbed most of the way home.

Chapter 79

Fall 1892

I squeezed my eyes shut and tried to pray, but the words wouldn't come. I had so much on my mind that to choose what to pray for first seemed like a daunting task. I was sitting at the kitchen table, sipping a tepid cup of tea and staring at a piece of dry toast on a lovely fall day. The air outside was crisp and the sight of falling leaves never failed to cheer me. Until that day. I loved all the seasons equally, although I wished March could be just a few days shorter than the other months. But this day, despite the beauty of a New England autumn, I felt bleak, sadder than I could remember.

The new cook, a young woman from Belfast who had joined the household just a few months ago, bustled into the kitchen. Sinead Feeney was tall and broad-shouldered, with a thick red braid hanging down her back. She was skilled in the kitchen and unfazed by the size of our household, which expanded depending on the day of the week. Weekends were usually hectic and since there was always room at the table for anyone who showed up at mealtime, menu planning could get very complicated. A roast for six might need to be stretched to a stew for ten with just an hour's notice. So far Sinead had proven herself up to the challenge of preparing meals for family and guests. I gave her the night off whenever it was just me and Fred or Marion and she enjoyed a social life, often going out with a few of the other cooks and maids who worked in the neighborhood. I had overheard Sinead telling Jenny, who worked as a chambermaid for the Farrells next door, that, in her mind, "Missus Mary was the kindest employer she had ever had the good luck to work for" and that "the Olmsted family was a loving, high-spirited group of hard-working people." *Nothing high-spirited today.*

"Now Missus, I'm heading to the butchers and greengrocers, but can I fetch you a fresh cup of tea?" I protested, but Sinead swooped over and grabbed the cup. Eyeing the plate of cold toast, she continued. "And how about a sandwich? You barely ate your porridge this morning and a woman as busy as you can't survive without a proper meal. There's lamb from last night. I could toast the bread."

"No, Sinead. I do not want a sandwich, delightful as that lamb was last night. The tea will be sufficient." I watched as she poured me a piping hot cup of tea, breathing in the spicy smell gratefully. "My goodness. Is there anything better than a cup of tea to cure what ails you?" Sinead stood nearby, unsure how to proceed. She had said she had errands to do, but…?

"Would you like to join me?" I asked. Sarah, our former cook, had been practically a member of the family, but Sinead was more reserved, especially with Fred and John. Her eyes widened as she considered the invitation. "Please, dear. I could use some company," I admitted, realizing how true the words were as I spoke them. Sinead did not need to be asked again. Turning on her heel, she grabbed a cup and saucer from the sideboard and returned to the table.

"One more thing." She hurried to the pantry, returning less than a minute later with a plate heaped with almond shortbread. "Do you mind?" she asked and without waiting for an answer, settled into a chair. She poured a cup, helped herself to a handful of cookies, and passed the plate to me.

"I really shouldn't," I protested even as I placed two cookies on my napkin. Sinead chuckled in response.

"Me mam always said I had the appetite of a workhorse," she admitted, only half apologetically. "I figure if some fella can't see past my broad arse, well then—" She stopped, blushing furiously. "Oh, Missus, I'm sorry. I don't know where my manners up and went to. I never should have…" I patted her hand.

"It's all right. Just remember when Mr. Fred is around." Sinead nodded her head.

"And Mr. John, too. I need to be on my best behavior around them both."

"After we plan the menus for the week, let's make a habit of sharing a nice pot of tea, shall we?" Sinead smiled and we sat for a few moments, enjoying the snack and each other's company. Then she stood and gathered up the cups and plates. I was about to tell her to leave it, but stopped myself. She would have plenty of time to finish her chores and get to the park to spend the rest of the day with her friends. No sense in overdoing the amount of time off.

With a wave, Sinead rushed from the room, presumably to grab her shawl from the hook in her room. Listening to her clattering down the stairs, followed by the sound of the door closing behind her, I let out a breath, once again alone with my thoughts. Fred's failing health and frequent memory lapses consumed me as did the fact that my three grandsons were growing up without their mother. So much sadness, but deep down I knew I wanted to be there for those I loved and enjoy every moment we had together.

I pushed my chair back, suddenly determined to get out and enjoy this beautiful day. I would place a quick call to Anne, who had moved with her family to the Boston area earlier in the year. It was wonderful living close to each other once more. Treating her to a delightful meal, followed by a stroll around the Common, would be the perfect way to spend the day. If Anne wasn't available, I could go to Macy's, look for some new gloves, and have a piece of their divine pie in the tearoom. Afterwards, a leisurely stroll and maybe a ride on the swan boats. Energized and looking forward to the day, I hurried to the phone.

Chapter 80

Spring 1893

Opening day for the World's Columbian Exposition, more commonly referred to as the Chicago World's Fair, had exceeded all attendance estimates. Only a few hours after the gates swung open, the original prediction of 150,000 paid attendees had already been met, and we were later told that by the time the fair closed for the night, paid attendance had soared to 200,000. Early reviews were enthusiastic. The preponderance of white buildings housing the exhibition halls dominating the fairgrounds had given Chicago a new name: the White City. Visitors returned and each day, the numbers grew.

I was thinking of Fred as I prepared to leave our hotel room and meet him for dinner. After spending the past three days touring the exhibits and marveling at all the exposition offered, I had begged off, insisting on a well-deserved lie-in. Fred left for the fair at the crack of dawn, accompanied by Rick and Marion, but promised to return at midday. John had caught an early train back to Boston yesterday, claiming at least one Olmsted needed to be on site at the office. Despite my best efforts, our grandsons had not joined us on the trip. John Bryant had insisted the summer months were much more convenient for travel and promised all three boys would spend some time at Fairsted soon. I was disappointed, but told myself it had been pure folly to think the boys could miss two weeks of school in the middle of the term to attend a fair. Fred had not raised an eyebrow when he saw the growing pile of souvenirs I had been collecting for them.

Realizing I was running behind, I hurried down the wide staircase to the lobby. I saw Fred sitting on one of the overstuffed armchairs near the center of the large space and rushed over to him. He was deep in conversation with three other men and all wore somber expressions. I wondered what was wrong as I approached them. Had ticket sales dropped? I stopped when I overheard one of the younger men say the word "murder." *What on earth?* Conversation halted as soon as I joined them. Fred was the last to notice, and he stared up at me, his normally twinkling blue eyes dull and unfocused. He stood, unsteady at first, and cleared his throat.

"Gentlemen, let me introduce my wife, Mary. Mary, this is Mr. Daniel Burnham, chief architect and the Director of Works. Surely you have heard me speak of him." I nodded and smiled graciously. I held out my hand, which Burnham grasped in his own for a moment.

"Ah, Mrs. Olmsted. This is a pleasure. I was just saying to my wife the other day, I said, we must have the Olmsteds over as soon as all of this settles down." He shrugged his shoulders. "And now all of this. No rest for the weary, yes?" I nodded again, having no clue what 'all of this' was.

Fred continued with the introductions. "Mary, I am pleased to present Mr. Louis Sullivan. He is a local architect and has been a valuable member of the team this past year." Sullivan silently held out a hand to me. "And last but not least, this is Mr. George Ferris, engineer and inventor —" I brightened at the sound of the man's name.

"Of course, Mr. Ferris. What an honor. Your wheel is a nothing short of a masterpiece. Why, our daughter Marion and our son Rick must have ridden it a dozen times or more this week. It's a marvel." Ferris looked pleased at the compliment and I started to add that if it were not for a persistent case of vertigo, I too would have gone for a spin, but Burnham spoke up.

"This is all lovely, but with my deepest apologies to Mrs. Olmsted, gentlemen, we need to get back to the matter at hand," he said with an air of mystery. Fred nodded knowingly, then turned to me.

"I'm sorry, my dear. I am afraid I will have to pass on dinner today. Something has come up. A most delicate matter. We're discussing how best to handle it, before detectives from the Chicago Police Department arrive."

"The police? Whatever for?" I asked. The men looked at each other, and by some unspoken agreement, remained silent. Finally, Burnham spoke up.

"In the strictest confidence, now," he said. "This is not to leave this room. It is imperative that—" Fred cut him off.

"For God's sake, man, this is my wife. She is the most circumspect of women you will ever chance to meet. You have my word that she won't speak a word of this to anyone." The younger man had the grace to blush at being chastised. "If you don't tell her, you can be certain that I will." Burnham's expression softened a bit as he regarded me warily.

"I understand and please, Mrs. Olmsted. Our need for secrecy was not meant as a slight. I meant no disrespect." He ran his fingers through his hair and shook his head sadly.

"Of course," I said, but Burnham was finally ready to break the silence.

"There has been a murder."

"But who? Someone attending the fair?" I stammered, feeling my knees go weak. Fred sat back in his chair, as did Burnham and Sullivan. George Ferris pulled a chair over for me and wordlessly, I sank into it. Grateful for the kind gesture, I smiled briefly, relieved I hadn't toppled over.

"We don't know as yet. The only report is that a 'woman of an indeterminate age' was found nearby the gate by a night watchman." I turned to Louis Sullivan when he spoke up.

"It's likely she was killed elsewhere and her body was dumped near the exposition. Not everyone in Chicago is thrilled with the spectacle this fair has been creating," he said darkly. Burnham glared at him.

"No more speculating, Sullivan. That detective we're meeting told me to keep all of this under wraps until we know more. The last thing we need right now is a rumor implicating the fair in this most unfortunate business. That it's not safe. It's bad enough our headliner Buffalo Bill Cody is threatening to cancel this weekend." He shook his head in bewilderment. "And he knows how to use a gun. If *he's* too afraid to join us, well…" Everyone reflected on that for a moment, then Fred turned towards me.

"This is a good chance to grab a bite to eat. When word gets out, chances are we'll be swamped by reporters and looky-loos. I recommend having a tray sent up. I'll send word to Marion to join you." I nodded mutely and stood. I bid farewell to the men and, as I was exiting the lobby, looked back to see a tall man in a long black coat leading a group of uniformed police officers towards Fred and the others. The cavalry had arrived. I trudged up the stairs to our room.

***

Fred's prediction that our hotel would be mobbed was accurate. By mid-afternoon, when Marion arrived at our suite, she reported a line of onlookers and reporters clambering to enter the lobby. They stationed police officers at every door to keep anyone but registered guests and those on official business from entering. I had ordered a tray of sandwiches from room service two hours earlier, but had merely picked at the food. As soon as Marion joined me, I ate with more enthusiasm. The pot of coffee had long gone cold and calls to replace it with a fresh pot went unanswered. Marion ran the water in the tap until it was as hot as it would get and attempted to make me a cup of tea with a tea bag left over from breakfast. I held her close, very aware that somewhere in Chicago, there was another mother who would never again have the chance to hug her daughter.

We sat side by side as the room grew dark, waiting for more news of the day's tragedy. Fred returned hours later, thoroughly exhausted with disappointing news. Despite an extensive manhunt, the killer had proven elusive. When we left Chicago later that week, there was still no sign of the man now being referred to in the newspapers as the 'Devil in the White City'.

Chapter 81

Spring 1894

Last night Fred had notified me of an appointment he had scheduled for this morning, and I decided it was time to have a conversation with John and Rick. A private one, so I could talk to them *without* Fred. I was troubled about recent developments and wanted to share my concerns, but as my sons joined me in the dining room, I was having second thoughts. *Who was I to judge?* I could be blowing a few minor incidents way out of proportion. But, deep down, I knew that wasn't the case. Fred had been slipping further and further away these last few months and it was critical to the future of Olmsted and Sons—as well as to the family—that action be taken. John cleared his throat and spoke first, sounding concerned.

"Mother, what is it? I canceled two appointments to be here. Can you please tell us what is going on?" Rick nodded in agreement.

"We're concerned, naturally," Rick said. "Our biggest worry is you, Mama. Are you all right? Is it Charlotte?" I winced at the sound of her name. By some unspoken agreement, we rarely spoke of her.

"No, dear. I have no change to report concerning Charlotte, and I'm certain Marion is still fighting the good fight in New York." I watched Rick's look of concern turn to a smirk. "Now believe what you will, young man, but your sister is passionate about women's rights and your father and I support her one hundred percent." The fact that our support included a generous monthly allowance to supplement Marion's pitiful wages as a part-time hostess in a mid-town tearoom was none of their concern. And far afield from my intended topic of discussion for today. I took a deep breath.

"I wanted to talk about your father. First, let me ask if either of you has noticed anything unusual about his behavior lately." John looked puzzled as he thought about the question, but Rick spoke up quickly.

"Other than he still prefers strong black coffee and pickles for breakfast whenever we're traveling," he said, knowing full well my idea of a healthy breakfast was porridge or eggs and toast. "Why he—"

"I am aware your father's diet is much impaired when he's out of the house, as well as the fact he claims to smoke one or two cigars a week, when it's probably closer to five. That's not what I wanted to talk to you about. I'm concerned about his mental health—his, well, state of mind." John's look of confusion deepened.

"Mother, I'm not sure what you're referring to. He is as sharp as a tack when it comes to the business and balancing all the projects we've got on the books." Rick was shaking his head, rejecting his brother's claim.

"Now John, you know Father has not been at the top of his game for some time now. You've been covering for him for so long you don't even realize how often he forgets things. Names of clients, details about projects, expenditures made." He nodded vigorously. "I hate to admit it, but I think you're right, Mama. Tell us, what have you noticed?" I started to relax. I had been worried about Rick's reaction in particular. He was always so quick to defend his father, who could do no wrong in his opinion. The fact he, too, sensed something was amiss was a relief. I knew I wasn't just imaging things, but what do we do about it?

"It's not so much he's been forgetting things," I said. "My concern is how vehemently he denies it when mistakes are brought to his attention. He flies off the handle with the slightest provocation. Why, just yesterday, he appeared in the kitchen not one hour after we had eaten and asked me when dinner would be ready. I reminded him he had just finished eating, and he became furious. He swore I was deliberately misleading him. Claimed to be hungry and reminded me how busy he was. I felt the only way to placate him was to fry some eggs and toast some bread. He grumbled the entire way through the meal. He pushed his plate away without finishing and hurried off without so much as a fare thee well. And that is only the latest." I stopped speaking, feeling overwhelmed as I recalled incidents occurring for months now. Fred frequently appeared confused, and it was getting worse.

Tears sprang to my eyes as I studied my sons' sad faces. "I can't begin to tell you how often this sort of thing occurs around here. I worry he'll get lost and not be able to find his way back home. When he travels overnight, I picture him wandering around a strange city by himself." John hurried to reassure me.

"From now on, one of us will accompany him on all overnight trips," he said. "And for day trips, a trainee can shadow him. We'll remind him how much knowledge he has to impart. How good the experience will be for their professional development. That way he can keep his dignity and you can rest easier, knowing he'll be safe." Rick nodded vehemently.

"Father can never know that we're worried about him or that he's being assigned someone to watch over him." He shuddered dramatically. "Let me talk to him, John. I can convince him our interns need more time with him, more on-the-job training. He'll be tickled pink to know his value as a mentor." I smiled in appreciation, but there was still one thought nagging at me.

"That sounds splendid, my dears. First rate. But there is one more thing." John spoke up quickly.

"What do you need, Mother?" he asked gently.

"I could use some help here at home," I admitted sadly. "I know you both have your own lives to lead, but if you could join us for supper more often, that would be much appreciated. When your father is tired, that's when he gets worse." At the look of alarm crossing both men's faces, I continued quickly. "I'm not afraid for my safety, but maybe one of you could get him settled with a book or a glass of port? He sleeps most nights in the loft over the office, anyway." That had been a fairly recent development. Fred, claiming his persistent insomnia robbed me of a good night's sleep, had been bunking downstairs, leaving me alone to lie awake for hours and worry. "You have more pressing issues, John, and I respect your right to carve out some privacy for yourself." Still living at home at forty-one, John frequently dined alone in his room, preferring to spend his evening reading or poring over plans for upcoming projects. "And Rick, the young women of Boston would be lost without you most evenings." Rick had the good sense to blush slightly at this. Sophisticated and good-looking, he was quite the catch and a very eligible bachelor. It was John's turn to smirk, but Rick quickly agreed to help.

"Of course, Mama," he said. "John and I will work it out and trust me, you'll start seeing one or both of us here most evenings, I promise." I breathed a sigh of relief and pushed my chair back before I walked first to John, then to Rick, hugging each in turn and kissing them on the cheek. With my boys on my side, we could weather whatever came next.

Chapter 82

Summer 1894

Fred was studying the large cake dominating the work table. Normally covered with blueprints and plans, we had cleared it to accommodate the cake, a stack of plates, a dozen forks, a bottle of port and a tray of glasses. Seated at the head of the table, he appeared to be counting the many candles, lit and glowing.

"There are thirty-eight candles, in case you're interested. We're celebrating your retirement, after all. One for every year of your employment as a landscape architect," I said with a teary smile. Rick spoke quickly to fill the silence that followed.

"I suggested one for every year of your life, Father, but a cake that large would be very hard to come by, don't you agree?" Everyone laughed at that, Fred the loudest of all.

"We could do one candle for every successful project you have completed, Mr. Olmsted," said one of the young apprentices, blushing wildly as he did. Fred smiled at him, shaking his head slowly.

"And that, Timothy, is the problem with retiring," he said sadly. "Everyone wants to focus on what has already been accomplished, but what of tomorrow? And the day after? If a man's legacy has already been established, what can he look forward to?" I groaned inwardly at that. Fred had been quite despondent lately. Despite acknowledging that his most productive years were behind him, he refused to engage in the plans for the future I tried to tempt him with. Marion rushed over to her father and kissed the top of his head, before kneeling at his side.

"Now Papa," she said in her most convincing voice. "You will continue as head of Olmsted and Sons, albeit in a slightly less visible capacity, for many years. Until one of my brothers is lucky enough to find a woman to bear his own sons, you have to remain in command." She smiled knowingly at John and Rick as she spoke. "And since it is unlikely John will convince a woman to go out on a second date, let alone marry him, and of course, Rick..." She continued in a hushed tone. "It's painfully clear he'll never be able to narrow down the field and set his sights on one particular woman, so I'm afraid, dear Father, you will be on the letterhead for the foreseeable future." I smiled gratefully at her. *Dear Marion always knows just what to say.* I wiped at my eyes and spoke up.

"We have much to celebrate, whether it's the number of years or the number of beautiful parks. Please, dear, won't you blow out the candles?" Fred leaned forward and attempted to comply. It quickly became clear he would need help, so his three children and five young apprentices came to his rescue. As soon as the smoke cleared, I motioned for Sinead to cut slices for everyone. "Rick, pour some wine for our guests, won't you?"

Soon everyone was clustered around the table enjoying their mid-afternoon refreshments. I whispered to Fred.

"Why didn't you tell everyone about our travel plans, my dear?" He let out a low chuckle.

"*Your* plans, Mary. I have yet to agree a voyage like you are suggesting is really the best course of action." I tried to count to ten, but only got to four before responding.

"We always said we would go back to England someday, Fred, and Ireland too. You know how much I want to travel to France again. And while we're there, it's just a hop, skip and a jump over to Spain and Italy."

"Of course, my pet. Whatever you say. A European vacation sounds like just the thing. Let's pick some tentative dates and get hold of the sailing timetables, shall we?" I breathed a sigh of relief. Now I had to convince Marion to accompany us, as I was certain I would fare much better with the help of another able-bodied adult.

Chapter 83

Winter 1894-1895

Fred and I had set off that fall without Marion, intending to travel for roughly three months, but returned home when Fred developed chest pains and shortness of breath. During our travels through England, Ireland, Scotland and Wales, Fred had complained of fatigue and often required a full day's rest between sightseeing excursions. The situation worsened after we returned to London from Edinburgh, with Fred experiencing sharp pains he was convinced were the onset of a heart attack. A former school friend of Fred's hastily arranged a consultation with his doctor, and although the doctor found no signs of a cardiac episode, he diagnosed dehydration and nervous exhaustion. Out of Fred's hearing, the doctor pulled me aside.

"Your husband's health is not good, Mrs. Olmsted," he had whispered in a tone that brooked no argument. "Unless you wish to see him in one of our fine British hospitals for a spell, I recommend you get him back to Boston as soon as possible." That was all I needed to hear, and I booked our voyage for later in the week. Fred experienced no further ailments while at sea, and we arrived home to rest up for the holidays.

In the three months since we returned, we developed a daily pattern suiting us both. In recent years, Fred had taken to sleeping in the loft above his office so as not to disturb me with his customary tossing and turning. Ever since his retirement, he had returned to the bed we had always shared, and I welcomed him happily. He was sleeping more soundly and—despite his recurrent snoring—so was I.

Each morning, I prepared breakfast for the two of us, usually something light, either porridge or toast with honey and plenty of strong black coffee. If Fred hadn't arrived downstairs by the time everything was ready, I assembled a tray and served him breakfast in bed, a practice he crowed about to his friends.

"Imagine that," I heard him say one morning during a phone conversation with his oldest friend, Charley Brace. "Being served a veritable feast by the love of my life." I shook my head at his silliness, but was pleased to indulge him, thrilled it made him happy.

After a leisurely breakfast, I did the washing up while Fred read two or three newspapers and occasionally smoked a cigar. Then we bundled up in warm clothes and set out for a walk which Fred referred to as our 'morning constitutional'. Depending on the weather and the condition of the sidewalks—Fred was terrified he would slip on ice and have to be carried home—we would walk towards the reservoir or, if feeling more energetic, to Hammond Park.

When we returned, I would discuss menus with Sinead, who, since her wedding to Danny Flynn, a ginger-haired patrolman for the Boston Police Department, was working for us just four afternoons a week. Fred usually wandered down to the office under the guise of needing a certain book or a favorite pen, but generally to kibbutz with the employees who were working feverishly at their drafting tables to keep up with the demands of the thriving design firm.

As soon as dinner was on the table, usually soup and sandwiches, I would ring downstairs and Fred would return, frequently with one or both sons in tow. The conversation was lively, allowing Fred to catch up on the latest news and progress reports on a myriad of projects. Often the conversation drifted to the latest gossip. The citizens of Boston were just as intrigued as the rest of the country by the stories coming out of Chicago, where the serial killer was still on the loose. More than a dozen murders had been attributed to the 'Devil', the first of which had occurred during the opening week of the Chicago World's Fair nearly two years earlier. Fred seemed particularly concerned about the Biltmore Estate, although both sons assured him that the project was complete. I was pleased to see the familiar gleam in his blue eyes during our midday meals.

After the boys returned to work, Fred would head upstairs for a nap, which, as the winter months continued to drag, often lasted several hours. I used this opportunity to catch up on my correspondence, writing to far-flung friends and family around the globe. Occasionally I would call on Anne or a friend in the neighborhood for tea or a game of cards, but more often than not, I would relish the quiet time, sitting at the desk in the parlor. I had taken to watching the birds congregate outside, vowing to install a bird feeder as soon as the weather allowed and frequently consulting a newly purchased copy of Audubon's *The Birds of America*.

If Fred woke early from his nap, he would join me for a cup of tea or a glass of port and a walk around the block before returning home to eat supper. It was usually a quiet affair, but I could occasionally convince one or both boys to join us, especially on the nights Sinead served a pot roast and apple cobbler. We spent evenings in front of the fireplace, both of us with our books. I still preferred the French novelists, while Fred worked his way through a dog-eared copy of Thoreau's *Walden; or, Life in the Woods*. By 10:00p.m., we were ready for bed.

Early one morning in February, Fred was sitting at the kitchen table, reading the *Boston Globe* and enjoying a third cup of coffee. I was used to him calling me over or reading an article at the top of his lungs as if I were the one who was hard of hearing. But that morning, I was returning from the pantry and heard him call my name. As I approached, I watched him thrust his clenched fist upward and let out a loud whoop.

"They got him. The murdering bastard. They got him and he'll hang for his crimes," he crowed.

"What is it? Who did they get?" Fred just shook his head and pointed at the paper. I leaned over and even without glasses, I could make out the headline.

"Devil in the White City Arrested!" It appeared the nightmare plaguing the city of Chicago was finally at an end.

"Oh Fred, that is wonderful news. I remember sitting in that hotel room in Chicago that day, when they found the first victim. And after all your hard work!" Fred squeezed my hand.

"It's the hard work of the police that should be recognized. They are the actual heroes." I nodded in agreement and kissed the top of his head.

But you're still my hero.

Chapter 84

Summer 1895

The heat that summer had been so oppressive we rarely ventured out in the middle of the day. We began taking a stroll around the neighborhood before we ate breakfast and although Fred often grumbled that in a civilized country, no man should be expected to walk, let alone interact with others before consuming a sufficient amount of coffee, he seemed to relish the opportunity to chat with neighbors during our walks.

The weather was the topic of the day, but news of H. H. Holmes, the Chicago 'Devil' and his murder trial often took center stage. While I preferred to ignore the gory details of the 'Murder Castle' where many of the killings were reported to have taken place, the trial fascinated me. There was already talk of a public hanging, should the thirty-five-year-old Holmes be found guilty.

This particular morning, we returned home later than usual and I went to prepare a pot of coffee, while Fred sorted through a stack of newspapers from earlier in the week.

"I am certain it's in here," he called out. I nodded absentmindedly, measuring scoops of coffee into the percolator. Fred seemed to take my silence as some sort of rejection, because he angrily added, "I'm telling you, Mary. I saw it just the other day."

"What exactly are you referring to?" I asked, straining to adopt a patient tone. "I'm sorry, my mind is elsewhere this morning." Fred studied me closely.

"You are pale, my love, and you've barely said a word. Usually when you run into the Browns, you're quite the chatterbox. What you and Mrs. Brown have to jabber on about is positively beyond me." I suddenly felt unsteady on my feet and Fred grew alarmed at the sight of me leaning against the sink, holding on for dear life.

"Mary," he called out. He reached out to me and I fell into his arms, slumping onto the floor as everything went black.

***

The next day, I stayed in bed. I had spent most of the preceding day in bed as well after being carried there by John, who had revived me with smelling salts. The doctor, who had shown up less than an hour after my fainting spell, had diagnosed dehydration and heat stroke. He had attempted to chastise me for our early morning walk during a heat spell, but Fred had cut him off.

"Not six months ago, you advised me to get more exercise. A walk is just the thing, you told me," Fred had said. "Now you are giving the exact opposite advice to my wife."

"Your wife's condition is totally unlike yours, Olmsted. And six months ago, it was forty degrees outside. It's more than double that today. We're expecting thunderstorms with significant flashes of lightning later this afternoon. Those storms plaguing the Midwest are apparently on their way here." I lay listening, my mind elsewhere. As if those poor people in Chicago don't have enough to contend with. A homicidal maniac had been terrorizing them, and now they had to fear being struck by lightning.

The doctor prescribed bed rest, fluids and a light diet for the next two days and I was happy to comply. I had no appetite, so chicken broth and a small scoop of homemade blueberry ice cream was a welcome sight on the tray Sinead had delivered last night. This morning, however, I studied the same tray with little interest. How had Fred managed to burn the toast *and* drench it in spilled coffee? He stood quietly, waiting for my reaction. In over thirty-five years of marriage, he had never brought me breakfast in bed.

"Oh, you shouldn't have bothered," I said. "I could have waited for Sinead," Fred shook his head glumly.

"It's Thursday, my dear," he said. "Sinead is off on Thursdays." My heart sank. Despite my sluggish appetite, I had no desire to starve to death in my own home. I took a sip of the now-tepid coffee with the consistency of mud. *What to do?*

"Well, if I had ever wished for more daughters or a daughter-in-law," I quipped, "now would be the time." I was craving a mug of hot tea and a slice of buttered toast, not one soaked in lukewarm coffee. Fred smiled at me.

"You sound better. You should be right as rain by this time tomorrow." I nodded, racking my brain as to how to get food delivered. I hated to bother Sinead on her day off, and Mabel Brown had told me yesterday she was escaping to Cape Cod to avoid the blistering heat in the city. Even if John and Rick were around, their culinary skills were no better than their father's. The sudden appearance of Anne Vaux interrupted my thoughts.

"My dearest," she called out, "It is positively stifling in this room. It's no wonder you're feeling poorly. Fred," she scolded. "Please fetch your poor wife a large glass of ice cold water." As Fred shuffled out of the room, she examined the tray balanced on my lap with amusement. "This will not do," she announced briskly, and after dumping the contents of the tray on the bureau, began unpacking a large satchel. The aroma of fresh baked bread filled the air. *Was that cinnamon?* Anne's cinnamon rolls were the stuff of legend.

"But—how did you know?" I asked. "I thought you were still in England with Cal's family."

"I got home last night in time to enjoy the remnants of this blasted heatwave. And the humidity! I barely slept a wink. And then first thing this morning, I got a phone call from Marion."

"My Marion?"

"Yes, of course. Fred had called her last night, worried sick about you. You fainted on the street I heard."

"It was, um, the kitchen floor, actually," I admitted sheepishly.

"At any rate, she was hoping I could bring you breakfast today. She said she would be here in time to make dinner. I would have thought Fred could manage a decent pot of coffee at least. Oh well, I'll leave you some cinnamon rolls and go down to slice up this bread and brew you some proper coffee. Unless you would prefer tea?" I nodded gratefully.

"Tea would be wonderful. I can't thank you enough..." I began, but Anne waved me off and strode out of the bedroom, nearly bumping into poor Fred, who was balancing a tray with two glasses and a pitcher of ice water in one hand and an ancient table fan in the other.

I watched her go with a smile as I reached for a warm cinnamon roll. I breathed in the spicy aroma and took a large bite. *Heavenly!* Angels come in all shapes and sizes, I decided.

Chapter 85

Fall 1895

The *Cephalonia* set sail from Boston heading to Liverpool with Fred, Marion, Rick and me on board. I was fully recovered and looking forward to an extended visit. We would be staying in England for an undetermined amount of time. Rick had rented a two-story house in the village of Lympstone in Devon, where Fred would undergo treatment with a nerve disorder specialist. Each day of the ocean voyage seemed to bring a new level of comfort to Fred, and by the time we arrived in Devon he appeared relaxed and eager to explore our new surroundings.

Despite quickly realizing this new treatment was no more effective than earlier ones, we prepared to celebrate the holidays in England. I was determined to make it a special time for the family and, at my urging, John arrived just a few days before Christmas.

One morning, Marion and I traipsed through the nearby woods, returning with arms full of evergreen boughs. Firm in my commitment to decorate our temporary home in a festive way, I didn't even miss the boxes of holiday decorations I had been collecting for years.

"We'll make new memories this year," I said to Marion as we arranged the evergreens, bright with red berries, on the mantel and she happily agreed.

"We'll make it nice for Papa," she said, and we did just that.

Everyone agreed the highlight of the holidays was when a group of neighbors came caroling one night. After listening to their beautiful renditions of "It Came Upon the Midnight Clear," "Away in a Manger" and Fred's favorite, "We Three Kings of Orient Are," I decided to join them. Hurrying to gather my cloak, I tried to coax someone to accompany me, but everyone was content to linger by the blazing fire, sipping mulled wine.

"We'll be here when you return, my dear," a slightly tipsy Fred called as I hurried out the door, eager to lend my voice to the chorus.

***

A few days after Christmas, we received word that Calvert Vaux had drowned. The seventy-one-year-old had slipped and fallen off a pier while visiting New York. His body was found two days later, missing his hat, one shoe and his spectacles.

"Don't anyone tell your father," I begged. His spirits were high despite his poor health, and I wanted to wait for the right opportunity to share the devastating news. I was beside myself as I tried to reach Anne. Phone service was nearly non-existent in the tiny English village, but Rick and Marion traveled to a nearby town to send a telegram expressing our condolences.

A few days later, I broke the news to Fred. At first, he seemed confused, not at all certain he remembered his friend and business associate. Suddenly recognition seemed to come to him.

"Cal Vaux? We worked together for a time, he and I," Fred said. "He was my friend." I squeezed his hand.

"He was your dear friend Fred," I said. "Do you remember when we shared a house with the Vauxes? That huge convent nearby to Central Park. Do you remember how much fun our children had playing with theirs?" Fred's eyes brightened as he seemed to recall those happy memories. Then his mood darkened.

"Charlotte used to play the little mother," he mumbled, his eyes dull. "Remember how happy she was when we had Marion? A sister for her. And Owen? So much like his father. He and John were so alike. All gone now," he said. Tears welling in my eyes, I tried to console him.

"Yes, my dear, but we have to remember the good times we had with those we love. And be grateful for those still with us. And here we are celebrating the holidays in England with our wonderful children." Fred nodded thoughtfully, but in a rare moment of total clarity, he turned to me.

"I'm going downhill rapidly, my love. We should head home early in the new year." I kissed his cheek and held him close. With my face buried in his neck, I assured him we would be home soon.

Chapter 86

Spring 1897
Convinced that Fred's mood swings could be managed better in a more tranquil setting, I purchased a plot of land in Deer Isle, Maine. With John and Rick both so busy, I asked Marion to draw up plans to renovate the tiny cottage that came with the property to allow for a weekend retreat. I was thrilled with her work. The layout made the most of the relatively small space. Within a few months, the place was ready, and we traveled north to spend a week in the new cottage I had named Felsted.

"I can't understand why you picked this place, Mary," Fred said as we stood on the front porch shortly after arriving. "We're in the middle of nowhere. Why, we passed Portland hours ago. Where in blazes are we?" I spread my arms around, showing the wooded areas surrounding three sides of the cottage.

"There are more elm trees here than you can count Fred," I said. "They're your favorite, don't you remember?"

"Of course, I remember," he said. "I'm not the doddering old fool you so regularly make me out to be."

"I don't think you're an old fool, my dear. But if you were, you'd be *my* old fool. Now, how about a cup of tea and then we can walk to the pond and you can tell me all about our new neighbors that live there." Fred brightened as he watched a school of ducks making their way across the water.

"I've loved ducks since I was a boy, Mary. Did I ever tell you how much I enjoyed spending summers in Deer Isle? Up in Maine? Why, there were more species of ducks than you can imagine. Now those ducks swimming toward us? They're called buffleheads. They are the smallest breed of diving ducks. Watch them vanish and resurface as they feed. Quite amazing they are," he said, sounding proud that he could share this. *We're here on Deer Isle, my love.*

I led Fred over to a large wicker settee on the porch. "You sit here and get ready to tell me all about the ducks while I make us some tea." Fred leaned back, his eyes brighter than I had seen them in ages.

"All right," he said. "But not too much milk. Last time it was too..." I left him to his grumblings and went inside to prepare a tea tray in our tiny new kitchen.

***

Despite Fred's initial misgivings, we spent many weekends in Maine over the next couple of years. While not the panacea I had hoped for, he seemed content most of the time and enjoyed afternoons napping on the porch and watching his beloved ducks.

Chapter 87

Summer 1899

"I'm just surprised you have adapted so well to this... change is all. Honestly Mother, it's as if you were pleased that Father is residing in an asylum." Marion's voice was cold and her demeanor stiff and formal. She had returned home the night before with the intention of talking us out of our plan to commit Fred to the McLean Asylum; the facility Fred had worked on years ago. Marion had been outraged when she discovered Fred had been admitted several hours earlier. She had immediately set off for the facility but arrived past normal visiting hours and had been turned away. When she returned to Brookline last night, she had ignored me and gone straight to her room. Apparently cooler heads prevailed this morning, and Marion's angry mood was replaced with frustration and disappointment.

"Surely there is a more humane way of taking care of Papa. If you need help, why can't you hire a nurse to come in a few times a week?" She sounded sad, and I knew she was concerned about her beloved father.

I watched her pace the length of the dining room, still in her dressing gown, her hair mussed from what looked to have been a very restless night. I had much to say, but how to explain my reasoning without breaking her heart? Marion thought the world of her father and probably could not handle the cold, hard truth. The reality I had been living with for years.

"My dear, will you please sit down? There's coffee, and it's still piping hot. I even put out some of those cardamom buns you love so—" Marion cut me off angrily.

"I don't want buns, Mother. I want answers. I want to know why you chose to have my poor father committed to an insane asylum. And further, why you aren't more upset with the decision. You sit there with your tea and crumpets or coffee and buns or whatever, as if everything is right with the world. How can you be so heartless?" Marion began to sob and buried her face in her hands. Although her words cut me to the quick, I wanted to comfort her and help her to see what was really going on.

"Marion," I said. She looked up and began to dab at her eyes with a napkin. I attempted to soften my tone. "Pet, you have not lived with us for years." Seeing her start to protest, I held up a hand to stop her. "I know what you're going to say. That you visit here whenever you can and when you're with us, your father seems quite normal. And that is true, for the most part. But what you haven't seen—and that's probably my fault because I hid it from you, sheltered you from the truth—is the fact that your father is suffering, and has been for years. His doctors suggested having him hospitalized years ago, for his own safety as well as mine. I resisted, certain I could care for him better at home. I told myself it wasn't all that bad. That I was only bothered by his angry outbursts when I was tired or feeling under the weather. But last week when he..." My voice faltered. I drew in a deep breath and continued, my voice a whisper.

"Your father disappeared one morning. He'd had his breakfast, and I went up to the bedroom to locate a book to lend to Sinead. I swear I left him alone for less than five minutes. When I came back to the kitchen, he had left. But before I could go look for him, I had to attend to another matter, a more pressing one." I took a deep breath, willing myself not to cry. Marion had stopped pacing and appeared to hang on my every word. "Your father had attempted to stub out one of his cigars, but he didn't use the ashtray. He stubbed it out in his pile of newspapers and the entire stack had burst into flames. By the time I stamped out the fire and doused the whole thing with a bucket of water, several more minutes had passed. I screamed for your brothers, and Rick and one of the interns came running. They took off in separate directions down the street, while I began calling the neighbors. No one was home at the first three houses I called, but I finally got hold of the Harris's maid and she said she had seen your father heading toward the reservoir." Marion nodded mutely, seeming to be incapable of speech.

"I hurried outside and I could see Rick heading in that direction. I hollered at him to catch your father before he reached the water. He could have drowned." *Like Cal*. Painful memories of the past week caught up with me and I sobbed, shoulders shaking with the release of pent-up emotion. "It's been a nightmare. Honestly, a living nightmare. To watch the man that I love disappearing in front of my eyes and to know there's nothing I can do to stop it. I pray you never have to go through this yourself someday, Marion." She bent to embrace me, her words muffled.

"I didn't know, Mama. I'm so sorry I doubted you. I know you wouldn't make a decision like this hastily. But why didn't you contact me? Or one of my brothers. Why didn't they tell me? I talked to Rick just the other day. He didn't say a word."

"I asked them not to bother you, my pet. I didn't want to worry you, and to be honest, I've kept most of this from them. The new *maid* we hired last year? She's actually a nurse brought in to watch your father, but he is so damned stubborn. Other than getting him to eat or cleaning up after him, there is so little she can do. Your brothers have been an absolute godsend. One or both of them is here most evenings and they help me get your father settled for the night. But he's getting worse, and they can't be here around the clock. I worry for his safety and the safety of all of us in this house."

"What if I hadn't returned to the kitchen straightaway that morning? An old house like this? It would have gone up in flames, trapping me upstairs and endangering all the fine young men who work for us? Believe me, this is the best option. McLean is a fine facility. Your father will be safe and maybe being surrounded by the beautiful landscape he designed over twenty years ago will soothe him somewhat. He was the one who proposed residents live in cottages on the grounds to feel less institutionalized. He always spoke so favorably about that project. It might spark some long-forgotten memory for him."

I did not add that while it was a hopeful thought, it was unlikely. Fred had all but stopped speaking over the last several weeks and frequently did not even seem aware of his surroundings. His blue eyes had lost their sparkle, and he seemed to find little joy in anything. Marion would find out soon enough just how much he had deteriorated.

"I want to see him as soon as possible. Can we please go today?"

"Let me call ahead and see if he can see anyone. Their policy is to limit visits the first week to get new residents situated. I'll go ring them right now."

Later that day, we sat in a large, well-appointed room at McLean waiting for Fred. He was living in a nearby cottage and would be escorted to the main building by one of the staff. I grew increasingly anxious as the minutes passed. Perhaps this was too soon. Maybe Fred didn't want to see anyone. *Would he even recognize us?* Marion had been chattering away while we waited, filling me in on all that was going on in New York.

"You should see how women are wearing their hemlines Mother. And you would be shocked at how simple their dresses are. No more draping, padding, ruffles or pleats. And everyone is riding bicycles. They're simply…"

I studied her closely. She had grown to be a handsome woman with bright blue eyes and light brown hair worn in a loose chignon. I wasn't aware that she had stopped talking until I realized she was waiting for a response.

"I'm sorry, dear. What is it now?"

"I was asking you to please come and visit me once Father is better. Maybe he could come too. A couple of weeks of rest is all he needs. Some fresh air, well-balanced meals…" I was about to protest that I had been providing all of that and more for years now when the door opened and a young nurse wheeled Fred into the room. We stood and watched him approach, waiting for a look of recognition, but his eyes remained glazed and unfocused.

"Well, look at who we have here, Mr. Olmsted. Your wife and daughter have come to visit. Isn't that just lovely?" The nurse was so cheerful. I couldn't imagine how difficult it would be to keep one's spirits up with patients so challenging. I leaned forward and took one of Fred's hands in mine.

"My dear, Marion has come all the way from New York to see you. Isn't that wonderful?" I realized my voice was pitched higher than usual, and I willed myself to relax. Marion was standing stock-still, perhaps wondering if her father recognized her. A hint of a smile formed on Fred's thin, parched lips and his eyes brightened.

"Of course, my dear Mary. And Marion. It is a joy to see you. And naturally I remember New York. People say I built a park out of some swampland there a few years back. Tell me, dear, is the park still standing?" he asked, and we witnessed the start of a twinkle in the blue eyes peering out of his dear craggy face.

Chapter 88

Summer 1903

Fred had remained in residence at McLean for the past four years, during which time John, Rick, Marion and I visited him regularly. He appeared overwhelmed and grew agitated the one time all four of us called on him together, so we went in pairs. Sadly, Fred's condition continued to deteriorate and his memory and mental state worsened. Increasingly, he could not recognize us, and during the last year, he kept silent during our visits. The staff reported his appetite was not very good, but he was generally agreeable and quite docile, a favorite patient among the mostly female staff. We had grown accustomed to his weakened state and frail appearance, but the occasional outside visitor's reaction was one of shock and dismay.

I continued to live quietly, splitting my time between Brookline and the cabin on Deer Isle, Maine. I spent my days reading and writing letters and had just taken up needlepoint, but I lacked the patience to complete most of the projects I began. My efforts at gardening produced only beds of weeds, so I gave up that pastime as well. I remarked to anyone who would listen that I must be the only Olmsted past or present lacking a green thumb.

I approached my visits to Fred with a steely resolve, always hoping for some small sign of recognition but trying to keep my expectations in check. During the time with him, I maintained an air of cheerfulness, but by the time I left the hospital after several hours, I was both emotionally spent and physically exhausted.

On August 27, 1903, John, Rick and I rushed to McClean following a call from Fred's doctor. His breathing was labored, and he wavered in and out of consciousness. We began a bedside vigil and for a short while it appeared as if he would rally. But, sadly, at 2:00a.m. Fred drew his last breath with the three of us at his side. John and Rick broke down and sobbed, and I tried in vain to comfort them. I had cried buckets of tears for years and had prayed to see an end to the poor man's misery. In all honesty, I had said goodbye to him years ago and his death was almost a relief. *Almost.* My darling husband. The love of my life.

"He squeezed my hand," I said to the attending doctor triumphantly. "He was saying goodbye, telling me it was his time to go." He had smiled sadly.

"That is a wonderful memory to console yourself with, Mrs. Olmsted," he assured me.

Three days later, we held a funeral service at Fairsted for immediate family and a few close friends. Through it all, I wanted nothing more than to feel Fred's arms around me, to lay my head against his chest and have him gently stroke my hair. I was numb, but afterwards, I overheard everyone saying how composed I was. Fred's body was later cremated, and we accompanied the ashes to Hartford where they were placed in the family vault in the Old North Cemetery. After a few days visiting family in the area, I returned to Brookline, alone and broken-hearted. I could not imagine a world without my larger-than-life husband. I didn't want to.

Chapter 89

I had grown accustomed to living alone with Fred in the hospital, but after his death, I found the house in Brookline too large for one person. When Sinead gave notice in her sixth month of pregnancy, I made the cottage in Deer Isle my permanent residence. My sons could better use the space without me rattling around. The family business had changed its name to Olmsted Brothers, and John and Rick had more work than they could handle. They immediately took over the living space on the main floor and converted the huge parlor and dining room into additional office space with large drafting tables.

Shortly before I moved to Maine, I invited Anne to dinner. It was Sinead's last day of work, and she came in early to prepare a special meal for us. At my suggestion, she joined us at the kitchen table and we enjoyed a meal of steamed cod with haricot verts and boiled new potatoes. After serving coffee, Sinead bade us goodbye and, with tears in her eyes, begged me to stay in touch.

Over coffee and a plate of anise shortbread, Anne brought me up to date on all that had been happening in her life since Cal's death. Finally ruled an accidental drowning after concerns it had been a suicide, Anne planned to collect the life insurance proceeds and move back to New York to be closer to her grown children and grandchildren.

"The only reason we moved to Boston was to be closer to you and Fred. With you moving and both of our husbands gone, there is nothing for me here." I nodded thoughtfully. It had crossed my mind to ask Anne to consider moving with me to Maine, but had realized it would probably not have worked out well. The small cottage was suitable for a married couple perhaps, not for friends who both enjoyed their private spaces.

"You're doing the right thing," I assured her. "Being near your family is a blessing." I shook my head slowly. "I envy you all those grandchildren. What I wouldn't give."

"It's true that Charlotte's husband remarried? He has a new wife?" I laughed bitterly.

"Apparently a wife in a mental institution is not exactly a feather in the cap of a prominent physician. He could divorce Charlotte on the grounds of abandonment; can you imagine? My poor daughter."

"And the boys? How are they enjoying their new step-mother?"

"To hear my former son-in-law, everything is hunky dory. And his wife is already pregnant. Just as the oldest boy is going off to college next fall."

"Have you seen them since Fred died?"

"Yes. Rick brought me to Cohasset a few months ago. The new Mrs. Bryant was indisposed, but we spent a lovely afternoon with the boys. Everyone seemed happy enough. John promised the boys would come to visit me in Maine this summer, so we'll see. Anyway," I said, "How about a pleasant walk to work off all of this food? I'm afraid I'll fall asleep in my chair if I don't get up and move around."

"I shouldn't," Anne said. "I need to continue packing. But before I go, are you sure about moving to Maine full time? Won't you get lonesome?"

"Naturally, but it will actually be a relief. This house has too many memories, too many ghosts in residence. Fred spent only a little time up there when we first bought the cottage and honestly, it never really held his interest. Other than the ducks in the pond… it was too isolated for him. But I'll be fine and of course I can come back anytime. There is a lovely young couple just down the road from the cottage. He'll maintain the grounds and fix whatever breaks, and she's a charming woman. Just a little slip of a thing. I've hired her to help with the cleaning and she will bring me my supper five nights a week. It'll be grand," I said with a smile.

"But at night? Are you prepared to be alone?" Anne asked.

I thought of all the nights I had spent with Fred in over forty years of marriage. Together in our bed, I had known the greatest joy and happiness I could have ever imagined. I would never be alone as long as I had my memories.

"I'm the luckiest woman in the world, my friend. Marriage to Fred was the greatest privilege of my life. If I have to live the next few years on my own until it is time to join him, then that's what I must do."

Epilogue

I spent most of the next seventeen years in Maine. In order to accommodate the family members and friends who came to visit, I had a large house built on the empty lot behind the original cottage. Especially in the summer months, it was frequently full of guests, including Charlotte's three boys and their step-sister. Our son John had married a widow with two young daughters, and the sounds of children playing filled my heart with joy. *How Fred would have loved this!*

I continued to live alone in my cottage, but mornings when there were children in residence, I left my front door open to allow for their visits. Early one morning, John's six-year-old step-daughter Kathleen showed up, and I prepared hot chocolate for us. Seated on the large wicker settee on the front porch, we watched the ducks swimming in the pond.

"I love ducks," Kathleen said. "Do you?" I got a lump in my throat, but nodded happily.

"I do, my pet. But your grandpa Fred loved them most of all." The young girl looked thoughtful, her large brown eyes watching me closely.

"What else did he love?" she asked. I smiled, blinking back my tears. *That's easy. He loved me, he loved his children, he loved making people happy…*

"He loved building parks," I told her proudly.

Death Notice

The Boston Globe

August 23, 1921

We regret to announce the death of Mary Perkins Olmsted, at her family home in Brookline, at the age of ninety-one after a brief illness. Her sons, John Charles Olmsted and Frederick Law Olmsted, Jr., partners in the landscape architect design firm Olmsted Brothers, and her daughter Marion Olmsted, a renowned photographer, were by her side. Mary was the widow of renowned landscape architect Frederick Law Olmsted, who during his nearly forty-year career was responsible for over thirty major city parks including Central Park in Manhattan, Prospect Park in Brooklyn and the Arnold Arboretum and the Emerald Necklace in Boston, and the US Capitol Grounds in Washington, D.C., Yosemite National Park, and dozens of college campuses, hospital grounds and private estates.

Mrs. Olmsted was predeceased by her first husband, Dr. John Hull Olmsted, two infant sons and her son Owen, who died in 1881, as well as daughter Charlotte Olmsted Bryant, who died in 1908 after a long illness. Orphaned at the age of eight, Mrs. Olmsted was raised by her paternal grandparents Dr. and Mrs. Cyrus Perkins on Staten Island. She attended school in New York City.

Mrs. Olmsted was devoted to her family and supported several charitable causes in the towns of Deer Isle, Maine, and Brookline, Massachusetts.

Calling hours will be held on Tuesday from 1:00p.m. to 4:00p.m. at the Wentworth Funeral Home in Brookline. In lieu of flowers, the family asks that donations be made to the Audubon Society for the protection of the American waterbird population.

About the Author

Gail Ward Olmsted was a marketing executive and a college professor before she began writing fiction on a fulltime basis. A trip to Sedona, AZ inspired her first novel *Jeep Tour*. Three more novels followed before she began *Landscape of a Marriage,* a biographical work of fiction featuring landscape architect Frederick Law Olmsted, an ancestor of her husband's, and his wife Mary.

For more information, please visit her on Facebook and at GailOlmsted.com.

Note from the Author

I felt compelled to write the story of Frederick Law Olmsted (FLO) and his marriage to his widowed sister-in-law Mary for one simple reason: To paraphrase writer Toni Morrison, "I wrote it, because I wanted to read it!" My husband Deane's great, great grandfather, Aaron Olmsted, and FLO's grandfather, Benjamin Olmsted, were brothers, making FLO a distant cousin of my husband's. I truly wanted to know more about FLO as he figures prominently in our family's history.

Landscape of a Marriage is a biographical novel, a work of fiction. I focused on Fred and Mary's personal relationship and reimagined or created certain elements to meet the needs of the novel, as I deemed necessary. My goal was to tell a love story set against a backdrop of the turbulent and exciting events of the second half of the nineteenth century in America. I stuck as close as I could to the actual events and timelines, but I embellished certain elements to create a more interesting narrative.

What is true: the dates and circumstances of marriages, births, accidents and illnesses, deaths, major events (the Civil War, Lincoln's assassination, the Gold Rush, the women's movement, the Industrial Revolution); and the body of work (parks, public lands, private estates, hospitals and universities) attributed to FLO during his career. The family really did make all those moves beginning in New York, then to Washington, California, back to New York and finally Brookline and Deer Isle, Maine. FLO actually was asked to run for Vice-President of the United States, he frequently subsisted on a diet of black coffee and pickles and he reportedly blamed a bout of illness on the wallpaper in the family's dining room!

What is imagined: the letters and notes, the dialogue, the reactions to and the personal impact of the historic events on the main characters.

Here is where I took 'significant liberties':

The romantic nature of the marriage: The true essence of Fred and Mary's relationship is impossible to know with any certainty. By all accounts, theirs was a 'marriage of convenience' and there are well-documented periods of long separation. I set out to portray them as a couple devoted to each other, with a shared vision for the changing American landscape. I felt their passion for work and family was the impetus for their love affair for over forty years.

The friendship between Mary and Calvert Vaux's wife: I created their lifelong connection, as I felt Mary Olmsted needed a best friend and confidante. My own friends are a never-ending source of joy to me, and I saw this relationship as an opportunity to reflect how Mary Olmsted was evolving as a woman, a wife and a mother. After reading the first draft of *Landscape*, my editor suggested I change Mrs. Vaux's name from Mary, as it got more than a bit confusing which Mary was speaking. I re-named her Anne, after my mother Anne Brennan Ward. If not with each other, I only hope that both 'Mary's' experienced a similar level of support and connection during their lives.

Katherine Wormeley's impact on the marriage of FLO and Mary: Katherine is an actual person, an accomplished nurse, writer and translator. There has been some speculation about the nature of her relationship with FLO, but I have no reason to believe that the friendship between them was a true cause for conflict in the Olmsted's marriage.

Marion Olmsted's interest in the suffragette movement: In order to provide a sense of the impact the women's movement was having on society at the time, I wanted one of the principal characters to become a staunch and vocal supporter of women's rights. I chose Marion for that role. I also refer to her love and devotion to her family, her compassion and her skills as a photographer, all of which are well-documented.

Despite taking place nearly one hundred and fifty years ago, the issues presented in the novel are still relevant today: gender bias and women's equality, balancing work demands with family needs, maintaining one's individual identity in a marriage, the impact that prolonged separations can have on a relationship, the need for meaningful friendships outside of marriage, the struggle of raising a child with mental or physical health issues and the heart-breaking challenge of trying to cope with the loss of a child. As I wrote *Landscape*, these were the central themes I wanted to explore from Mary's point of view. She had a profound influence of FLO's career as a landscape architect, first as a sounding board and cheerleader. With her growing self-confidence and burgeoning sense of worth beyond her roles as wife and mother, all evidence points to her critical role as creative influence and partner.

I hope you enjoyed *Landscape of a Marriage* and would appreciate it greatly if you were to leave a rating or review online. I welcome your comments and questions. You can reach me at:

gwolmsted@gmail.com
Facebook @ gailolmstedauthor
Instagram @ gwolmsted
Twitter @gwolmsted

Check out my other titles on
www.GailOlmsted.com

Thanks!
Gail Ward Olmsted

Thank you so much for reading
one of our **Historical Fiction** novels.
If you enjoyed our book, please check out our recommended
title for your next great read!

Fateful Decisions by Trevor D'Silva

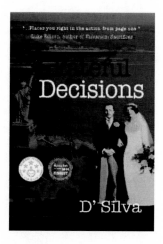

"...Places you right in the action from page one."
-Luke Edison, author of *Valcarion: Sacrifices*

View other Black Rose Writing titles at
<u>www.blackrosewriting.com/books</u> and use promo code
PRINT to receive a **20% discount** when purchasing.

Made in United States
North Haven, CT
07 January 2024

47168937R00188